THE WORLD
BEAT

**Other Mitch Roberts Novels
by Gaylord Dold**

Rude Boys
A Penny for the Old Guy

THE WORLD BEAT

G A Y L O R D   D O L D

ST. MARTIN'S PRESS
NEW YORK

Design by Basha Zapatka

Library of Congress Cataloging-in-Publication Data

Dold, Gaylord.
   The world beat / Gaylord Dold.
         p.   cm.
   "A Thomas Dunne book."
   ISBN 0-312-09945-2
   1. Roberts, Mitchell (Fictitious character)—Fiction.
   2. Private investigator—England—London—Fiction.
   3. Americans—Africa—Fiction.   I. Title.
PS3554.O436W67   1993
   813'.54—dc20   93-29085
                                                           CIP

10 9 8 7 6 5 4 3 2

PART ONE

KWENDA NZURI

EUROPEANS FLEEING ZAIRE
Kinshasa, Zaire

Belgian paratroopers were evacuating more of their citizens from this violence-torn nation Wednesday, defying an ultimatum by President Mobuto Sese Seko for foreign forces to immediately pull out.

French soldiers, meanwhile, prepared to leave Zaire after taking the last French nationals out of the country.

AP

1

ALREADY HE HAD COUNTED SIXTEEN soldiers, ten beige-clad paratroopers sleeping under a big umbrella tree down by the river quay where there was some shade. On the taxi ride away from Brazzaville, along the dusty road where the plateau broke down to brown grassless hills, he had seen maybe six soldiers marching wearily, looking sad-eyed and stoned on *bangi,* crazy from the canopy of unrelieved sun. Roberts had been relaxing in the back seat of the old Renault, glad to be getting away from the center of the *ville,* even though there were parts of the city that were quite beautiful and very pleasant, when he saw the soldiers through the window in a glaze of heat and red laterite dust, carrying their automatic weapons. At first he thought they were African women carrying laundry on their backs, far away through the brown atmosphere, and then as they drew down the slope toward the river he could see they were soldiers wearing beige camouflage khaki, packs on their backs, and they were stoned. Some of them were actually smoking the heavy bush reefer, staring at him with unfocused red eyes as his taxi whooshed past in a cloud of rising dust. Mostly he had felt amazed and a little lucky to be in Africa, but just then he felt afraid, as if a little bubble of balance in the middle of his head had suddenly been tilted to one side, and the soldiers knew it.

. . . .

3

Roberts paid the taxi driver and watched the man drive away uphill toward Brazzaville, the city on the plateau above the river. He tried to keep one eye on the sleeping soldiers, waiting to see one of them awaken, and in a drunken anger, start to hassle the white American for bribes called *matabish,* his papers, some French francs, whatever. When it didn't happen, Roberts skirted the concrete-bunkered ticket office that was built just over the river where the ferry stopped, and found some shade under the tin roof of the quay waiting area. It was a rectangle of reinforced plywood with a dirt floor, buttressed halfway up by rotting hardwood sides, and Roberts could look out over the river to Zaire and back toward Brazzaville, which was a patch of brown and green far away. There was a deafening silence and no breeze, and when Roberts gazed out over the river he could see planks of heat rising from the ochre surface of the water through which a few crocodiles seemed to glide. He couldn't see very well though, partly because of the heat, partly because of the glaze of light that poured down from the tropical sun. Gradually a vision of *mangungu* groves appeared on the opposite shore and Roberts wiped his forehead with a handkerchief that was already soaking wet.

He rested on the concrete rail that ran across the top of the buttress so that he could see directly down the riverbank toward the Kinshasa ferry—the corroded rust bucket of a boat—the milling crowds waiting at the customs stalls, and a few police smoking cigarettes while eyeing the citizens. All at once the diesel ferry belched a cloud of black smoke and Roberts could see the brown water at her stern begin to boil, the boat buck slightly and move away from the wharf, circling slowly once as she left the bank and made way toward the channel between two sand islands. Her bells clanged and the

Africans on shore began to shout and wave as a shower of white egrets erupted on the near bank.

For some reason a feeling of intense malaise crowded in on Roberts, a feeling that he couldn't escape the heat and the sound of the droning insects, compounded by the raw smell of garbage he could see floating in the river. The light was coming off the river as sharp as a bullet, goats were bawling, and now Roberts could hear the soldiers who were coming awake, laughing, beginning to play cards and drink again. He moved away, behind a wood pillar, keeping watch on the soldiers while at the same time marking the passage of the ferry across the river toward Kinshasa docks, maybe two miles away. Roberts was impressed by the absolute anarchy in the look of the soldiers, a graceful malignity that was composed of languid stares, gestures with automatic weapons, cigarettes poised artfully from pouty lips. When Roberts had come onto the quay he was afraid some of them might be awake enough to look at him and talk to him in Swahili. For just one moment he thought one of them had opened his eyes, began to mumble and was going to point his weapon. But the soldier hadn't; everything had happened inside Roberts' imagination, and he thought it was vaguely racist, this dread of blackness.

He was trying to declassify his dread when he saw two soldiers down on the mud plage beating the tiny figure of a man who lay face down in the muck. One soldier had the poor bastard by the ankles, and had pulled him into some shallow water where the man had to crane his neck back just to catch a breath, while the other soldier stood just above the victim's head, pulling his ears for sport. Like a crazy marionette, the stick-figure African face down in the mud would raise his head and let out a scream—and then one of the soldiers would pull his ears, the other step on his ankles. The African would plunge his face down into the muddy water, then raise it again and howl, and the charade would begin again, suffering, pleasure, suffering, pleasure. Roberts walked all the way to the end of the shelter where a storm had torn away part of the tin roof and stood there watching in rapt surprise, the scene in full sun as the ferry became small against the backdrop of the mangungu swamps.

These soldiers aren't official, Roberts thought. *They're different,* wearing green fatigue pants and black T-shirts, sleeves rolled up over huge muscled arms, short-cropped hair and gray berets and combat boots, guys that could have hopped right off a postcard of the Third World. There was an *espalier* that Roberts was trying to hide behind while he watched, trying to think what he should do; maybe he could help the poor stick-figure African down on the riverbank—but he saw that the soldiers were extremely large men, and maybe they weren't soldiers at all. Suddenly, one of them caught his eye, transfixing the space between them and locking onto Roberts like radar. Roberts wiped his forehead and pretended to look away, as if his previous enchantment with the scene had been accidental, perhaps his neck had been uncontrolled for an instant in time. Roberts thought that the stare of the soldier pierced through him, it was that intense. He heard another howl escape from the tiny African, the man's head smacked down against the shallow water, and then he was silent. Down by the ticket office there was laughter, some dogs barked and the bells of the Kinshasa ferry sounded again, this time far away and metallic. What really got to Roberts when he looked down at the riverbank again, at the man's tormentors in their black T-shirts and green fatigue pants, was the fact that both of them were wearing necklaces made from razor blades.

Now in the gray heat-glazed distance, across the brown placid surface of the river, Roberts could see the ferry churning the water as it backed in toward shore. It was an antiquated three-deck steamer, jammed to its rafters with passengers, animals, baggage, cargo. Roberts recalled that he had seen two or three black men jump overboard just as the ferry left the dock, scrawny men who pushed one leg over the side, then fell like rags into the water. For a moment he wondered about them, but then his attention was caught by two fish eagles screaming overhead, the birds swooning up and down looking for food. A few gulls scattered, diving once or twice to pick at bits of garbage and flotsam. He was fascinated by the eagles, their grace and danger, the wide ragged wingspread. These huge ugly graceful birds with thick bodies and feathers puffing, dove and swirled, wings tucked.

Down on the mud plage the two soldiers were picking over the tiny African like a bone. They had turned him up like a turtle on his back, the spindly legs splayed, the grizzled gray hair full of wet muck, his pants now down around his knees. A soldier yanked them off entirely and the man was naked. The soldiers laughed, the man crouched in shame and then scurried off through the mangungu grove, his naked buttocks flacid, scrawny legs pumping. Roberts turned his back to the espalier and sighed, still dazed from the heat even though he was standing in full shade. This was a situation he was going to have to get used to, he thought, authorized violence that was random as well, unfolding in unexpected places, the unfairness of it. A fountainhead of concentrated guilt washed over Roberts. In his head were all the confrontations he had already seen, shards of complex violence that would break off and enter his bloodstream, feel their way toward his heart—cabbies, goatherds, bus conductors, soldiers prowling sullenly, police in their dusty blue uniforms with rifles slung over their shoulders, everywhere in the Brazzaville scene. Every time Roberts saw such things his consciousness entered a new phase: Something turned down in his head, as if he might become inured to the malaise, and then he would see something like two soldiers with necklaces of razor blades beating a scrawny citizen.

Yeah, well, he thought, *there was plenty of good too:* the gentleness of the women in line at the market stalls, kids with their wide happy faces kicking soccer balls in dusty alleys, sounds of music in the morning and the huge frangipani blossoms floating through the evening breeze, smells of charcoal and river water, and the steep cobbled streets in the old ville where kids would polish your shoes and there were herds of goats wading through the doorways. This could get under your skin, too. This could go to your heart and imbed itself there, but just now all Roberts could think about was the old man running bare through the mangungu groves, his skinny cheeks lapping, spindly legs millwheeling wildly in the oozing mud of the beach.

Roberts focused his mind's eye back. He could see the ferry leaving the dock, its naked rusty hulk, and the white paint flaking off: *Kwenda Nzuri,* "go well" in Swahili, which Roberts had learned from a Swahili traveler's guide he had purchased in a shop along the Seine. Such a lovely name, but now there was irony in it: Go Well! From even this far away, Roberts watched the boat follow its diagonal course toward shore, far away, but he still thought he could hear the goats bawling, the few cattle on board lowing, and he thought he could see the animals on the below deck, moving, heads bobbing up and down. This phrase kept coming back to him: Go Well.

On the night flight from Paris, leaving just as the sun was setting down on Orly, Roberts had stared through the port-

hole at the pink-tentacled Montmartre, the rainy tarmac un-
raveling behind him at one hundred miles an hour; the
smoked-glass feeling he got looking at the airport complex
and all the traffic, this bit of Europe that smelled of cheese and
gasoline. He had flown all night, sleeping fitfully, his belly full
of beer and cheap *cordon bleu,* until they had landed in Libre-
ville, the capital of Gabon. He waited in a dusty, fly-ridden
airport lounge while the passengers went through customs
and the jet was refueled, delayed for hours in the heat and
green-insect droning, soldiers and customs officials arguing in
schoolboy French. Roberts had waited in the chafing heat,
buying a ham sandwich, exploring for a bit the single-story
airport. Outside, a line of rusty Renaults with the taxi drivers
asleep, drunk, somnolent with inactivity and sloth, the huge
palm trees and stunted brown hills in the distance. A long arc
of sunlight seemed to be everywhere; the buildings of the
airport brown with mold and mildew. And then when they
took off again, after hours of delays, Roberts couldn't relax or
begin to sleep. He felt nervous and confined as a captive tiger,
too distressed to give up his consciousness of Africa, and so he
studied his Swahili phrasebook, coming across the words
Kwenda Nzuri, "go well," something he thought he might
use.

And even after the big Air France jet had landed at Maya
Maya Airport, Brazzaville, where the police wore square kepi
hats and saluted with white gloves, and after riding across the
ville in a battered taxi, through the traffic and along the
disused expressway with its broken concrete, and lines of
women and children laboring up and down the shoulders, the
phrase kept coming back to Roberts, *kwenda nzuri,* until he
had checked into the Hotel National and tried to sleep the
better part of the day. Only then had he forgotten the phrase,
lying there on his soggy hotel bed in the damp chugging

atmosphere of partial air-conditioning, with the sour smell of beer and cigarette smoke on his clothes, the music hammering up from the bar on the mezzanine just below him. When he woke up in the late afternoon he was wearing prisoner's stripes of jalousied sunshine and he had forgotten the Swahili phrase entirely, and so he went downstairs to the lobby of the hotel for the first time. Wearing his khakis, white socks and the jungle boots he'd bought on Oxford Street, he now felt perfectly stupid and out of place because all the Africans were wearing suits and ties, two-piece pinstripe suits that looked French-tailored.

The lobby was full of potted palms and pouty boys who seemed to bear a film of grit that had seeped out of the threadbare green carpet. There was an African behind the desk and when he took the room key from Roberts he looked up with a soulful doe-eyed brilliance, saying, *"Kwenda nzuri,"* which made Roberts start for a moment. The clerk had a pale brown face and a tubercular chest, a circular crown of jet-black hair slicked down with cream. Roberts thanked the man, admiring his snappy red uniform and beret, and managed to engage the clerk somehow with his eyes, thinking that this was his first human contact on the continent. Roberts smiled and nodded, trying to catch himself in the act of speaking Swahili, but it didn't happen. He noticed the stupefying heat, the light pouring through the glass doors of the lobby, the green carpet that was tearing away from the walls. And he now realized the chain of coincidences linking him to Paris, the *Kwenda Nzuri* chugging away toward Kinshasa, the doe-eyed clerk, the Swahili phrase book on Roberts' knee while a fat Arab in the seat next to him snored and smelled of garlic.

Roberts was still waiting in the shade when he saw another swimmer near shore, some kid who must have jumped overboard and had been afraid to come onto the beach because of the soldiers, just dog-paddling, treading water, and now he was tired and didn't have any choice but to come in to where the soldiers could see him, fear on his face. The two soldiers waded out into shallow water and dragged the boy in, their expressions worn away to nothing but smooth masks, like Easter Island idols, and then one of the soldiers kneed the boy in the groin, then again just below the heart and the boy went down to his knees in the mud, trying to catch his breath while another soldier searched his pockets, cuffed him on one ear. Something forced Roberts up through himself, through his layers of fear and distance, until he could tell there wasn't a deafening silence anymore, but a tesselation of sounds, so many that he couldn't distinguish one from another, so many that each disappeared behind the other in a wall. He detected the tick of heat against the tin roof of the shelter, the drone of millions of swamp insects in the mangungu, the steady thump-thump of the diesel engine on the ferry far away, these sounds striking at him with a dreadful clarity.

Leaning over the buttress, looking down at the soldier kicking the boy, Roberts yelled, "Hey la, citizen, *citoyen,*" now pitifully aware of himself as one of the sounds, like an insect, *"qu'est que vous faites là-bas? Arretez. Vous le tuez!"* Roberts angled his body out of the shade and into the full sun so that he could be seen, no longer hidden under the tin roof, but fully visible to the soldiers who were both staring at him. One of the soldiers struck the boy a glancing blow as if in answer to Roberts' pleas for them to stop. *"Arretez,* okay?" Roberts said, calmly now, trying to defuse a probable situation, something he knew nothing about, but was deathly afraid of anyway. One of the soldiers hadn't bothered to look; he was busy taking some money from the boy. *Goddamn thieves,* Roberts thought to himself, luckily not knowing the

French word, or maybe just common thugs who would come up here and kick my ass, leave me naked to hobble off into the mangungu. The scene took on the elemental gestalt of an ancient stele, Roberts thinking these guys could be damn near anybody—private militia, special military police, secret police. Hell, they could be regular Army for that matter, come down to the waterfront for an afternoon of kicking native ass. One thing he knew: They weren't part of the Presidential Guard, Moroccans who were Israeli trained, guys too bad to wear razor blade necklaces, beat up old men and boys. These guys could be customs or rogues, but Roberts didn't know if customs officers carried automatic weapons.

The big soldier who had hold of one of the boy's legs let it drop and pointed his weapon at Roberts' head, cutting a rigorous smile.

"Hey," Roberts said calmly again, *"il est un garçon, comprenez-vous?"*

Both soldiers laughed roughly. Roberts had created a loop, only he was outside it now, trying to think of a way to communicate his feelings in worried French. He didn't know if he had helped the boy or not, or if these two soldiers would come up the mud plage, or even if the two guys spoke any French. One of them was growling at him in an African language that wasn't Swahili; it didn't have that East African pop and click. So, here was Roberts on the opposite side of a language from an African soldier who was wearing razor blades and pointing an automatic weapon.

"Il faut être diplomatique, n'est pas?" Roberts asked hopefully as the soldiers stared up at him. One of them made a slow circle with the barrel of his weapon, a signal to finish the boy, turn his pockets inside out. The boy rolled away, exhausted from his swim and his humiliation, elbows resting in the mud. Roberts could see his thin face, its reflection in the shallow

water, all the hurt ebbing away. *"Pardon, pardon,"* Roberts called out. *"Je suis un ètranger. Je ne comprende pas, non?"*

Roberts looked at the ferry, which was two miles away. The gulls were diving for garbage on the near shore, but Roberts couldn't see if any of the soldiers under the umbrella tree were awake. Roberts thought that if it was going to happen he was going to let it, let them drag him down to the mud, beat the shit out of him and take his money, which was about seventy-five French francs. He only hoped the other soldiers wouldn't get involved; he didn't like the thought of a crowd scene. As if moving could do any good, Roberts began to edge down toward the ticket office, away from the soldiers on the beach, and he was about ten paces down the shelter when he saw another African.

One arm cocked against the sun, the other palm down against the rim of a metal brace encasing his left leg, the man hobbled down the shelter, the brace banging against the wooden board sides. He was wearing a shabby black suit coat covered by red dust, shorts, a white shirt without a tie and a beaded Nigerian skullcap. For some reason Roberts thought about the ferry, the long brown stretch of water, and wondered what this guy was doing down here long after it had departed. The thought crossed his mind that this African was his contact, his man in Africa, the one his London people told him he would meet if he came down to the Kinshasa ferry every afternoon at four o'clock. But as Roberts assessed this man, the one stiff leg in an iron brace, muscular arms, round jovial face, the laugh wrinkles in the corners of his eyes, it didn't compute.

Roberts took a brief inventory of the terrain just in case. There was a vast mud plage stretching about six miles away to the Pool Malebo above Kinshasa, the shoreline thick with green mangungu groves, above that the treeless cliffs and grassy plateaus. Behind him was the empty parking lot, the dusty road back uphill toward Brazzaville—about three miles to the first African village—the petrol station, some cattle pens, vegetable gardens. Roberts thought he might run, or make a surprise grab for one of the weapons, but he realized he might be trading a beating for a gunshot wound. Growing so hot he was almost cold and numb, Roberts realized he had bargained everyday dullness for this danger. Hearing the excited voices of the soldiers brought back the meaning of life.

"Danger, monsieur?" Roberts heard the African say, the clank of his brace interrupting the words as the man leaned on the barrier, looking down at the soldiers. The soldiers themselves had backed away, just to get a better look at the European, and were still exchanging words in an African language. To his surprise, and before he could answer, Roberts heard the small African beside him conversing with the soldiers below, an exchange that he couldn't understand, though he did pick up the French words *laissez passer, citoyen,* words buried in a long African argument. Roberts fell away into all the available shade, part of his disguise now, so that he wouldn't compromise the deft flow of things, so that he couldn't see if the soldiers were still waving their weapons at him, so that his presence wouldn't give them a target for their anger, their glares, the present tense of their passion. In the corner of his eye, Roberts saw another swimmer emerge from the river, gasping for breath, staggering upright and walking toward the shelter of the groves. To his delight, Roberts knew this other victim had captured the attention of the soldiers, that they'd be going now with some other object.

"They go, monsieur," the African said.

With this sudden reprieve, Roberts felt his heart beating, pounding against his chest. The source of his life was flowing back, but it was causing him pain.

"Thank you," Roberts muttered, truly grateful. He didn't know what the African had said or if it had helped, but it struck him that these gestures had qualities, that they had made a difference.

"I am Adam Mbenga," the African announced. Roberts shook the man's hand, which was strong, despite the fragility of his crippled leg and his short height.

"Who are those guys?" Roberts asked.

"A part of the landscape," Mbenga said.

An unsteady wind kicked laterite dust down the hills, across the empty parking lot. It settled onto the surface of the river. In late afternoon, with the sun about to go behind the cliffs, the whole sky seemed filled with burning ash. The banana palms down by the ticket office were burdened with the wind, the film of ash on the fronds turning the green fronds gray. It was very hot, even though the two men were standing in shade and there was a breeze. Mbenga supported himself on one elbow, leaning against the concrete rail. "You must have drawn the attention of these soldiers, no?" Mbenga said.

Roberts licked his lips. He was thirsty. He hadn't had a drink of water since he left the hotel, and he'd been standing under the tin roof for about an hour. "They beat and robbed an old man. Then they did the same thing to a boy."

"Of course they did," Mbenga said. "It is what these men do."

"I presumed I was next."

"It is possible," Mbenga said.

"What did you tell them?"

Mbenga glanced back at the ticket office. "It is better we stay here for a time. The soldiers there are drinking now and playing cards. Pretty soon they will be tired, and they will go to sleep again. This is what they do as well. But still, it is better if we keep away for a time."

Roberts agreed. He didn't know why, but he felt that he was safe in this man's hands for now, and it didn't bother him at all. "All right," he said, smiling. He could hear the Kinshasa ferry blasting its horn, turning toward the Zaire dock. Without the sun the river looked absolutely red.

"But let me see," Mbenga said, returning to Roberts' question. "I told these soldiers that you were an important man. I told them that you were an important dignitary come to speak with the President about a matter of grave concern for him." When he smiled, Mbenga revealed a lack of incisors and one gold tooth in front. "I told them that you hadn't meant to meddle in their business and that if any harm came to you it would be serious business to the President." Mbenga pulled his leg up behind him and balanced on the railing with both elbows, now looking out over the river which had turned deep vermillion and blue. A white powder of insects drifted down through the breeze and the palms were clicking like mad. "Even so, I don't think this impressed them much. I think they gave you up for the citizen who swam out of the water just a few minutes ago."

"I tried some French," Roberts said. "Do they speak French? I didn't even know, but I didn't want them kicking that boy and I told them so."

"Those kind don't speak French," Mbenga said. "They speak Kikongo, some French phrases, but no English."

"So who are they?"

"Kikongo, private police, thugs, who knows? Those two people you saw swimming away from the ferry, they were *fradeurs.*"

Roberts shrugged in puzzlement.

Mbenga said, "They are smugglers, monsieur. Those swimmers you saw in the river were trying to take something over to the Zaire side of the border. Maybe bars of soap, some French francs they earned here shining shoes, or some toothpaste. When the customs men find them out on the ferry, the ones who can get away fling themselves overboard and swim to shore. That way they can save themselves for another day, try to sneak back on board the ferry again tomorrow where the game is played all over again. Our Kikongo come down every afternoon and wait on the shore for these fradeurs and then they rob them of all they have. It is impossible to say who they work for, but it is perhaps that they are part of the Army, men who aren't paid, or who need money to support their habits." Mbenga shrugged as if to emphasize the ordinariness of the situation, its implacability and inevitability. These Kikongo were as much a part of the landscape as the red laterite ash suspended in a film over the river, the screaming insects in the mangungu swamps, the dark smell of charcoal fires at night. "The irony is," Mbenga continued, "that these Kikongo smuggle the same francs, soap or toothpaste into Zaire themselves when they can. I wanted to tell you that there wasn't much danger to the smugglers, because the Kikongo don't want to kill them. They want these smugglers to come back and play the game again, next week maybe, next month."

"Still, I want to thank you," Roberts said seriously. "I think I was about to become part of the landscape, too."

"Who knows?" Mbenga replied.

"You speak excellent English," Roberts said. He was still thinking this small African might be his contact.

Mbenga paused, noncommittal. "For some years I was a clerk in the office of an English oil company in Kinshasa.

Because of my education, I helped with the correspondence."
Again he shrugged, this time dropping his upper lip. "But
now you see I am officially dead."

"Officially dead?" Roberts said.

"Mort civil, actually. Banished."

"I'm sorry," Roberts said stupidly.

"It is nothing," Mbenga said cheerfully. "In fact, after
Mobutu, it is quite commonplace. One day you are a citizen
of the country of Zaire, and the next day you are not. You
become something else, a man without a country, without
civil rights and without a home. It is nothing to take too
seriously."

Mbenga was wiping red dust from his eyes while Roberts
studied him, trying to guess the man's age, which wasn't easy
because he seemed both young and old. He had a few grizzled
gray hairs behind the ears, but a smooth unlined face, and the
brace, which was unplaceable in time. Mbenga looked over
his shoulder at the soldiers who were spread out under the
umbrella tree, some of them asleep, others still playing cards.

The fish eagles were screaming and Roberts wanted it to
happen right now. He thought the moment had come. The
fine red ash was sifting down, the soldiers were playing
drunken games, the simmering green mangungu was rasping
in the wind, and now this guy Adam Mbenga would an-
nounce that he was Roberts' African contact. Roberts wanted
it to be, even though the guy was wearing a brace on his left
leg, even though he was officially dead. After a single day in
his new environment, Roberts was ready for reality to reveal
itself, for the new structures to pop into being and force a
major transition. Roberts wanted to be done with the surface
and get to the bones underneath, the skeleton of Africa, not
just the postcard image. This impatience was his worst trait,
a character flaw that made him miss the slower events.

"How did you happen to be on the quay?" Roberts asked self-consciously, aware of his complicity. "I'm glad you were here, of course."

"My sister," Mbenga said. "She visits me here in Brazza-ville. She brings me clothes she has made. I give her soap and toothpaste and toilet paper, things that aren't available in Zaire. I give her shreds of material for her sewing machine. And so when she returns to Zaire, I have some new clothes, and she has some soap."

Mbenga smiled gently, and gestured across the river as if to leave Roberts with some impression of the country. Now that the Kikongo thugs had gone, Roberts could see some skinny children playing in the water at the edge of the plage, and their voices percolated up at him. They were throwing rocks at some gulls, ripples in the surface of the water radiat-ing out, the gulls crying, swinging up into the dusty evening air.

"And did you see your sister?"

"Yes, she is come here."

"My first trip to Africa," Roberts said, hoping to keep the conversation alive.

"I see," Mbenga said.

"Just here on business," Roberts added, nearly interrupting the African. Now Roberts was sure of his disappointment. "I have to go back to my hotel now. Can I give you a taxi ride?"

"I have a bicycle here," Mbenga said, probably noticing the surprise on Roberts' face. "It belongs to my uncle but he let me ride it. My sister has gone on in a taxi. I'm afraid we can afford only one fare." Roberts was following the African slowly down the shelter, staying slightly behind the man and on his right shoulder.

Roberts was surprised, but when they got to the ticket office the soldiers didn't pay them any attention. He didn't know if they were drunk on palm wine, or stoned on the Zaire bangi, but they looked like rags scattered willy-nilly. Mbenga offered his hand, and the two men shook hands politely. Then Roberts watched the other clamber laboriously onto his fragile English bike and pedal uphill along the dusty roadway toward the old ville. He stood there until the African disappeared around a corner of one of the barren hills, and then he waited for a taxi. When no taxi came he had to walk about two kilometers to a bunker petrol stop before he found one finally, and even then he had to wait about fifteen minutes. When he got back to his hotel in Brazzaville, he was very tired, soaked through with sweat and caked by dust. It also turned out that there was no running water in the shower, so he had to dab himself with towels dampened from the sink. He changed into clean underwear and white cotton socks.

He was not hungry and it was too early to sleep, even though the night was pitch black. He recognized his unpreparedness for night's sudden drop, its tropical depth, the lack of warning or any compromise between day and night, light and dark. One second there is brilliant sunshine, and the next there is a completely sullen blackness without shadow. Roberts stood at his hotel window, trying to estimate the numerous powers he was experiencing: the steady downpour of dead insects, the implicit beat of the music in the city streets and far away, the sulky charcoal smell of smoke from cooking fires. He was finally forced back inside himself by the dark and his inability to see. His bed smelled of damp pissed beer and roaches were eating the peeling wallpaper.

2

ONLY A SUNRISE FROM LONDON, and already Roberts felt as if he had been transported to another planet. Clocks turned clockwise, smoke rose skyward, and his sweat fell to earth; everything was in its place except his consciousness. Just the week before he had been living peacefully, almost somnolently, in a basement flat along the Kensington Road in London, a few short steps from the Portobello, trying to scrounge a few odd jobs to keep himself busy and his spirits elevated. He would drift upstairs to have dinners in the late, long spring evenings when the sun sifted through the chestnuts and it stayed light until nearly nine o'clock, and you could hear the sounds of children playing in the common across the road. He was trying to love Amanda as best he could, but he felt ensconced in an atmosphere of permanent self-delusion, doubt mixed with his demeanor of a permanent expatriate. Often, during those weeks of early spring, and even later when the unmistakable stamp of summer had descended on London, and the chestnuts were beginning to bloom, and the streetlights glowed against the permanent evening light, he would escape the city to wander by himself in Wales, through the high mountain passes and vales. Or he would fish in Hampshire, or comb the chalk countryside of the Downs

· · · · · · · · · ·

21

above Brighton, keeping on the lookout for red foxes. Isolated and comfortable with himself, he would return to London much refreshed, and make love to Amanda in that cool, detached manner they had achieved with their mutual embarrassment and passion, lying together for hours in the back of her row house, in a room with flowered wallpaper from which they could see all the old ladies of the neighborhood tending their roses. It was the ballyhooed English summer, with periods of dull gray and listless drizzle followed by low scudding clouds, then puffy white ones, and then clearing azure skies with nervous thunder rolling away.

The man named Thomas Slade came to see Roberts late one afternoon, just after six, when Roberts was sitting in the patch of garden in front of his flat. An evening wind had bulked in the chestnuts across Kensington Road, and there were black cabs stalking down the streets. The surface of the city seemed silent, as if for a single moment every living thing was frozen to its spot, and the only sounds were natural ones: the wind leaking through the branches of the trees, church bells tolling. Roberts was thinking about drinking a cider, just one draught before an early supper, but he watched Slade get out of his taxi, a Cratchett character in a shiny pinstripe suit, stooped because of his extreme height. He walked to Amanda's door and stiffly rang the bell. Amanda answered and spoke to him, and then Slade walked down the garden steps about six feet to where Roberts, dressed in jeans and short-sleeve shirt, was lounging in a rattan chair. Roberts slipped his feet into a pair of Indian moccasins while Slade took off his suit jacket and draped it over his arm.

"Slade," the man said diffidently in a Yorkshire accent. Before Roberts could respond the man put out his hand to shake. "Mrs. Trench directed me here, hope you don't mind." Roberts recognized this kind of formal English friendliness. It made you want to cut your throat in deference.

"No bother," Roberts replied, recognizing that he was on the defensive for reasons he didn't understand. Perhaps as an American, he was inured to easy amiability, something the English found vaguely embarrassing. "I was just sitting out enjoying the evening."

Slade paced one step back, as if busy reformulating his approach. There was a silence and Roberts tried to place this guy, the slightly rumpled blue suit that looked like Fleet Street, the worn shoes that needed new soles and a coat of polish, the narrow-set yellow eyes and pointy nose. Slade offered Roberts an Oval, lit one himself. "Where I come from we call this porch-sitting," Roberts sighed. "It's considered an honorable devotion."

"No doubt," Slade said.

The sky had become furry with indistinct clouds. There was a promise of weather. Roberts had been hoping for a storm with lashing rain, lightning.

"What can I do for you?" Roberts asked. In the back of his mind Roberts wondered if this were a policeman, though Slade didn't have the straightforwardness. For months now, Roberts had been working without a permit, illegally, and he could see himself detained and deported. And he had no money for a lawyer. "If you don't mind talking out here," Roberts added for no reason.

"I'm with Lloyd's," Slade said.

"Of London," Roberts added.

"Right then," Slade said. "Are you engaged?"

"If you mean am I working, the answer is no." Roberts excused himself, went into his basement and came back with two ciders. Slade calmly refused the drink. He did produce a business card and handed it to Roberts. Some children had commenced a football game in the park and were screaming happily.

"Then let me come to the point," Slade said.

Roberts shrugged and sat down in his rattan chair. An air of expectancy had enveloped the men, Slade standing with one shoe on the stone step above Roberts. The two men hardly looked at each other. Something would have to slide into place, like a Chinese puzzle box, for another something to take its place. Roberts was certain there were structures to this event he wouldn't comprehend right away.

"By all means," Roberts said, mimicking the English phrase.

Roberts agreed that he had heard of Lloyd's of London, of course, who hadn't? Slade referred Roberts to the business card again, and the twenty on-staff years it represented. The man smoked his Oval down to the filter and tossed it away into the garden border of daisies. He went on and on about his years with the company.

Roberts regretted this, the time wasted here on the garden steps with an insurance man. "I thought I might go up to Notting Hill and see a movie," Roberts lied, hoping he might get rid of the guy. Roberts was so near to being broke, the promise of a small sum of money made no difference to him. He was as near to being free as he had ever been in his life.

"Please, my company," Slade said, again repeating the word *Lloyd's,* "carried a very substantial policy on one of the largest copper companies in Europe. At present we are in danger of paying a rather sizable claim. Naturally, we should like to avoid that if at all possible."

"I don't blame you," Roberts said.

"Then you've done insurance work before."

"Quite a lot actually."

Slade grinned, probably thinking he had made an ally. "I'm afraid the problem we have is rather unusual. You might even call it unique. And it is rather urgent."

Roberts leaned forward in his chair and drained the cider. He was hoping that Slade would sit down on one of the steps, do something to achieve some familiarity, anything to promote confidence, a sense of trust. But the man remained standing up, looking over Roberts' shoulder.

"Let me explain something so there isn't any misunderstanding," Roberts said. "I'm an American and I have no work permit. I'm an experienced investigator, but right now, every quid I earn in Great Britain is an illegal one. If that's a problem, then you might as well find someone else."

Slade nudged himself forward onto the balls of his feet, as if a shift in mood had unbalanced him. "Well, I don't believe that is a problem."

"For you, maybe not. But for me, who knows? I don't like getting off on the wrong foot with anyone."

Slade nodded vaguely. "If you were engaged, your work would be perfectly legal, I assure you. This task would not take place within the boundaries of the United Kingdom, and you would not be paid in pounds, nor even to an account in this country. It would involve some travel."

"What kind of work are we talking about?"

"I'm not at liberty to say."

"How did you come to find me?" Roberts asked.

"You are known around Lincoln's Inn."

"And you'd just as soon have a foreigner do the work."

"I'm not at liberty to say."

"What kind of pay are we talking about?"

"I'm not at liberty to say," Slade insisted.

"In what country?"

"I'm not at liberty to say."

"Mr. Slade," Roberts said, "I'm very interested in doing honest work for honest pay. But I don't have the slightest idea what the hell you're talking about, or what all this secrecy is supposed to mean. I'm a direct sort of person."

Right then Roberts wanted to beg off, maybe just to prove that he could say no to something like Lloyd's of London as a kind of moral guffaw. He thought it would be nice to sit in the garden and listen to the sparrows sing, while the sun went down through the chestnuts across the street. He was looking forward to dinner with Amanda, the Satyajit Ray film at the Odeon up the hill, five or six whiskeys then a cold chicken sandwich at midnight. Slade preempted this peace by putting on his suit jacket and lighting another cigarette.

"Speaking directly," Slade said curtly, "one of our managing directors is waiting at a branch office in Mayfair. If you wish to speak with him, he will tell you all the pertinent details." Slade added that he would hire a cab and see to it that Roberts returned from the appointment. "We can pay you for your time, of course," he added as a challenge.

Roberts didn't understand the hurry, but he shrugged and went inside his flat and changed into some wool pants and a blue dress shirt. He telephoned Amanda upstairs and told her to wait his supper, or to eat without him if she got hungry, that he wanted to see her later if he could. He went back out and locked his door, noticing that a cab was waiting at the curb, probably meaning that Slade had told the driver to wait around the corner. Roberts felt a flush of anger at this audacity, the certainty that he could be relied upon to react, but then he realized he had no ground for his anger.

Roberts piled in beside Slade and they rode silently up to Notting Hill, past Hyde Park and the Mall. The cabbie pulled to a stop just beyond Grosvenor Place, a block of expensive white flats with Georgian fronts, black iron fences and well-tended window boxes where red geraniums were like splotches of blood. This was where money and privilege whispered through the cobbled streets, glanced off the curved Queen Anne windows, and reflected back for a fleeting instant, just long enough for someone sharp-eyed to catch a glimpse. Slade paid the cabbie and ushered Roberts up some stairs to the parlor of one of the flats. The polished wood walls were like mirrors and the carpets deep and plush. Down at the end of the hall, someone with silver hair and wing collars was waiting. Slade disappeared down a hallway.

Simon Reynolds motioned Roberts into a room that was entirely hushed, except for two parakeets chirping in a cage. There was frost-beige wallpaper, emerald-green carpeting and bay windows that sliced onto a view of the Palace Gardens in the late summer sunshine, entirely empty. Roberts noticed the rows of leather-bound books on the walls, the mahogany and brass fixtures, a ficus tree in a pot. Roberts accepted a cut-glass full of dry sherry. He tasted it, finding the hint of sea salt that told him it was Manzanilla.

"Please accept my thanks for coming," Reynolds told Roberts, as he sat down in his chair. The silence of expensive London threatened a deep, narcotic sleep. The sidewalks outside were vacant and there was none of the hubbub of the suburbs: the buses chugging up and down, newspaper vendors, underground diesel engines.

"No problem," Roberts said stupidly.

"Slade will see you home later."

"I appreciate that."

"I hope this doesn't disrupt your evening," Reynolds said.

"Could we get down to business?"

Reynolds laughed. "You Americans are abrupt." He produced a manila folder from his teak desk and played with its contents, pretending to read from them. Roberts was embarrassed to find that he had drained his sherry in one gulp.

"I'm a managing director for Lloyd's," Reynolds said, peering from the top lens of his bifocals. "Not on the Board of Directors, mind you, but one of ten district managers for this area. You can accept my word that I have full authority to bind the company to a contract for your services. My word will be kept."

"I understand."

Reynolds seemed to relax. The parakeets were making a merry racket in one corner of the room. "Are you familiar with a company called EuroCopper?"

"Not really," Roberts replied.

"Well, this is a very old and valuable concern. EuroCopper is the largest mining company in England. It got its start as a consortium of English and Belgian interests during the period of the Congo Free State."

"King Leopold's fiefdom."

"If you wish," Reynolds said, annoyed. "The company was moribund for some time after the Free State became a colony of Belgium, but was reorganized and revitalized after World War Two. For many years, the company was involved in mining and smelting copper in the southern province of Katanga and transhipping the ore to Stanleyville in the north. From there the raw ore would be shipped down the Congo River to Kinshasa, and from there to Europe and Asia. During the 1950s, EuroCopper also became involved with mining and smelting in Canada. Perhaps this jogs your memory, does it?"

"Slade told me nothing, but I've some idea of what you're talking about."

"The markets are worldwide. The insurance premiums paid by a company like EuroCopper are enormous."

"And the coverages are large as well. Any loss might be huge."

"Yes, quite right," Reynolds said.

"Do you know that I'm an American on a tourist visa?"

"We are aware of that."

"Slade told me this work involved foreign countries."

"And indeed it does," Reynolds said. "But we're getting slightly ahead of ourselves. For now I must ask that everything I tell you here today be held in strictest confidence. If word of what I say here were to get to the newspapers, I fear that loss of life might result."

"You won't have to worry about me," Roberts promised. "I don't have anyone to tell." This wasn't quite true, but both men let it pass. Reynolds poured some more sherry, though he had hardly touched his. Roberts took a gentle sip.

"Then I can count on you . . . good," Reynolds said. Roberts thought he detected a compliant condescension, something escaping the man like an aura. "It would be a terrible shame to breach the company's faith."

"You don't have to worry, Mr. Reynolds," Roberts said.

"Well then," Reynolds continued, "EuroCopper has many company sites throughout what is now the country of Zaire. After independence in the early 1960s, many of the local names changed. The Belgian Congo became Zaire." Reynolds raised an aristocratic eyebrow as if displeased by the thought. "At present there are perhaps fifteen mines throughout the southern part of the country where copper is dug from huge pits. It is transhipped to Kisangani, which used to be called Stanleyville. The ore is tugged down the Congo River. Some of it is smelted in Kinshasa, some is taken directly to South Africa and elsewhere. But for now, the most important town on this route is Kisangani, perhaps fifteen hundred miles upriver from the capital, Kinshasa."

Roberts said he'd heard about the cities, and took another polite sip of sherry while Reynolds continued to lecture. The man spoke in a clipped old-boy voice, occasionally tugging at his bow tie, running one hand through his thick silver hair.

"You probably know that after independence Zaire was plunged into virtual anarchy. There was no stable political element in the country, and Mobutu emerged as a strong man. I'm afraid the economic life of the country stagnated, and then fell into chaos itself. In the early to mid-'70s, there was one bright spot and that bright spot was copper. The price rose to record levels and there was an influx of Europeans to work with EuroCopper. There have always been Belgians and French in Zaire, but now many more left Europe to work there."

Roberts closed his eyes, and when he opened them again he could see pigeons rising in the towers of Belgravia. There was a thin dreamy white light sifting through the empty streets and the parakeets in their cage had quieted. It was a moment full of tension, with the echoes of traffic rising far away.

"What is your trouble, Mr. Reynolds?" Roberts asked.

"There's been a kidnapping," Reynolds said dully, running a wet finger over his upper lip. For the first time he looked directly at Roberts and the two men stared at one another. The light and silence in the room vectored suddenly. "EuroCopper runs a clinic for sick workers at the Kisangani site. One of the doctors, or I should say the only doctor, at the clinic was taken off last week. I'm afraid she hasn't been heard from since and there is a bit of bother about it."

"She. . . " Roberts said.

"Yes, she. A woman."

For a moment Roberts was stunned.

"Why me?" he asked. "Slade didn't say."

"Your last work at Lincoln's Inn was not without notice. The first requirement of this job is that it be handled without publicity. That is an absolute *must*. If there is any publicity connected with this operation, it could be fatal. Despite our best efforts at intelligence gathering, and despite help from the Foreign Office, we've had no good luck identifying the parties with whom we're dealing."

"Terrorists?"

"I don't know."

"You intend to pay a ransom?"

"In a reasonable amount."

"And the ransom demand? How large is that?"

"Somewhat over the policy limit." Reynolds finally sipped some of his sherry. "Still, it is a rather large amount we are prepared to offer the kidnappers."

Roberts drained his drink. "Let's see if I understand this well enough. You hold a substantial policy of kidnapping insurance on behalf of the company, in the name of this doctor."

"All of the major employees," Reynolds said, now annoyed, looking out the bay window.

"You hope to ransom the victim, for a sum less than you'd have to pay out if she were killed."

"Well, of course. Nothing wrong with that."

"Nothing wrong," Roberts agreed. "How much larger is the life insurance policy than the ransom benefits. Ten times? Twenty?"

"Substantial," Reynolds said.

"So, we'd rather save this woman's life than pay a death benefit for the family and the company."

Reynolds feigned a nod.

"And you'd like to bargain with the kidnappers. Offer them less than the ransom demand by telling them that you've got policy limits. Give them the old bum's rush."

"I'm afraid I don't understand," Reynolds protested.

"It doesn't matter." Roberts had a feeling that everybody understood perfectly well. These guys wanted an obscure American to try to deliver a ransom and free the doctor in Zaire. If he were killed or the ransom went undelivered, then no English daily like the *Mail* or the *Observer* would scream its headlines all over London, there would be no missing Englishman and no hell to pay. What Reynolds wanted was a stalking horse, some stooge to take all the risks. "I guess you have your reasons for wanting to keep this thing quiet."

"Any publicity could stir up a wave of kidnappings of Europeans down there. EuroCopper has many employees."

"And the insurance company could pay many ransoms."

"Of course. This is a business."

Roberts relaxed. He was being too hard on Reynolds. The man had a job to do. "All right Mr. Reynolds, say I'm interested. Say I might be willing to handle this thing for you. But the price has to be right, and you have to be able to meet my terms."

"We can certainly discuss this. I'd like to formulate our arrangement tonight. Time is of the essence."

"Tell me who did the kidnapping? Do you know?"

"BaLese tribesmen, we think. They're a poor northern tribe who've been in a state of unrest for some time."

"And these people, do they have political motives? Are they fanatical, terrorists. . . . Do they have a history of violence?"

"I know very little at this point," Reynolds said slowly. "The kidnapping occurred just last week. Our main office has learned that the group is probably being exploited by the central government. The doctor is being held somewhere in the area of Kisangani. The single ransom note was delivered simultaneously to the consulate in Kinshasa and the company offices there, saying only that there had been a kidnapping and that the doctor was being held for payment of ransom. It stated that if the ransom was not delivered, she would be killed. Although I don't have any information on the political orientation of this group, or if they even have a political orientation, it is safe to assume they're very dangerous."

"I agree," Roberts said. "Did the note make other demands?"

"Generally, yes. This group demanded that a single Westerner bear the ransom to Kisangani, that he stay at the New Stanley Hotel and there would be further contact at that point. I'm afraid it's all rather vague, except that a time limit of two weeks was placed upon the transaction. After that time, they vowed to kill the doctor."

"So, you want me to go to Kisangani and check into the New Stanley Hotel and wait for these people to contact me?"

"I'm afraid so. The town of Kisangani is already in some turmoil. As a Westerner, you'd be very easy to single out and contact."

"But you know nothing of the trustworthiness of this group?"

"Absolutely nothing, I'm afraid."

"And this doctor, who is she?"

"Now Mr. Roberts," Reynolds said, with an air of quiet rectitude, as if he were sharing a secret, "the fate of this one doctor in the whole scheme of African political life and economic destiny is relatively unimportant. But assume Euro-Copper allows a single kidnapping to dispel the notion that the company can continue to operate in absolute safety, and then you can see that they may have a wave of kidnappings on their hands. It could become another Brazil during the reign of the Generals, another modern Beirut. This is the puzzle of modern terrorism. Our values tell us that the individual is the highest good, while the forces of history tell us that the individual is utterly without significance."

"But the name of the doctor," Roberts insisted. In the back of his mind, something wasn't computing for him. The fact that the kidnapping had not received worldwide news coverage was an item. If the kidnapping were strictly political, then the group responsible would have broadcast the news to every bureau in Europe and Africa. "I think we're dealing with a crime here, not a political act."

"Very well," Reynolds agreed, "but this must remain absolutely confidential." Roberts agreed. "This doctor's name is Elyse Revelle. She's Belgian and she's been in Doctors Without Borders for some time. Ten years ago, when the AIDS epidemic first became known worldwide, she left to take a permanent job with EuroCopper. She's been working in the forests around Kisangani, and now with the border people in Rwanda and Burundi, even Uganda. I'm afraid she's rather expanded the initial operation envisioned by the company. They were interested in treating company employees and their families. Now the clinic is a regional medical center of sorts, costing the company a lot in resources I think they'd rather use elsewhere."

"How long has she been at the clinic?"

"Going on ten years now."

"May I see the ransom note?"

"It's a dispatch really," Reynolds said, handing Roberts a Xerox copy of a note written in poor French on tablet paper. Roberts could read enough French to realize the group was asking ninety thousand English pounds for the release of the doctor.

"Suppose I do this," Roberts said, putting the copy in his lap, "how do I get the money inside Zaire?"

"You'll have to be somewhat inventive on this. I can assure you a letter of credit will be deposited with the central bank in Brazzaville, capital of the Republic of the Congo. You would be authorized to withdraw the funds in cash upon presentation of the proper identification. I'm sending Slade on to help iron out the details of getting the cash into Kinshasa itself, although this is very tricky indeed. The country is riddled with corruption and theft. But if you work closely with Slade, and if you are willing to suspend your disbelief about things African, then we'll find a way to get you and the funds to Kisangani."

"Wire transfers won't work?"

"I'm afraid every minister and junior minister in the whole country would have his hand in the till."

"It will be a dangerous trip."

"Of course," Reynolds agreed.

"And you'd allow me absolute control of the operation?"

"You'll consult with Slade."

"And what about my fee?"

"Ten thousand pounds."

"Paid when?"

"Paid half now, half when you return. Into your international account of course. What you do with the tax authorities is up to you entirely." Reynolds grinned for the first time, as if they had just shared an old-boy joke.

"A lot can go wrong," Roberts said. "The people we're dealing with are probably volatile." Roberts leaned over the desk, careful not to disturb the organization of papers and family pictures. "And what are the insurable limits for the ransom?"

"You're very clever," Reynolds said. "Seventy-five thousand. It's all the policy allows."

"You want me to go there fifteen thousand pounds short of their demands? That's asking a lot."

"I'll see what can be arranged." Reynolds met Roberts halfway across the desk. "But you have to understand. If I myself were being held captive, I doubt the company would break the policy limits. You can see the dangerous precedent that it would set."

"EuroCopper can make up the difference."

"Perhaps, yes."

"Do we have any way of contacting these people prior to my arrival? Just to let them know that their demands are going to be met, so they won't harm the doctor. Maybe so they would relax a little bit. We don't want any trouble, do we?"

"I can look into it. But I doubt it seriously."

The summer twilight was now frosted with a luminous glow. The streets had achieved a state of suspended transcendence, holding the trimmed sycamores in a light breeze. Roberts took a deep breath, lost in his own calculations. He was on the verge of something unknowable.

"First of all," Roberts said, "my fee will be twenty thousand pounds, payable to my American account in advance. This isn't refundable, and I want that in writing. I want my cash expenses taken care of on a *per diem* basis."

"Anything else?" Reynolds remarked dryly.

"You've probably had me investigated, but just so you'll know, I'm going to explain myself to you. I'm a combat veteran and I know explosives and weapons inside out. I speak schoolboy French and some German, but no Swahili. I've never been to Africa. I'll need a few days, maybe more, to study the doctor and her background. I want maps of the countryside surrounding Kisangani and all the photographs you can find from the company of the clinic, the compound and its staff. I want to prepare a dossier on the political situation in Zaire, and in Kisangani in general, along with names and histories of the political officials and the police. I want to spend some time with experts at the University who know the area, and I want deep background on Zaire. I want carte blanche to create any plan I wish, to my own devising, on how to get the money into Kisangani, how to pay the ransom, and how to achieve the release of the doctor."

Reynolds folded his hands into a chapel, then smiled benignly. "Agreed," he remarked wearily, with a tone of resignation, as if he was doing Roberts a favor. "I also think you'll need a briefing on the health situation upriver. We don't want you falling ill, do we?"

The question had a barbed fishhook tone. "No, we don't, do we?" For some reason Roberts had taken a dislike to Slade, perhaps his crouched appearance, the pinstripe suit dotted with cigarette ash. If so, then it was rubbing off on Reynolds too. "Do you have a photograph of the doctor?"

"You'll have one," Reynolds said. "I'm sure it can be arranged."

"When can the ransom money be transferred to Brazzaville."

"In the next twenty-four hours."

"Do, please. And make it the ninety we spoke about."

"We'll do our best, of course."

"Just so we understand one another," Roberts said, nearly whispering. "I know what's happening here. I know why you want me for the job, and not an Englishman. If something goes wrong and things get messy, there won't be much about it in the local press. I'm an American, no wife, no kids.

If I'm erased, not a single light goes out in the universe. But in return for this, I want your absolute support in money and information, and I don't want any interference from you or Slade in how I do my job, or what arrangements I make."

"I understand perfectly," Reynolds said, clearly annoyed. "But there is something you should understand. The price of copper in the last five years has dropped through the floor. There are no markets even if there were a profit in it. I have information that the clinic facility in Zaire was ordered closed two years ago, as part of EuroCopper plans to abandon all their operations in Katanga, including closing down the transhipment point in Kisangani. The doctor has prevailed for two years against all odds to persuade the directors to fund her clinic. By all rights, she should be out of there and the clinic should be closed. So you see, these fine moral distinctions you're making here about policy limits and ransom payments are a bit two-edged." Reynolds swiveled around to face the window again.

"Where's my contact in Kinshasa going to be?"

"You wait on the Brazzaville side at the ferry dock. The company in Kisangani is sending a man down from the transhipment site. I don't know who it is yet. If you go to the dock every day at four o'clock, the man will contact you."

Roberts stood and the two men shook hands perfunctorily.

Slade appeared and escorted Roberts out to the front stoop where he could see a cab waiting.

Slade threw down a lit cigarette. "It's all arranged then, is it?"

"You'll help me with my expense money, plane tickets, immigration problems and shots?"

"Absolutely."

Roberts had to smile. "Reynolds is really something," he

said. "He agreed to twenty thousand pounds as a fee. I was ready to take fifteen."

"He was ready to pay twenty-five," Slade said.

Roberts declined the cab and walked four or five miles back to Notting Hill Gate, through Hyde Park and along the Serpentine where children were sailing boats and the geese were being fed by pensioners. He didn't want to think too much right then. He just wanted to walk under that pale summer curtain of light.

3

FOR A SINGLE INSTANT THAT first morning in Africa, Roberts imagined himself back in London. But then he was aware of the sound of wings and a sensation of aloneness swept over him, a backdrop to a ruffled hum arrowing across the sky outside. He realized he was really in Africa; he could see a flight of marabou storks in a curved formation going away over the tin roofs of the old ville, their shaggy bodies totemic and unnerving. The storks were flying in the direction of the river, and when Roberts finally came fully awake he recognized the outline of Brazzaville, the heat lying like a blanket over the city, the red dirt streets, the sheltering palms and the high hazy clouds in spatulate forms over the barren hills beyond.

Lying there in his soggy bed, he was thirsty and his neck hurt him terribly, the pains surging down into his spine. He remembered that he had fallen asleep in the woven rattan chair, sitting next to the window where he had spent the evening watching this strange city, like a mirror against his face, wondering what he would do next. He hadn't wanted to go to bed, partly because of the alien feelings welling up inside him, and partly because of the roar of the insects and the constant pounding of music; it came from everywhere all at once, as if the city were bleeding music. He was kept awake also by the overwhelming problem of finding a weapon here in Africa, where weapons were treasured, feared and hunted, like elephants. This African world, Roberts knew, was screwed down tight by Big Men and their security forces, men like those he had seen down on the mud plage by the river, men with necklaces of razor blades. Even so, Roberts knew that he wasn't thinking straight, that his mind had been dulled by the long flight across two continents, by the desultory wait along the quay for his contact who never arrived.

Whatever the reason, as if it mattered, Roberts had remained sitting in the chair beside the window while insects fell through an unutterably black night, powdering the streets with a fog of their dead bodies. When he awoke, just then, there had been marabou storks flying in formation just beyond his reach, as if a dream had transformed his sleep, and now Roberts felt forlorn and dislocated, terribly alone, like a lost glove. *And just at that moment* between being fully awake and still asleep, Roberts suffered a *déjà vu* and he knew how he was going to get a weapon, here in this strange country of contradicting evil and great beauty. He walked in his undershorts across to the window, next to which he'd slept most of the night, and looked down on the square in front of the Hotel National, the plaza ringed by dusty banana trees and a few old Fords and Lincolns, and he perfected his insight. He knew how he was going to get a gun.

Back in London, the *plastique* had been easy, no problem. In London Roberts had met all kinds of people: Irish gun runners, gamblers, pimps, prostitutes, petty thieves. It was run-of-the-mill stuff, life on the street. He remembered one Pakistani who moved guns to the Mujahadeen, Dover to Geneva to Peshawar, then up the hills across the Afghan border. There was money in that sort of thing. For a few hundred pounds, the Pakistani put him onto the plastique, probably destined for the Irish Republican Army, and that's what started Roberts on his career collecting plastic explosives, detonators, timing devices and transceivers. One day Roberts drove to Swansea and picked up the plastique, a single kilo for six hundred English pounds, which was certainly outrageous, but it wasn't Roberts' money. Besides, he didn't need more than a single kilo, which was enough to blow the shit out of a warehouse, much more than he thought he'd need.

When Roberts got back from Swansea, he bought some packages of saltwater taffy and unwrapped it by carefully steaming open the packets. He flattened the plastique into two bars, then varnished it and after a few hours used model airplane paint to make nice red and white swirls on the gunmetal-gray explosive. Then he rewrapped the plastique in the saltwater taffy packets and steamed the packets closed again, putting them in his overnight bag. He knew he would fly to Paris, and then to Maya Maya Airport in Brazzaville. He figured he was about two customs searches away; most of the time the Africans didn't care a damn what you brought in as long as it wasn't guns. It was only going out that they gave you big trouble, but by then Roberts thought he'd be clean. And that was when the part about the guns started really worrying him, knowing he couldn't try to smuggle a weapon into Africa, and especially onto the plane bound for Brazzaville. His mind started working overtime on the problem of guns and ammunition.

The same Irishman who sold him the plastique in Swansea sold him a half-dozen electronic detonators, about the size of American nickels, the kind detonated by remote control with a radio transceiver. Roberts broke down his electric shaver and put a few of the detonators inside the works, then put the rest in his pocket along with his spare change. They looked like slugs anyway, and he didn't want to lose the detonators if he lost his shaver. About the same time, Roberts thought he might need a good timing device, so he bought a chess clock on Oxford Street, one of the most expensive and accurate clocks made, along with some spare batteries. There was no doubt he could get the clock into France and Africa, and into the Congo too for that matter, and if he needed wire when he got there, he thought he could surely get that in Kinshasa. Later, he bought a book about African birdlife, some good 35X German binoculars with a wide-angle attachment, and made Reynolds supply him with ten gold sovereigns, which he sewed into the lining of his canvas safari belt. He thought it might happen that he would lose everything—plastique, detonators, wire, clock—and if that happened he wanted something to fall back on. If he lost his belt, then it would be too bad, wouldn't it?

He got the maps from London University. He had hoped to find waterproof maps, but couldn't so he bought waterproof rubber bags from an outfitter on Sloan Square and spent several hours with a Scotsman at the University who was an expert in topography and climate. For the next few days, he read everything he could find about Zaire, the politics and history of the place. He spent time brushing up on his French, studying Swahili from a traveler's handbook, trying to learn all the phrases he thought might come in handy, things like giving and getting directions, asking for food, rehearsing two- or three-dozen lies to tell if he got in a tight spot. He thought he could fake being an American birdwatcher on a self-guided safari, this wide-eyed Mr. Magoo, and he practiced being a World Bank official making a spot tour, and he also practiced the truth, but he wanted that to be a last resort.

Finally, he spent a day at the School for Tropical Medicine, trying to find out about Elyse Revelle, all he could about malaria and cholera and dysentery, the myriad ways Africa could cut you down. The Bursar provided him with a student photograph of the Belgian doctor and he made fifteen copies of the woman and her delicate cheekbones, long mannered neck, luxurious red hair. In about a week of effort, he managed to pack all his gear into two bags: his clothes, boots, books, the plastique, detonators, his chess clock.

In the back of his mind he formed a mental image of the woman, not just her face, but the soul behind the face, this woman who'd studied tropical medicine, and who had spent her adult life in the forests of Burundi and Rwanda, on the salt plains of southern Chad, in the high mountain passes of Asmara, and for the last ten years, in the forest clearing just northeast of Kisangani, Zaire. He had an idea about the woman, something that burned just behind the point in his neck where it met his back, and he knew that she might be dead, that this was all just a charade, but he knew he'd go in after her anyway. If he needed help once he got there, well, that was another reason for the ten gold sovereigns.

Roberts picked up plenty of medicines, antibiotics, vitamins, something to counteract the viruses and retroviruses, all the bugs that could get inside your body. He took paregoric to make him sleep and ease his pain. He bought Lomotil for diarrhea, and plenty of chloroquine tablets for malaria. The doctors told him the chloroquine didn't work much anymore because there were new strains of the disease, but it was worth taking along just in case. Even if he got malaria, the chloroquine would make his spells of chill and fever easier to bear. He also bought a supply of Aralen and Fansidar, just in case he got the disease and needed tried-and-true treatments. If he did contract malaria, he was told he'd be down for about a week during the first attack, unless he was lucky and had some kind of unique resistance. If worse came to worst, he could get bombed on paregoric and sleep for a week, and when he woke up he would be better, not exactly perfect, but able to move. He read enough about Africa to know that just about anything could happen to your body: You could get a scratch and the next morning it could become a festering open sore, and the morning after that you could have tetanus and your body would swell, your tongue would turn black and you could have a temp well over one hundred. And if he got cholera, then he would dose himself with Lomotil and try to find a doctor and a place with clean drinking water, because if he didn't he would die. He would shit out his life through his ass, and that would be the end of it. There would be no getting out of bed later, his long intestine would snake outside, he would turn inside out.

Now Roberts was standing at his hotel window with a view of the colonial parts of Brazzaville, looking down one of the five hills of the city, toward a shoulder of the river and the cité. He was facing south and already the sun slanted down through the room, filling it with heat, like a soup of heat, and below him was a mass of yellow-and-blue plaster buildings, tin roofed, some with central patios. Here and there were tulip trees and the true colonial buildings with green shutters on all the windows. The sun was reflecting from the tin roofs, caving in through the hollows of shadow, and already Roberts could hear it clicking on the metal surfaces. Now in the early morning was the sound of goats, and chickens crowing, and in the far distance the smell of the river which was deep and heavy, like loam, and the charcoal smoke still hovering somehow in the air. Now that he had discovered how he would get a gun, his mind felt clearer, even though he was sore all down his neck and back. His room was painted a plain light brown wainscot, with peeling wallpaper to the ceiling. Like an egg, he thought, a cubicle of warmth.

Roberts found a thin flow of water from the sink tap and washed his face, arms and chest. He stripped off his under-shorts and gave himself a sponge bath, but as soon as he put on his clothes he began to sweat. He tried the ceiling fan, and its movement stirred the dead air. He went downstairs and had some arabica coffee and rolls in the lounge. From behind some dusty palms in the lobby he watched Africans marching up and down the hilly streets carrying bales and bundles, pushing wheelbarrows, leading animals. There were a few Europeans, mostly French and Belgian, and some scattered squads of city policemen, and even a few tourists, probably Germans bound for the game preserves in Tanzania. Roberts had more coffee mixed with goat milk, and when he felt hungry he ordered some oranges and two boiled eggs.

Roberts spent the morning in the ville, walking five or six miles through the steamy morning, orienting himself to the wavelength of Africa, the rhythms of life, the colors, the density of woven textures. Hiking up the tallest of the five hills of Brazzaville he discovered a wooden Baptist church, which had been built during the nineteenth century. It was an octagonal haven of quiet and shade, surrounded by ceiba trees, which spread their limbs over the whole structure. It was cool there, and from its vantage point Roberts could see all of the modern cité, with its jumble of concrete bunkers, warehouses down by the river, bars and restaurants, sterile avenues built by the President, and the white plaster govern-ment buildings at the hub. Thin clouds banked up over Zaire to the east and there seemed to be a permanent mist on the river, like exhaust that had turned a shade of burnt orange. Eastward beyond that, there were emerald green and broken

brown hills and a blue horizon which lent everything a perspective, a shape, something to which Roberts was trying to
adjust. Sitting in the shade, there on a mahogany bench under
a ceiba tree, drinking a lemonade, Roberts knew that he
didn't want to exercise too much judgment all at once. It
would louse up his perceptions, the way your vision is loused
up by too much booze. If he needed anything, he needed to
be clear in his head. That way he could give Africa a chance.

By the time he got to the French Bank of Commerce it was
nearly two o'clock. He presented his identification to one of
the clerks and was told that the deposit in his name had been
made. He put the cash in his overnight case and walked down
the hill to his hotel, realizing that he'd startled the clerk. He
had lunch at the hotel, washed up again and took a taxi down
to the ferry dock to again wait for his contact on the ferry
dock.

Walking down through the dusty parking lot, with the
black valise under one arm, Roberts saw something that surprised him. The man called Adam Mbenga was standing at
the ferry dock, just under the shaded tin roof of the shelter,
his back turned, looking at the river. A crowd of Africans
milled around the ticket office and there was a squad of
soldiers under the umbrella tree. Mbenga turned and raised an
arm in greeting. He was wearing the same dirty slacks and
white shirt he'd worn the day before, his left leg braced.
Beyond him, the ferry was chugging black diesel smoke and
some thunderheads were lifting out of the forest of Zaire.

"Bonjour, mzungu," Mbenga said when Roberts reached
the shelter. Hello, white man.

"Bonjour, ndugu," Roberts said. Good day, brother.

Some soldiers shouted down by the ticket office, making
Roberts glance nervously. Mbenga motioned Roberts away
toward a pool of shade on the river side. Now that Roberts

looked at him carefully, he realized how small the man was, barely up to Roberts' shoulder, with small strong hands and two webbed fingers on his right hand. Roberts knew he had found his African contact, this tiny fellow with a bad leg, bad teeth and two webbed fingers.

"Why didn't you tell me yesterday?" Roberts asked.

"I wanted to see what kind of man you were. Do you forgive me this small indecision?"

"How did I turn out?"

"Oh, very good indeed," Mbenga laughed. "You were crazy indeed to talk to those Kikongo." Mbenga turned and leaned against the abutment, resting his leg. "Someone so crazy has to be a little good, no?"

Roberts had to agree. "But you have to be a little crazy too, taking a job like this."

"Not too crazy like you," Mbenga said. "I work upriver at the clinic in Kisangani. When the company sent word that they needed someone to meet you at the ferry dock, I was only too willing to come. There is a great need to help the doctor. She is in serious trouble. You must tell me what you need. I am here to see to your needs."

Roberts was hesitant to confide in this man just yet. He'd seen enough to measure him, but he wasn't sure. Just now he thought Mbenga might be a good man to have along.

"What I need is a weapon," Roberts said flatly.

"A weapon," Mbenga said quietly, snatching a quick look back at the soldiers on the loading dock. They were herding passengers through the turnstiles, up the gangplank and onto the lower deck of the ferry. "This is not so easy," he continued. "I can get you most everything you might need— soap, rice, air and steamship tickets. But weapons, that is another thing, don't you *comprenez?*" Mbenga brightened suddenly. "But I have a car here. We can go back to your hotel in Brazzaville and discuss these matters. No?"

"Not just yet," Roberts said, touching the man's shoulder, a gentle reprimand. "I tell you, ndugu, my friend, I'm not going upriver without a weapon. This is not a country to go through without protection. It would be very stupid, and I can't help Dr. Revelle without some protection."

Mbenga nodded a reluctant yes. "It is possible always to do the *margoulinage* in this country, to bypass all the rules. We have these rules to remind us that they can be bypassed, that they exist to make Mobutu rich. In all sorts of ways, there is the matabish, this petty trading of favors for all kinds of commercial goods and services, the underground without which there would be no sunshine. In Zaire, it is possible to find diamonds, cobalt, francs, women, the ivory of murdered elephants, even babies and wood products just the same. This involves finding the right fradeur and having some good luck."

Mbenga stopped speaking, leaning his head back with his neck against the rail abutment, in the shadow of a frangipani, its red flowers tearing away in the hot breeze. "Weapons," the man sighed to himself, a look of perplexed wistfulness on his face, "these are impossible to trade for, to purchase, or to steal." He pointed toward the soldiers. "Yes, there are a great many weapons in this country, as in any other. One can turn one's head and one can see a weapon. But it is absolutely forbidden for a citoyen to possess such a thing. There is no trade in such things and the authorities are terrible in their consequences." Mbenga shrugged as if the matter had been closed.

The breeze was sliding up from the river now, through the dense mangungu groves on the bank. Already the Kinshasa

ferry had turned on its keel, heading out toward the two sand
islands in the channel, where some crocodiles were sleeping.
A pair of fish eagles screamed and gulls puffed up from the
ferry decks, disturbed by the noise and sudden movement. In
the far distance, behind the shimmering outline of Kinshasa's
skyscrapers, clouds had bunched along the eastern horizon
and lightning licked down. The forest had turned cobalt blue
and the air became suddenly dense and electric, like wet
wool. Now Roberts was deciding how far he could trust this
African, how much trouble he could lead the man into without breaking his present bond, this total stranger who had
maybe saved his life. And what was there to make this African
trust this mzungu, this Westerner?

"Would you get us two beers from the lounge?" Roberts
asked. Mbenga looked surprised, then nodded and walked off
in the direction of the ticket office.

While he waited Roberts tried to spot the man's car, deciding it was a battered Peugeot parked forty meters down the
road from the parking lot in full sun, near a pile of construction debris and downed banana palms. Now Roberts smelled
the first rain-scented ozone. He watched Mbenga disappear
inside the ticket office lounge where the soldiers had taken up
residence under their umbrella tree, drinking and smoking
bangi. Out in the main channel, the ferry turned and skirted
the two islands. In a few minutes, Mbenga returned with two
paper cups full of Primus, the Belgian lager.

Roberts took a long drink and watched the clouds over
Zaire. He thought he could see the forest ooze toward him,
a perceptible movement, and there were more fish eagles
now, five or six diving and spinning in the gathering wind,
drawn, he thought, by the changing pressure, the tide coming
up all the way from the Atlantic, six hundred miles away.

Roberts touched the man's cup. "For the next half an hour we have to trust each other implicitly," he said.

"This is my mission, mzungu."

"Later we talk, get to know one another better. But right now we have one thing we have to do together."

"I am ready for that."

"We're going to get a weapon."

Mbenga stiffened, touched his leg brace. "This is very dangerous," he said quietly.

"The soldiers," Roberts said, motioning to the umbrella tree just outside the station house and ticket office. "Pretty soon these paratroopers are going to be stoned on bangi and palm wine. We wait here just a while, and they'll be mostly asleep, or so stoned they won't know what is going on. You don't think any of them are doing *mira,* speed?"

"No mira, just bangi," Mbenga said.

"Pretty quick now," Roberts said calmly, "I want you to go up the hill, get in your car and start the motor. Just start the motor and watch for me in your rearview mirror. Be ready to move, to come and get me."

"What are you going to do, mzungu?"

"Get a weapon."

Mbenga crossed himself quickly. "From the soldiers?" he asked helplessly.

Roberts drew strength from Mbenga's very real fear. He could see the man tremble. Their eyes met, and Mbenga began his clanking gait down the shadowy shelter, then across the parking lot, and up the dusty path toward his old Peugeot. For the first time Roberts sensed the breeze cooling down, and he knew it was the rain drawing toward the river from the forest far away. He remembered his first morning in Africa, climbing down the gangway from the Air France jet, plunging into a heat that took his breath away, and a noonday brilliance of color and resonance. He looked at the soldiers sprawled under the umbrella tree, then back at the splotch of purple on the horizon, rain in Zaire.

Roberts waited until Mbenga reached his car and then he walked down the shelter and into the ticket office. A portrait of the President looked down at him from the pink-plaster wall: sunglasses, square chin, a muted glare. The ticket agent had gone, and he could watch the soldiers from barred windows, a dozen of them asleep in the shade. Pretty soon he went outside the office, down the wharf where the river lapped against the pylons beneath him, and around the back of the umbrella tree where there was a tangle of mangungu and piles of concrete rubble. He could smell the river now, and the leftovers of bangi smoke, and somewhere he could hear toucans in the brush and palm trees. He was nervous and sweating inside his khaki clothes, feeling disembodied, as if someone else were performing his actions for him. He stood in the shade like a cat poised about to cross a busy street, all the stiff energy coiled inside his muscles, electricity slicking toward the tips of his fingers. He studied two soldiers asleep, separated a bit from the rest of their troop, one cradling an empty Primus bottle and a snuffed bangi joint. He kneeled down and picked up a single chunk of concrete, about the size of a fist.

When he walked over to the two soldiers he could see that one of them was awake, the man looking confused, without pleasure or pain, his red eyes unfocused. Roberts bent over slightly, and hit the man hard on the forehead, just behind the right eye. Then he hit him again at the base of the neck as the soldier slumped over. Roberts felt cold and clear and very good as he watched the soldier relax away. He realized that he had made almost no sound. Just as he looked at the soldiers' two weapons, he heard the first raindrop touch dust and Mbenga in the Peugeot hauling ass downhill fast.

4

ALL THE WAY BACK TO his hotel, Roberts was giving shape to his disappointment. He told Mbenga goodbye, then went up to his room and took another sponge bath. He lay down on his bed and began to assess the damage. "Raw shit," he muttered to himself, as the mosquitoes banged against the hotel window. He opened his overnight case and put on some clean underwear, hoping to be dry and cool, even if for only five or ten minutes. Even that would be a blessing, even that might enable him to think clearly while his nerves settled.

It was deep night in Brazzaville, and the music was eerie in its ubiquity, another thing that was giving shape to his disappointment. He had hoped for some real firepower, an automatic rifle with hitting punch, and a machine pistol that was clean and accurate, and here he had this pseudo-NATO junk that the French Generals ordered on *spec* to keep the French arms industry rolling. He picked up the Model 1950 pistolet with its nine-round detachable box magazine and low muzzle velocity, this toy that drug dealers in Houston would toss away in the junk heap. But even worse to his mind was the FAMAS 5.56 delayed-blowback semiautomatic rifle. Roberts thought it was amazing that any master of war thought a paratrooper would jump out of a plane with this thing in his hands, hopping into a pitch black night, ready to kill Russians with a toy. Roberts wrapped the guns with hotel towels, and dropped them back into his black leather valise, beginning to work on the real problem at hand.

Mbenga had done his job that afternoon, for sure. Roberts remembered stripping the guns from the two soldiers, looking up to see Mbenga's sweat-streaked face in reflection in the rearview mirror, this look of terror in his eyes that told Roberts the man was dealing as best he could. When Mbenga pulled up and stuck his head outside the window, Roberts thought he looked like he might faint, but then Roberts hopped into the car and they were speeding uphill toward the barren brown rises, bouncing over the unpaved laterite road—mud-rutted from long-forgotten rains—throwing up huge clouds of dust and particles of gravel behind, just as raindrops began to dot the road. Roberts watched the buildings of the quay grow small, and then he could see the river widening in profile behind the wharf, winding back north and east toward the Pool Malebo, with Kinshasa in the middle distance like a tower of glass overlaid with turquoise rain clouds. Beyond that were the green folds of the forest, and even farther away the uplifted cliffs where Roberts knew there were cataracts. Then rain engulfed the quay docks, turning the river into a black slash, engulfing the ferry too. Where the rain touched Kinshasa it was turning a smoky gray and rising as steam from the garbage dumps, slums and skyscrapers of the city. It was utterly fantastic to Roberts, like science fiction, but it was real, and he couldn't discount his perceptions.

Before they went around a last bend in the road, Roberts saw one of the soldiers get up, stagger, and look after the Peugeot in surprise. Mbenga turned around to Roberts, who was sitting in the backseat, tourist-style. *"Nous avons besoin d'un miracle,"* he said fatalistically.

"La, la," Roberts responded in Swahili, making half a joke, still trying to encourage Mbenga. *"Les soldats dorment."* The soldiers are sleeping. This seemed to calm Mbenga, who turned back to his driving, grabbing the wheel with both hands as if it were a ship's wheel, a vessel on the high seas. Really, Roberts wasn't sure about the soldiers, but he wanted to soothe the African, so that he could think. Mbenga wiped his face with an oily rag, driving with a fierceness that was urban, surprising Roberts with its recklessness. They drove west and north and west again, through bouldered hills where there were women carrying loads, children leading geese and chickens and old men pedaling bicycles. All the trees had been cut from the hillsides, and you could see erosion destroying the hills an ounce at a time. Back away toward the river it was raining, but on the road it was blazing hot, with clear skies.

"These soldiers," Roberts asked, "do they have radios? Or is there a radio in the ticket office?"

"Maybe so, mzungu," Mbenga answered. Roberts thought that meant *probably so*. Maybe right now the soldiers were erecting a wall against them, to keep them out of Brazzaville, where they could lose themselves in the hordes of bicycles and taxis, all the peddlers and street people.

The road took them up through rounded knolls until they crested a series of steep hills and ran through a bucket of humpbacked rims, stunted acacias and bush that divided the river valley from the bowl in which Brazzaville had been built. Now when Roberts turned back to see where they'd come from he could really grasp all of the river winding north and east between masses of green mangungu and dense forest, with the city of Kinshasa spread out on the horizon in the

near distance. It had something of a coda, but Roberts didn't
have the experience necessary to decipher it yet, these strange
apparitions so foreign to his eye.

Just then he was reliving the whole creative text of what
he'd just done: the long walk down the shaded quay to the
ticket office, his wait inside the concrete bunker, the picture
of the President staring down at him from those sunglassed
eyes, until he had seen the two soldiers drowsing, high on
beer and bangi. Roberts felt the dead weight of the concrete
clod in his hand, the memory of it heavy in his head, and he
remembered the dead uncomprehending eye of the soldier he
had hit, the quiver in his cheek as consciousness left him,
something like a moment of recognition.

The soldier was a large man, maybe twenty years old with
a black beret on his head and it had slid to the left side as he
slumped. For an instant Roberts was certain there had been
comprehension in the man's gaze, and he was glad for it.
Roberts had taken away his rifle and pistol, in addition to as
many clips of ammunition as he thought he could. And then
he had seen the Peugeot moving downhill fast, the face of
Mbenga through the windscreen and big, blue raindrops
splattering in the dust.

They reached a crossroads where there was a petrol station
and a country market. One road, an asphalt section lowered
through some palm groves and finally wound up to the
sprawling African part of Brazzaville; the other was a new
concrete expressway that went north toward the ville where
the French and Belgians lived.

"But my hotel," Roberts began to say, as Mbenga turned
toward the African part of the city, away from the ville.

"We go down to the cité, mzungu," Mbenga said, interrupting. "If the police are behind us we can hide in the cité
with my uncle there. The first thing the police will do is

come to look for you at the Hotel National, you this Westerner, that is where you would stay, no? This matter of weapons is very serious. We must take a certain amount of care."

Roberts nodded, relaxed. It didn't matter, now that they were driving along the asphalt road, hidden in acacias, the road growing crowded with women carrying bundles, children on bicycles, old men, too, scatterings of goats and chickens. Behind them Roberts could smell the rain, but it didn't look like it would rain in Brazzaville just yet. Maybe tonight, he thought. Maybe the rain will cool the air and he could get some sleep.

"If they find these weapons," Mbenga was saying, "they will not ask us any questions, you know? They will put us in two holes and the next morning we will be taken someplace outside the palace and the Moroccans will stand us against a wall and that will be the end of us. You must trust my word on this, mzungu. Such things are very common." Mbenga looked at Roberts, a look that seemed to put an end to the conversation.

"I don't want to endanger your family," Roberts said.

"My uncle is an old man. He has seen too much to be terribly frightened by things like this. But me, I am frightened by things like this. It is best we hide in the cité for a time. There will be a time to go back to your hotel."

"Your uncle," Roberts asked, "is he *mort civil?*"

"One of many," Mbenga said. "But my uncle has no love for soldiers on either side of the river. But he is a Balubu, and he would do anything for the doctor who has been kidnapped. Besides, he is my family and we are used to such dangers. It is part of the landscape."

Roberts stifled his many questions. Now it was a time in which he would have to trust Mbenga, keep away from his checklist of suspicions. After all, hadn't he driven his Peugeot downhill when he needed him? There had been a moment when Roberts expected to be left alone with the soldiers, when he thought he would see the Peugeot speed uphill through the barren red hills, leaving him alone with a dozen drunken troopers. But it hadn't happened.

"Don't worry about my uncle, Mbenga said. "This old man has seen many bad things and he knows that this is another bad thing that will pass." Mbenga smiled, looking back at Roberts in the mirror. "And besides, you would rather have company against the wall, no?"

Roberts admitted that he would. He said they could have some conversation before the soldiers fired.

Mbenga steered slowly through a herd of ragged goats, and about two kilometers later they were in the slums of the cité. Roberts was appalled by the sea of concrete bunkers, bare dirt and scraggly bush. There were some hevea trees, and at every corner a bar or market. The air was full of dust and Roberts could see the hills visible in the north with their hint of coolness, frangipani, and the wooden church where Roberts had rested that first day. Now though, he knew he was in the middle of five square miles of concrete *shamba,* this dirty slum full of children, a few scrawny cattle, and a few fields of manioc and maize under an awesome sun. Everywhere he looked there were women and children and animals, but the only men were at the corner bars, clots of them drinking beer and smoking hand-rolled cigarettes. Mbenga took them down narrow lanes and alleys, and they pulled to a stop beside a square bunker with a blanket over the doorway. Way back in this maze it was very quiet and hot.

Mbenga locked the weapons in the trunk, and led Roberts inside the shamba. There was an old man sitting in one corner. He was very black with a smooth face and grizzled hair. His arms were no more than spindles and Mbenga spoke to him in a language Roberts didn't recognize, not French or Swahili. The old man listened patiently and motioned for Roberts to sit down at the square table in the center of the room.

The old man was named Masala, one of Mbenga's Balubu who had escaped across the border from Zaire during the civil war many years ago, during the fight over independence when Mobutu and the northern tribes had terrorized the whole country. Mbenga had been a child then and was protected by his family in Katanga, until even that province was drenched in blood after secession, when the crazy *Simbas* went on a rampage of kidnapping and murder. Some of his family, Mbenga explained, had escaped, like Uncle Masala, and would never go back to Zaire. But Mbenga himself had gone back, even though he was *mort civil,* and now he traveled freely because the customs and immigration in the country were so disorganized and riddled by corruption, and because Mbenga had a good job with EuroCopper. Mbenga had cousins and uncles all over the country, scattered in shambas in Kinshasa, in Kisangani. Even now his sister lived in Kisangani, at the clinic, even though they were all officially dead.

The old man offered Roberts some warm lemonade which he drank gratefully. Mbenga pulled the Peugeot around to the back of the shamba and the old man led Roberts outside to where there was a dusty acacia tree, some kitchen chairs and a pot of boiling vegetables beside a cardboard table. They sat together in the heat drinking lemonade with a sea of shambas spread out behind them, children playing in the dust, chickens scratching.

"Have you told your uncle about the weapons?" Roberts asked Mbenga, who had come back from the Peugeot and was sitting across the table in dusty shade. The old man was stirring his vegetables over a charcoal fire. Some dogs began to bark.

"He understands these things," Mbenga said. "We wait here until dark. Then I take you back to your hotel. My uncle will fix us something to eat."

Roberts thanked the old man in Swahili. These things were now a matter of unspoken trust.

"We have to make some plans," Roberts said to Mbenga, while the old man worked over his pot of vegetables.

"However you wish."

"I have to get the money across the river. And I have to get these guns across the river too."

"What is this money?"

"French francs. I drew it out of a bank in Brazzaville."

"This is the ransom?"

Roberts nodded.

"You didn't send it to Kinshasa?" Mbenga asked.

"We can't trust the banks there. I was told that if we deposited the money there that Mobutu's men would know all about it as soon as it hit the vault. Then we'd have to deal with the treasury officials and who knows what other bribes and deals. EuroCopper doesn't have much influence anymore because they're winding up their operations. The government doesn't want them to take out any cash."

"It is true," Mbenga said. "Everything is controlled by *Le Gros Legume.*" Behind them Masala laughed at the French words for Big Vegetable, what the people had named Mobutu. Mbenga exchanged some words with his uncle. "But now your money and your guns are in Brazzaville," he said to himself.

"I thought you might have some ideas," Roberts said, sipping his warm lemonade. The setting sun was making long strings of light in the acacias, dust-ridden rainbows of color.

"I thought I could take the cash across the river on the ferry, but I hadn't expected there to be so many fradeurs. Those Kikongo are dangerous."

"*La,*" Mbenga said in Swahili. No. He had become thoughtful, staring away at the dust circles. "This will take some trick, no? But I think as a mzungu, they won't bother you too much. But, I don't think you should take French francs across the river on the ferry even so. The customs would stop you and take this money away and you would be tied up in paperwork for many months. Something like this calls for *margoulinage.*" Roberts smiled at the French word for *the bypassing of rules.* "We must make the *brouillardise, l'affairisme,* no?"

"*Comprend,*" Roberts replied. "*Mais, je nais pas d'idée.* Maybe we could cross the river at night. Float over."

"No, no," Mbenga said quickly. "This is much too dangerous. There are many soldiers on watch, just like the ones you saw today. Not all of them are smoking bangi and drinking *pomba.*"

The old man sat the table with wooden bowls and spoons. He served the vegetables and they began to eat. Mbenga said, "There are only two things the soldiers are looking for hard. They don't care much about soup or rice. What they seek are French francs and diamonds. You must understand, the people smuggle francs into Zaire, and diamonds out of Zaire."

"The Kikongo were beating boys and old men for a few French francs?"

"The customs officers on the ferry find them out. When they jump overboard and try to swim back to shore, the Kikongo take them and their francs. These Africans are trying to take a few francs home to Zaire, where it is the only currency that is worth anything at all. This is a shameful thing, no?"

"It's shameful, yes." Roberts had seen the Zairian currency with its snarling black leopard about to spring, a black hand holding a torch. He ate some of the sombe, boiled greens, tamarind, hot pepper and corn. Masala had finished his meal already and was busy feeding tobacco into a homemade pipe. The sun had gone behind the shambas now and the crows were screaming. Roberts could smell thick charcoal smoke hovering over everything. The children were quiet and he could hear music. Something was giving him a longing for Amanda, but then he began to think about what Mbenga had said, francs into Zaire, diamonds out, and it was giving him an idea. He was touching an edge of margoulinage.

"Suppose we smuggle diamonds *into* Zaire," he said to Mbenga. The man was helping his uncle string a hammock between two acacia trunks.

"*Hatari,*" Mbenga whispered under his breath. Danger. Mbenga helped his uncle lie down, took the pipe out of his mouth, and pretty soon the old man began to snore softly. Roberts was trying to finish his sombe, but it was spiced very hot and he was having a hard time with it. Now that it was getting dark, there were mosquitoes in the air, a thin gauze of them competing with black flies for space. Even so, a cool breeze swept over Roberts and he felt suddenly relaxed. "To find diamonds we must deal with the worst sort of people in Brazzaville," Mbenga said, sitting down again.

"But it is possible?"

"*Oui, c'est possible,* yes."

"Do you know these people? These people who would sell us diamonds for my French francs?"

"I have heard of someone."

"Then we buy diamonds for my francs. Then I smuggle them across the border on the ferry. It makes sense to me. I can use the diamonds for the ransom. They'll be easier to carry than francs anyway. I think our kidnappers would find diamonds very valuable."

"You would do well with diamonds, mzungu," Mbenga said. "If you are fortunate enough to be able to buy diamonds in Brazzaville and if you are lucky enough to smuggle them across the river into Zaire, and then if you are strong enough to make a trade for the doctor in Kisangani, then you would find these diamonds most valuable." Mbenga smiled sadly. *"Comprenez?"*

"All right, it's done then. We buy diamonds in Brazzaville and we smuggle them across the river into Zaire and use them to pay the ransom. This solves two problems at once."

"I tell you, mzungu," Mbenga said, speaking slowly and distinctly now, as if trying to make Roberts understand every phrase and nuance, "this is a very difficult and dangerous business. I truly believe that a mzungu could smuggle diamonds across the river on the ferry. The customs would not expect this, and they would not be looking, no. Not on the ferry at any rate. And when you get to Kinshasa, I think that EuroCopper is expecting to fly you upriver to Kisangani. But even so, once you get to the clinic, anything can happen."

"I know that anyway. Having the diamonds doesn't make it any more dangerous once I get across the river. Less so, if anything. The main thing is to trust *you*, ndugu. I must know deep inside myself that you will help me on this journey."

"Of course, mzungu. I know the clinic and I know the countryside around it. I have worked there for more than five years now. I know the doctor very well."

"I have to understand this," Roberts said. "Why you are doing this? I know how dangerous it is for you."

"The doctor, she is important for my people," Mbenga said suddenly. Roberts fingered his empty lemonade cup.

The air was full of an intensity of sounds: dogs barking, monkeys, birds chattering in the trees.

"Why don't you tell me about it?" Roberts asked. He wanted to trust this African.

"I will tell you, mzungu, because these actions come from my heart." Mbenga looked at his uncle who was asleep in the hammock, snoring peacefully. Roberts was amazed that the old man could sleep this way, a car with automatic weapons in its trunk just outside the boundary of his shamba and this Westerner eating his sombe. "I was a village boy in Katanga just before the civil war," Mbenga explained. "This is a very beautiful and prosperous country and my tribe, the Balubu, are a very intelligent people. Most of my family were farmers who had cattle and goats, raised some chickens. They were very attached to the land, you see? I lived with my father and my brother and my sister, and my mother and two aunts and uncles who were old. And then came the announcement of independence. You know what happened then, no?"

Roberts said he had only a vague idea.

"Well, you see," Mbenga said, "the Belgians and French had many copper and diamond mines in the south part of the country. They wanted to keep those properties for their own. Independence was inevitable, but those two countries gave guns and money to the politicians among the Balubu, and to political groups in Katanga, in order that they should separate from the central government. And then the war of separation began, and soon became a tribal conflict of great cruelty. Katanga was supported by the Belgians and the French, while the Russians supported the central government. My people were destined to lose this conflict, mzungu, for we are not so many as the other tribes."

There was a wooden pitcher of lemonade on the table and

Roberts poured out two cups, giving one to Mbenga. There was a sudden silence in which Roberts could hear melodies coming from the corner bars, radios and tape players meshing in the evening.

"In this war," Mbenga said, "the Belgians and French hoped to keep their mines after independence. My father and my older brother went for soldiers and were killed together near one of our villages. I have never seen their bodies, nor has my family been able to properly bury them. At the time I was in the Belgian mission school, and the nuns sheltered me and my mother and sister from the marauding army of United Nations troops, Simbas and Mobutu. For a time I continued my education and then went to work for Euro-Copper, who continued to employ me despite the *mort civil* I've told you about. There is a great shortage of educated people who speak French and English and they needed me then. And so for many years while I pretended not to exist, I worked for the company in Kinshasa doing translations. During the last five or six years it became obvious that the company was going to leave Zaire, because of the corruption and the drop in copper prices. They sent me upriver to Kisangani to the transhipment site, and about five years ago I began to work at the clinic with the doctor."

"Tell me about her, can you?"

"Oh yes," Mbenga said. "I knew of this woman when I worked in Kinshasa. She had a very great reputation as a healer among the workers. This is something the people talked about all the time. They were very worshipful, no?" Here Mbenga stopped for a time, listening to the toucans far away, and the shrill cry of some pied crows fighting in the heveas. Some of the heat was leaving the day too. "When she came to Kisangani ten years ago, there was a great cry from the workers for some kind of medical aid station in Kisangani.

Copper prices were very high, and everyone knew that the company was making very great profits, you see, and yet there was no medical care for the workers at the warehouses and docks in Kisangani. When the doctor first came there was nothing, just some raffia shacks and a small dispensary. The workers and their families would come and she would examine them and dispense some drugs, perhaps wrap an arm or a leg, and that was all. Back then there was a smelter and she would treat industrial accident victims, too. It was very small, and there was not much money in it."

"Where had she come from?"

"I think Chad, but I could be wrong."

"She was with Doctors Without Borders?"

"Oh yes, I think so," Mbenga said. "You must understand this, mzungu," he continued, looking at Roberts now. "Pretty soon the people in the region began to bring their children to the doctor as well, and she could not turn them away. And then more and more the whole countryside began to treat this small dispensary as their only place of medical treatment for hundreds and hundreds of miles around. As the Belgians and French left, the roads went unrepaired, the rivers undredged, everything went back to the wilds. In this situation the doctor began to treat everyone who came to her. And as she did so, she began to press the company for more money and more staff to treat these people. She had to keep this development a secret, but it was not easy. It was hard to make the company give her the money necessary, even though they were making tremendous profits. Almost all of this was going back to France and Belgium, or to England. About five years ago she asked me to come to work for the clinic, because I knew French and English, and could write. I have been there ever since."

"And the doctor, were you there when she was kidnapped?"

"No, I am sorry. I was in Kisangani."

"Do you have any idea where she is being held?"

"No, mzungu." Mbenga went over and gently took the pipe from his uncle's mouth. He turned back and said, "I know only that we must take this ransom up the river before they harm her. I am sure these people will release her without trouble. We must not make any trouble. *Comprenez?*"

"Do you know this group? These people?"

"Only that they may be BaLese. Very poor and hungry."

"Anything more specific?"

"They are probably bandits. With the French and Belgians gong now, there is nothing but chaos and anarchy in these regions. It is wild country. The central government has no control any longer. The soldiers riot and loot. The *commissair* of the region is corrupt, and has no power."

Roberts thought for a long time about the conditions around Kisangani, the terror and unrestrained atmosphere of need and violence. It would only make his job more difficult, being next to this kind of political rupture. He had been near chaos before and knew its touch. "All right," he said to Mbenga, "now we trust one another completely, yes?"

"Yes, mzungu," Mbenga said. "You will find that I have the courage."

"I already know that," Roberts said. They shook hands spontaneously. Roberts felt a peace of mind now, something slipping over him like frost on a windowpane. The sky was dark, ineffable and perfect, with touches of rose hues from all the charcoal fires in the cité. Mbenga woke his uncle and thanked him, Roberts shaking his hand too, though the old man was sleepy. Mbenga put away the wooden bowls and spoons. Roberts followed him inside the shamba and noticed the single iron bed in one corner, a crucifix on the wall above it, the dusty earthen floor.

"Just drive me toward the ville," Roberts said. "Let me out someplace and I'll walk to the hotel."

"I know a way around the hills," Mbenga said. He pulled the Peugeot around to the front of the shamba and they drove through the alleys of the cité, honking at goats, weaving around clots of children playing on street corners. It took about half an hour for them to drive to a quiet, palm-covered hill above the hotel where there were some embassies and private residences.

Roberts had taken the guns out of the trunk and put them in his black valise. "You walk straight down the hill to your hotel," Mbenga said. Below Roberts a hillside dropped to the lights of the ville, and beyond that the glow of thousands of fires, a few orange flares at intersections. Now Roberts could hear frogs singing in the trees, so loud he could barely hear the motor hum. His stomach was upset, probably from the sombe, he thought.

"And the diamonds?" Roberts asked.

"There is a dirty Frenchman," Mbenga said. "His name is Raymond. I will make some inquiries tomorrow."

"Be careful. There may be police waiting for me at the hotel. If there are, then go back to Zaire. Forget you ever saw me."

"I hope that is not the case, mzungu."

"And there are these guns," Roberts said, tapping his valise.

"I have thought of them," Mbenga replied.

"I'll take them across."

"They can be broken down?"

"Yes, I'm sure."

"Then my sister will take them across."

"Your sister?"

"She is here in Brazzaville. She will take them across for you."

"No, it's too dangerous. Besides, your sister is not part of the plan. I can't allow it."

"She is part of this landscape," Mbenga said. Roberts looked at the small African, a man with a crippled leg, shabby white shirt and polyester trousers. "We are all part of this landscape now," he said.

Roberts got out of the car and watched the Peugeot sputter downhill. Mbenga would be coming to the hotel before noon, but just now Roberts wondered where this man would be tonight among the thousands of shambas of the cité, how he would sleep, what he would dream. Roberts walked down to his hotel, wondering about this, and whether there would be police and soldiers in the lobby, waiting for him.

5

Roberts had a very bad night, even though there were no police or soldiers waiting for him in the lobby. He went straight to his room and undressed, standing for a long time in front of the hotel window, watching the lights of the ville and listening to the sound of music. Some time while he was standing there a storm stripped across Brazzaville, scouring the hills with strong gusts of wind and a brief driving rain, but then it was hot and still again, and hours passed without a breath of air. He could hear the mosquitoes in his room. Just as he was trying to get some reading done the lights dimmed and he was left in a brown glaze, with no running water, and roaches coming out of the walls, prowling the toilet basin, skittering up and down the bedposts. For a long time he watched the roaches and then he fell asleep in the chair beside the window, which was the only place where he could catch a breeze. In the late morning he went downstairs and tried to eat, ordering some hard rolls and butter, arabica coffee and two boiled eggs that didn't taste fresh. He went back up to his room and bolted the door and studied his guns.

He knew the M1950 pistol had been around for years, part of the shoddy NATO arsenal, back when the French were part of the alliance. It was a popgun, about seven inches long, weighing about a pound and a half with a nine-round single-column detachable box magazine. Roberts thought that the weapon fired a lot like a Browning .45 caliber automatic carried by American troops, except you couldn't fire the weapon without the clip. Roberts tried his hand at field stripping it, realizing that it broke down just about like the Browning, no barrel bushing and recoil spring plug. He removed the slide from the receiver, then the hammer assembly, finding that the spring and lever and seat dropped out of the housing so that he could lift them all out as one piece after the slide. He sat on the bed in his hotel room and counted ten basic components, some small set screws and pieces of butt. Not counting the clips of ammunition.

But the Fusil Automatic was something different altogether. He knew it was French, but beyond that it was like nothing he had ever seen. So he took it apart carefully, feeling his way, starting with the operating parts, bolt, bolt carrier and delay lever, then the trigger assembly and carrying handle group, the buttstock and cheek, and finally the bayonet and sling. He looked at the fifteen components, wondering in his own mind if he could reassemble them, trying to figure the thing out. He finally decided it was a delayed-blowback weapon with a flash suppressor, firing twenty-five rounds at about one-thousand rounds a minute, and that it would be a trick to put it back together again now that he had it broken down. But the real trick would be getting these guns into Zaire, then putting them back together without running into some crazy Kikongo who wore a razor blade necklace and drank pomba for lunch. If that happened, Roberts knew he would be in shit so deep he would never see over it.

This thing about Mbenga's sister worried Roberts. He didn't want to involve anyone with weapons in Zaire who didn't have firsthand knowledge of the stakes, who wasn't really a player. Mbenga was a player now, and Roberts appreciated that, but that didn't mean his sister was a player too, just because she was part of the landscape. These were not only moral categories, they had to do with levels of commitment, solidarity that could mean facing a firing squad. You couldn't expect that kind of devotion without something special happening inside a person. Roberts looked at the weapons on the bed, these black components broken down, and he thought about the old man, Uncle Masala, and wondered if he was a player now. It wasn't easy to protect people like that when things got wild and speedy.

Roberts wrapped the components in a hotel towel and put them back in his black valise. He went downstairs and had a beer on the hotel veranda, sitting in the shade with his Primus and a bowl of groundnuts, watching the sun wash the streets of the ville. The night rain had washed away some of the dust from the trees and the acacia leaves were shining. South toward the cité the sun was streaming through a bank of low white clouds and Roberts could see the outline of the slums and the river in the far distance, the slums a haze of pastel cubicles with the river a brown slash. There were only a few people in the streets: some African women, a few government officials, taxi drivers on the corners waiting for fares. In the lobby behind him, ceiling fans stirred warm air and flies, the palms rustled. Roberts sipped his beer and ate some peanuts, thinking about the plastique and the detonators and his transmitter, how he hadn't told Mbenga about these things yet. How maybe that was okay because they were his responsibility anyway, he'd carry them across the river himself and let the wild and speedy people hassle him if they were going to. He had another beer, watching the street for Adam Mbenga.

Mbenga walked by his hotel on the opposite side of the street just before noon. He went by again, then crossed the street and came and sat down at the table with Roberts, who had finished his second beer and had a stomachache for his trouble. Roberts watched the man stroll down the street in his black pants and dirty tennis shoes, then come across to the table with a smile on his face. Mbenga ordered a lemonade from the waiter and Roberts another beer. Now at noon the streets were nearly deserted, sun-drenched.

"I have been afraid for you," Mbenga said. "I didn't know if the soldiers had come for you. I thought maybe they made you sit here at this table waiting for me. Then they would have both of us, *comprenez?*"

"Nobody came," Roberts said. "Just the roaches, a part of the landscape."

Mbenga laughed. "Better than the soldiers," he said.

Roberts had to agree. "I've broken down the guns. They're dirty, but they'll work if we can get them across."

"You know these things, huh?"

"Two guns, about twenty-five components. The largest is about the size of a baguette, most very small, some tiny. Altogether they weigh about eight pounds, four kilos. I've wrapped them in hotel towels and put them in my valise."

"My sister will be ready," Mbenga said seriously.

"You've told her about this situation?"

"Yes, about the guns. She is very prepared for this, *comprenez?*"

"But I'm not sure I am. As you say, this is very hatari. I don't want to involve her without a good reason."

"But there is a good reason," Mbenga said, touching Roberts' arm. "Please believe me, mzungu."

Thunder creased the horizon from Zaire. There were big storms brewing over the *cuvée*. The sound rolled across the horizon and stopped.

"When do we do this?" Mbenga asked.

"When we have the diamonds."

Mbenga leaned over so that he could whisper with Roberts. "I have made a contact already. This morning. But I am afraid you must do the business yourself. This dirty Frenchman named Raymond is expecting to speak with you. But like everything in this landscape, the suspicion level is very high. I have done what I can do to put my finger in this dike of fear, but I am afraid he is a very distrustful person." Mbenga shrugged as he had done so many times. "It is a pity, no? All this suspicion."

"C'nest pas une dommage," Roberts said. "There is much at stake and this is as it should be."

"Huonekana itanyesha," Mbenga remarked offhandedly in Swahili, words Roberts didn't know. "It looks like rain." He leaned over the table, his voice suddenly hard. "I have given Raymond word that you wish to buy seventy-five thousand pounds' worth of diamonds. The money is in French francs, he knows this. He has requested a meeting on the main square of Brazzaville in front of the Presidential Palace. There will be many people in the square at this time. Perhaps this is what he wants, a crowd."

"Do you know this man?"

"I have seen him, that is all. I know only his reputation."

"And what is that?"

"A trader of guns and diamonds and francs."

"He has the diamonds, you think?"

"Probably so, yes."

"Anything else?"

"But mzungu, do you know diamonds?"

"No, not a thing."

"I do, mzungu," Mbenga said. "If you grow up in Katanga you will know diamonds. In this I can help you, no? But in order to make this sale, you must appear confident."

"You've dealt with Raymond before?"

"Only a few times, through some of his people, this is all. He tries to be the businessman, not the fradeur. It is all the same here." Mbenga told Roberts that he had parked the Peugeot around the corner from the hotel. They could drive down to the cité and meet Raymond in the park; Mbenga could watch and check the diamonds. It would not be good to take weapons to the meeting because there would always be soldiers and police near the Palace. "There must be no violence, now. This must be commercial, no?"

"Don't worry, I don't want any violence," Roberts said.

"And then later, when we buy these diamonds, we can put them in a bar of soap or in a tin of tooth powder and you can take them across the river yourself. Nobody from customs will check these things for diamonds. The real danger is in this transaction with Raymond. The money is very great and so is the danger."

"I'm not going to give him seventy-five thousand pounds and just walk away."

"Of course, I will examine the stones."

"You know this much?"

"Yes, I assure you, mzungu. Katanga is full of diamonds and people smuggling them. This knowledge too is part of the landscape. Like the Big Vegetable and those Kikongo."

"What time exactly is this meeting?"

"Five o'clock. Very busy."

"I'll be back down here at four-thirty," Roberts said, paying the bill. The two men shook hands, and Mbenga hurried across the street and disappeared down an alley.

Back in his hotel room, Roberts tried to sleep. He tossed and turned for an hour, then took a sponge bath. He counted his francs in the black valise, and then he rigged some plastique in the lining, along with detonators he could explode by remote control, using the transceiver. The range of the radio transmitter was probably half a mile, and there was enough plastique in the load to blow off an arm. He went downstairs and waited for Mbenga, who showed up in front of the hotel in his Peugeot. They wound around the ville for about fifteen minutes before going down the hills to the flats where the Africans lived in the cité. The late-afternoon light had taken on a flat-red density, as if someone had spilled zinc-based cambric paint, strings of light coming through the acacia trees, the heveas, with Africans moving away from the market stalls at the end of a long day. It was terribly hot and there was no breeze, not a hint of rain from Zaire now.

Going down through the hills of the ville Roberts thought about Raymond and the hundreds of ways this guy could rip him off for his francs. Mbenga was driving while Roberts sat in the backseat, going down through the crumbling colonial section of town, through the seedy villas and government houses, stucco peeling from the buildings and the facades rusted from so much heat and damp, the tin roofs rusted. This was all building to something, he thought, and he was sure of it when they got down past the shambas to where the newer government buildings were situated. Here there were empty dusty spaces and wide concrete avenues, just the right size for tank movements, and white plaster buildings with black-shaded windows. When they finally got to the square in front of the Presidential Palace, Roberts was surprised at how quiet it was, an almost supernatural silence, rectangles of shade and dusty pepper trees, some blooming mimosa that created a faint perfume. There were a few soldiers clustered around a statue of the President, some bureaucrats in blue suits and a few children kicking a soccer ball along one of the avenues.

The banks and shops were closed, and Roberts made Mbenga go around the square three times before they stopped

and parked. He was looking for Raymond, trying to decipher
the ambush before it actually happened, but all he saw were
some American trekkers with backpacks, a Catholic nun leading some schoolchildren in uniforms and one or two diplomats on the steps of the Palace. The sun was blazing down
through the pepper trees and tiny finches splashed themselves
in the dust. Mbenga hadn't said a single word on the trip.
Roberts leaned over the seat and tapped the man on the
shoulder. "Take it easy, *mon ami,*" he said. "You see Raymond anywhere?"

"Not now," Mbenga said nervously. "But the man is supposed to be reliable. As these things go."

"As these things go," Roberts sighed. He was trying to
soften the atmosphere, ease them through to the other side of
what was happening right now. "We'll wait for the guy for
a while. When he comes, if he comes, you wait right here for
me when I go across the square and talk to Raymond. I'll do
the deal and bring back the diamonds and you can look at
them. Don't move and don't panic. If something goes wrong,
then you drive away quick. Don't try to do anything brave
and stupid, just let me go and get out of here. Don't even
think about being a hero. Just drive away. That's the only way
you can help the doctor. *Comprenez?*"

"This worries me, mzungu," Mbenga said.

Roberts shrugged and wiped his lips, which were parched
now with the heat and tension. After two days in Africa he
was beginning to feel his fatigue and estrangement as real
illness: an upset stomach, shaking hands, eyes that burned
when he tried to wipe away the dust. He hadn't slept well in
days, and now with the sombe and mafuta, all the sour vegetables and rancid cooking oil, his gut was hurting him. Late at
night he had tried drinking two or three Primus beers, but
they had given him a headache, and again he had fallen asleep

in the rattan chair, worrying about Raymond, about being short-circuited by the guy. And here Roberts was, two days in-country, and he was reaching critical mass already. Up the river in Zaire, it would get worse, but this was bad enough.

They waited, drove around the square again, just to be on the move. Less than half an hour later, Roberts saw a white Mercedes pull to a stop under a pepper tree. The car was being driven by an African, but in the backseat there was a Westerner wearing a white suit. He had thin blond hair and a wispy mustache. The man got out and walked over to a bench under the pepper tree and sat down, crossing his legs. The thrushes and finches in the pepper trees were singing madly. Roberts took in a deep breath for courage, and then walked across the park toward the bench, through the mimosa shadows and rising dust. He could see the man Raymond following him with his eyes, like radar.

Whatever Roberts had expected, the guy Raymond didn't fit the bill. They were locked onto one another, Roberts standing in the shade while Raymond sat still, legs crossed, a faint smile creasing the thin, aquiline features. This guy, Roberts thought, could have been a beach bum in California, his wavy blond hair going thin, square shoulders inside a wrinkled blue-linen suit, and steel-gray eyes that must have been pellucid once, now sunken. The man had a faintly rumpled air, as if he had been sedated for years, and was just now coming out of some deep somatic coma. But here he was, smiling benignly, a slightly comic bent to his shape, and this wavy blond hair. The only problem was the cruel eyes and the two-day stubble.

"Jambo," Roberts said, *"ninapesa kidogo."* Hello, I have a little money for you. Roberts recited the prepared speech he thought might break the ice, get them on track to serious business. Roberts stood away from the bench, one eye on the

African in the Mercedes, the black, smoky glass behind which he could see a shadow and the pale-gray leather interior. The birds were so loud it was hard to hear.

"I don't speak Swahili," Raymond said. *"Jambo* I understand. But I speak good English."

"You're Raymond," Roberts said, trying to place the man's French accent, southern he thought, or maybe Corsican, or Sardinian, something not quite on center, certainly not Parisian. "I'm here to do business."

"I'm Raymond," the man said. He slid down the bench, by implication offering Roberts a place to sit. The Mercedes was fifteen meters away, motor running, parked in the shade of a pepper tree and the trellis of an undernourished frangipani. "You have a name." Roberts recognized this as a statement, not a question, something emphatically deadpan, the source of an awesome boredom.

"What's the difference," he said.

"So," Raymond replied, with a shrug. *"Ça va,"* he continued, "I receive a telephone call. There is a message. Who knows what the situation is, no?"

Roberts didn't sit down. "There isn't a situation. I have the equivalent of seventy-five thousand English pounds in francs. You have diamonds. I want to buy."

"I see," Raymond said. Raymond sat still and surveyed the park, children playing soccer in a far corner. A border of cloud had rumbled over toward the river side of Brazzaville, turning dark at the bottom. Roberts hoped that it would rain, cool down, that he could escape the landscape for a while later. Roberts took another step. "Just so you know this, my friend, there is a man in that Mercedes with one of those terrible Israeli Uzis and he has it pointed at you right now. If we are to do business on the street, then I must have some insurance, don't you agree?"

Roberts studied the man's face, something slightly deca-
dent in the sharp features, the strong white teeth. He snapped
open the black valise and gave Raymond a look at the money.

"Very nice," Raymond said.

"And the diamonds?"

"Still, I am curious my friend. This matter of diamonds and
francs, it is my business. But you, I have never heard of you.
I could easily have you shot. Then you would have nothing."

Roberts was worried about the eighty-five ways he could
lose this proposition. He didn't think the African would
shoot, right here in the park across from the Presidential
Palace, but it was a possibility. Roberts was comparing this
feeling to his first emotion at Maya Maya Airport, that brief
roaring moment he'd stepped into the sun on African soil and
had seen a row of vultures perched on the roof of the weather
station, how he'd given himself a spot-check and recognized
an ominous mood, and now here it was happening. "I don't
think so," he said. "But, I don't know. If it's going to happen,
then do it."

"My friend," Raymond said. "I'm just curious. And I must
protect myself."

"Sell me the diamonds. I walk away. You have the francs."

"So simple," Raymond replied. "You are going to smuggle these stones to Europe?"

"It isn't important."

Raymond waved the comment away. "This talk of violence is so needless, don't you agree? I only ask because if you
are thinking of smuggling these stones to Europe, then perhaps I can be of further service to you. I have many friends
in the government of the Republic of the Congo, and I have
many friends who work for the French airline. I only wish to
warn you that if you are an amateur, you will find this matter

of smuggling gems to Europe not such an easy matter. I could be a good friend to you, no?"

"Let's do the deal," Roberts said.

"But you could lose the francs and the gems."

"Ça va," Roberts said.

Raymond nodded politely. Roberts wondered how the man managed to sit there so calmly in his linen suit without breaking a sweat. The air was still and hot, streaked with red from the setting sun.

"Very well then," Raymond said. "I think you are an amateur. You don't have the look of Interpol, or the French police. And I think you are an American. I have heard the Americans are, how do you say, very amiable and undiplomatic." Raymond took a velvet sack from his suit–coat pocket and handed it to Roberts, who opened the string, looked at the milky white stones, rough in texture. "Direct from Katanga province. Uncut and very valuable. With the political situation as it is, these stones are becoming very hard to get. You must consider yourself very lucky to have these. I must congratulate you."

"How many stones?" Roberts said, drawing the string.

"Thirty–seven, more or less. At the current price, I think you are getting a very good price. But I don't think this plaza is the place to conduct an examination. Perhaps we should go to your hotel so that you can make certain of your bargain? After all, I want you to be satisfied, no?"

Roberts opened the valise and placed it beside Raymond. The man looked inside, stirred the francs. "Count it if you like," Roberts said.

"In this place, it would be unwise."

"Then you can trust me."

"I don't think that would be appropriate. Perhaps at your hotel."

"Here's what's going to happen," Roberts announced. "I'm going to take these stones across the square. You're going to stay here with my francs. Count the money, no problem. If the diamonds are acceptable, I'll nod to you from there. You get the money, I get the francs."

"But monsieur," Raymond said.

Roberts took a few steps. "Just so you know," he said, "there's half a kilo of plastique in the valise you're holding. Stay sitting on the bench. If I see you move, or if the African in the Mercedes gets any ideas, I detonate the explosive. You might get lucky and lose two legs. I need some insurance, as you say."

Raymond squared himself as Roberts walked across the plaza, which had become a mosaic of color, hevea blossoms in the red laterite dust, pink mimosa flowers, the streaky sunset filtering down. Above the government buildings were the brown hills. Roberts put the diamonds in his pocket, walked across the park, not looking back, just walking toward the Peugeot. He stopped about fifteen paces away. "By the way," he called to Raymond who had turned gray-faced and expressionless, "I have a friend across the way who's an expert in these matters. If these stones aren't what you say they are, we'll blow you to shit. Are you understanding me, *monsieur?*"

"I think so my friend," Raymond said.

"You want to call this off, we do it now."

"*Comprend,*" Raymond called.

"I just want you to know, so that we can be friends. Speaking as an amateur."

Raymond said something Roberts couldn't understand, under his breath, and Roberts continued on his way. The Peugeot was parked near a newspaper kiosk, on one corner, heading away from the square. Roberts got to the car and slid in beside Mbenga. Raymond was sitting on the bench.

"What happened, mzungu?" Mbenga asked.

Roberts opened the velvet bag and showed the diamonds to Mbenga. "Look at these stones, quick," he said. Mbenga fumbled at them, but Roberts was surprised when he took out a jeweler's glass.

Mbenga studied the stones. "You are surprised," Mbenga said without looking up. "One comes from Katanga, one knows diamonds." Roberts kept his eye on Raymond while Mbenga did his work.

"Are they worth the price?" Roberts asked finally.

Mbenga poured the diamonds back into the velvet bag and shrugged. "The price is so liquid, you know? But I am very surprised, mzungu. I think you have made a very good purchase with those francs. And, you can't take francs across the river, so why not?"

Mbenga started the Peugeot and they went up a broad avenue away from the square, leaving Raymond to wonder. Roberts sat back in his seat, really admiring Mbenga: this guy one day in from Kisangani, already driving a getaway car from the quay where Roberts had stolen some weapons, sitting around in the hot sun while a diamond deal went down, driving with his shoulders arched back and calmly telling Roberts how they were going to smuggle diamonds and guns across the river into Zaire, how this could put them into prison for a long time and maybe even get them shot by Moroccan security forces. It was amazing, Mbenga driving one-handed, an arm slung over the seat, calmly cruising between crowds of soccer-playing kids and a few herds of goats, almost enjoying himself, as though he understood the developing pattern. Roberts knew he had developed trust, at least that was how he interpreted what was happening, and before they had gone halfway across the cité, through the evening crowds of drinkers and herds of animals, Roberts had decided to go across the river the next afternoon.

"We go tomorrow," Roberts said.

"To Zaire," Mbenga said.

They were stalled by animals. "If it can be arranged."

"Yes, of course. We go to my uncle's shamba. My sister will take the guns and the diamonds. They will be quite safe."

"I'm worried about this, my friend. Your sister."

"Please," Mbenga said.

"One more thing," Roberts said. "I don't want to take these diamonds back to my hotel with me. There may still be police or soldiers to deal with. They may come for me, you never know."

"Maybe so, I hope not."

"Take these diamonds to your uncle's shamba. Keep them for me tonight. Hide them. Just bring them when you pick me up tomorrow at my hotel. Or we can make our arrangements at the shamba. I leave these matters to you, my friend."

"You trust me with this, mzungu?"

Roberts shrugged and smiled. Mbenga made his way through the cité and let Roberts off five blocks from the hotel, on a hill above the ville. It had gotten dark, and there was charcoal smoke in the air already. All of the shops were closed, and it would be two or three hours before there were people back in the streets again. For now, he was alone, walking down through the palm-shaded villas and shops, in the curved roads lined by banana groves and frangipani. Roberts almost laughed to himself, thinking about Raymond, wondering how the guy had planned to rip off the amateur, but not really worrying about it now that everything was over and done.

Back at the hotel Roberts got his room key and walked up

the stairs and down the hall to the end, where he went inside his room. All he wanted was a short nap, and then a decent dinner, not sombe or fried bananas, but some decent lamb or goat, maybe a Primus and some apple pie. Already his stomach felt queasy, and his head ached from the lack of sleep and the stress, the wet sheets and the roaches eating wallpaper.

Once he got inside his room he relaxed and closed his eyes and smelled something that wasn't mold or charcoal, another *presence* that cooled the elocution of his thoughts. He had a click of recognition, something preternatural. Then he had a good look at a face inside his room, a pudgy oval in dim light, a man holding a small-caliber gun in his right hand, saying something in French Roberts readily understood, *silence, soyez tranquil monsieur,* when a hand pushed him down to the floor. An African was kneeling above him, one knee pushed down on his spine, one foot on his head, something that reminded Roberts of the scene on the mud plage, a posture he'd seen from the Kikongo.

Roberts could feel his own heart beating, lying there on the floor with the African kneeling above him, and it was humiliating, making him frightened beyond all measure, that feeling of being in a place where nothing would do any good at all, of falling in space. *Donnez-moi les diamants* was whispered in his ear, and Roberts smelled sour garlic, sweat. *Je n'ai pas les diamants,* Roberts heard himself saying, conspiring in his own debasement. Like a madman, Roberts kept talking in French, a voice above his own wordless fear: "The diamonds are on their way to Europe. See for yourself." Roberts could feel the gun's barrel at his skull.

While he lay there the African searched his room, going through the bedclothes, drawers, even Roberts' maps and papers. Roberts was still, listening to the dark night outside and the music coming up from the hotel disco. Sweat rolled down his face and he heard the African mutter to himself in some language he didn't understand, maybe Swahili, he didn't know. In his own mind, he knew he had underestimated Raymond, that he was the pro, Roberts the amateur. Here was this African in his room, and it was just luck that had kept Roberts from bringing the diamonds along, just a matter of trust. A few minutes later the African kneeled down again and hit Roberts just behind the right ear. Roberts saw a meld of stars and felt a sudden shock; his consciousness leaked away.

When Roberts woke, the African was gone. He was lying in a circle of cockroaches and he nearly panicked. A million tree frogs were singing in Brazzaville, all of them inside his head.

6

It was a sere African morning and Roberts was very ill. He was aware of his own nightmarish sleep, an embrace of wet sheets and the sensation of a bleak wave of sound suffocating him. Then he was sitting bolt upright on the bed in a streaming glow of light pouring through the hotel window, a shower of color that was hollow and piercing, too bright to understand. And in only a few minutes, Roberts recognized his nausea and he vomited into the sink.

Looking at himself in the mirror afterward, he came to remember how he had gotten the brown, blood-black bruise above his right eye, back toward the temple where his hair was thinning, and the two-day beard and the bleak eyelidless stare, almost as if a stranger had crawled inside his mirror and was daring him to acknowledge the resemblance. Roberts balanced himself on two hands above the sink, the vomit refusing to drain now, simmering before him like a green swamp, this stamp of his own illness that stank and stewed. He felt intensely light, as if his insides had swallowed themselves, or had flown away like a soul in the night, or as though his stomach had been drawn out from between his legs by some horrible succubus.

Outside it was diurnal Brazzaville, taxi horns tooting riotously, pied crows fighting over bits of garbage, the steady clump of the laterite-borne breeze banking through the groves of banana palms. For a moment, standing there in front of the mirror, Roberts felt as though he was going to lose consciousness. He could feel his legs give way like thin pegs, then his dizziness passed and he went to the window. He looked out over the ville, its mass of green-shingled colonial villas, the rusted tin roofs, the dull-white hills covered by brown grass in the distance, the stunning blue sky.

Wanting to wash, to have a hot shower, was his innermost desire. He stripped off one of the bedsheets and wet it in the thin flow of the faucet showerhead, and wiped himself down from heat to foot. He had a moment of nostalgia for the dewy gray mornings of summer in England, those monotonies of light and tone, something so contrary to the chaos of shades and colors in Africa.

He had shed his clothes in a lump at the foot of his bed. Wrapping himself in the damp sheet, he stood at the window for ten or fifteen minutes, trying to orient himself again. He marveled at the rows of vultures on the tin roofs and on telephone wires, sometimes flapping off in alarm or surprise, settling back down, flying up like question marks against the blue sky. Again he remembered being vaguely haunted by these vultures when he had stepped off the Air France jet at Maya Maya, this Westerner wearing the inevitable tourist khaki and hiking boots, taking those first faltering jet-lagged steps down the ladder after an all-night flight, eyes burning. At that moment, his first on African soil, Roberts was startled by the vultures which jolted him out of a present reality, dreamlike, but too real and dangerous to be a dream, and just at that moment he came to realize the challenge of Africa. The thought startled him, just as it had startled him while he stood, sick and tired, in his hotel room, looking out at the ville, down the windswept dusty streets of this African city. He knew he was going to have to redefine his perceptions, his whole conscious life, to transform his expectations from the commonplace and comfortable, to an acceptance of the untranslatable. Everything in Africa would be endlessly new.

He dosed himself with paregoric and began to feel better, still light-headed, but steady and reality-based. At the same time he tried to remember the night before, the details that would allow him to reconstruct the drama. He remembered the door to his hotel room opening, the first momentary feeling of strangeness, another presence, a smell that was off-center, and then almost immediately he had been pushed from behind—perhaps kneed—and he had felt the African's hand against his back forcing him down. Then came one knee against the small of his spine, the low growl in a language he didn't understand, and then the first few schoolboy French phrases that were so clear, pellucid. Rummaging through the pictures in his head, Roberts couldn't find one of the African. There was no real map to the guy's face, nothing directional at all, just the sour smell of garlic and sweat, and the feel of steel against the back of his neck. He remembered the feel of the man as he went through the room, the waves of fear he trailed, and the African going through Roberts' pockets, picking up the mattress, opening the dresser drawers, searching the bathroom, the shower stall, the medicine cabinet. The realization that he might be shot had coursed through his body like electric current, how he might have a flash of death as the bullet entered his brain, smashing through the skull, that flick of pain and the light going out forever. For some reason he didn't understand, the fear had died, and had been replaced by anger and resentment, a burning shame of humiliation Roberts shared with those boys and old men on the mud plage down by the river.

That goddamn Raymond, Roberts thought then, like a mantra that was keeping him alive. It was too predictable, these two guys, Roberts and the Frenchman, Raymond, trying to think of ways to outsmart each other. Roberts was satisfied that he'd won, and perhaps he had, but still, the humiliation ached inside him.

Roberts hadn't thought the African would shoot him. He wouldn't find the diamonds, which was why he'd come, and he wouldn't find them by shooting Roberts. He had begun to imagine confusion in the African, his frustration. That was when he began to realize he might live through the experience.

It was getting troublesome in Brazzaville, that was one thing for sure.

Roberts took some megavitamins and dried himself with the one hotel towel he was allowed. He went through his weapons, inventorying the parts, finding them all there, not surprising because the African was looking for diamonds. He probably didn't even recognize what he was combing his hands through when he'd rifled Robert's overnight bag. Roberts wrapped all the loose parts in old newsprint, tying each package with string, and then he dressed and went downstairs to the lobby restaurant and ordered orange juice, hard rolls, and some arabica coffee. He sat in the window of the restaurant so that he could watch the street, the Africans and their animals, a few businessmen and European tourists. He wasn't even aware of the time until he saw Mbenga on the other side of the street, looking at him nonchalantly, nodding, coming inside and joining him at the table.

"Jambo, mzungu," Mbenga said cheerfully. Two bored waiters in white smocks took his order. They seemed to be competing for whatever tip might come their way. Mbenga

spoke to them in Lingala and they went hurrying away. "Are you all right, *mon ami?* There is a bruise on your head."

Roberts touched his wound, which still ached a little. "I'm shaky inside. I've been vomiting all morning." One of the waiters brought coffee for Mbenga, the other following with hard rolls. An African woman was washing the tile floor on her hands and knees. With the brilliant sunshine splashing in, the hush of the ceiling fans, and the overpowering smell of disinfectant, Roberts got an institutional feel, as if he were sitting in the foyer of an insane asylum. Mbenga now nibbled at his roll, for the first time looking a bit scared, his eyes sheenless and wide, sneaking glances at the bruise on Roberts' temple. Roberts thought to himself that Mbenga could have been circling the hotel for hours, waiting for Roberts to appear in the restaurant.

"I am frightened for you, mzungu," Mbenga said at last.

"Last night when I came back to the hotel after you let me out, there was an African in my room. I don't know how long he'd been there, probably only a few minutes. He pushed me down on the floor and searched the room. And then he tapped me on the forehead with his gun."

"This is terrible," Mbenga said quietly.

"He didn't get the diamonds, did he?"

"You think this is the work of Raymond?"

"Yeah, Raymond," Roberts muttered. "He was pumping me yesterday about my hotel. He wanted to come back to my hotel and talk things over. But as you say, Westerners always stay in the National, so it wouldn't be hard for him to figure that out. His friend probably slipped a few francs to the bellboy, or the clerk, and went inside looking for the diamonds. I came along and surprised him, and he searched anyway."

"You don't blame me, mzungu?" Mbenga said cautiously.

"Of course not, my friend," Roberts said. "I expected Raymond to try something. I even planned ahead for it. Only I didn't plan far enough ahead. I'm grateful you kept the diamonds. Otherwise, your doctor would be in serious trouble right now."

"But I knew this Raymond only as a businessman. I am sorry I led you to him now. This is very dangerous for you."

"I don't blame you. We made our deal, and as you said, it was a good one." Roberts smiled at the African. He realized the matter of trust was now the key to their whole relationship—not race, not courage. They were finding their common ground now. "You do have the diamonds," Roberts added.

"Oh yes, of course. They are safe at my uncle's shamba. My sister is there with him. There is no problem with this arrangement. Your guns are undisturbed?"

"No problem there either. The guy wasn't looking for dismantled NATO shit."

Mbenga cackled openly. He covered his mouth with a look of apology. "I know what we can do, mzungu, just in case you think this Raymond is still following you."

"I was about to ask. I don't have any doubt that somebody is going to be following me around all day." Roberts gestured out the window as if to say it could be anybody, with hundreds of Africans in the street, all the police and diplomats and bankers.

"So you see," Mbenga said, "I have my cousin's taxi parked above the hotel as before." Roberts knew the place— in a clutch of banana palms on a steep hillside. "Now here is what I think. I will leave the hotel without you. Nobody knows me and they will be watching you, yes? When you leave you walk downhill through the ville, all the way to the end of the Avenue of the Republic. Just before you come to the edge of the cité there is the main market on your left." Roberts told Mbenga he'd seen the entrance to the market, an inverted *U* of shaggy palm fronds. "You walk down the Avenue to the market, and we hope this Raymond is following you. You go in the entrance to the market and all the way to the back of the sellers. There you will find the fetish sellers, with their markets of snake skins and potions. If you go through the stalls you will find an empty lot and a wide avenue. I will be waiting for you on the avenue behind the fetish stalls. You come to me and whoever is following you will be left behind. This would be very deft, no?" Mbenga smiled widely, proud of his deductions.

"I like it," Roberts said.

His nausea had passed, but he could tell that it was going to be hard keeping down the roll and orange juice. Some German tourists had come into the restaurant for lunch, and were making a noisy fuss with the African waiters. Roberts had seen these tourists in the hotel the day before, half a dozen red-faced louts come to see the last wild animals in Gabon, or the Central African Republic, snap some photos, and go back to Europe and their expensive cars. Somewhere here, Roberts thought, there is a real African experience, something outside international politics, the World Bank, all the human suffering and drama. There was something beyond tourist buses and photography kiosks, all the complaints about the food, the service and the heat. More and more Roberts wanted to be outside these standardized response levels, to tune himself to the real music that was beating all around him. While he was thinking, he suddenly realized that Mbenga had been talking, that he was telling Roberts about his cousin and the taxi. They shook hands, and Roberts watched Mbenga disappear down the Avenue of the Republic, and then turn up an alley.

Roberts paid his bill and sat at the table for a long time, thinking about Raymond. He wanted to give Mbenga time to be on his way, and he wanted to give Raymond some thought as well, just in case he'd have to deal with the man again. Then he went upstairs to his room and packed his bags, including the guns in their newsprint. His vomit was still stewing in the sink, refusing to drain, and the lights had dimmed again. He didn't want to pay his bill at the front desk because he thought that word would get back to Raymond, so he left his key and a packet of francs for the clerk to find later. He located a fire exit, and went out the back way and around the side of the hotel, keeping in the shade, away from the front lobby windows.

All the way down the broad Avenue of the Republic, Roberts hopped from shade puddle to shade puddle, just trying to keep his illness under control. He was surprised to find so few people on the streets, especially when just an hour before they had been swarming with men and women. He thought maybe it was the heat and the blowing dust, or just a custom after lunch, but now there were only a few Europeans and some sleepy-eyed children, along with the police. Once or twice he stopped in the shelter of a pepper tree to catch his breath against the terrible closeness of the afternoon. Resting, he began to think about how frail he felt, as though he had lost ten pounds already, as if his skin had been poached and was flaking away from his bones. He also stopped because he wanted to spot the African, and he did, about ten minutes later, a muscular Kikongo riding a minibike, dressed in a white undershirt, gray fatigues, and pink Converse tennis shoes.

Almost accidentally Roberts had crossed the avenue because his shade had run out. The road had narrowed to two lanes as he approached the cité, about two miles downhill from the Hotel National. One side of the street bordered a row of old colonial villas shrouded by banana trees, behind plaster walls topped by broken glass shards. Roberts had come down that way under the shelter of some hevea trees where an old man was sweeping the sidewalk in front of a bar, and then he had run out of shade, hearing guard dogs behind the villa walls, and had crossed the road to an apothecary. He stood in the brilliant sunlight, looking through the windows at an African druggist dusting shelves. He caught the reflection of the Kikongo, the big guy on his bike about fifty meters down the avenue glancing at Roberts through mirrored sunglasses. Pink tennis shoes? This guy who looked like a soldier down on the mud plage? Roberts smiled to himself, thinking that the Kikongo probably had a gun now, following behind only a shout away. Suddenly Roberts felt strong and alive again, as if he had touched a hot wire.

Roberts turned and walked downhill where he could see the concrete bunkers and garbage dumps of the cité, some smoke rising from one of the refineries. He estimated that it was about six hundred meters to the Ouzey market, that he would be there in about five minutes if he kept walking at this pace. The Kikongo behind him paused to roll a cigarette, then picked up the kickstand and rolled slowly down the hill. It was funny how this was all working, Roberts thought to himself, how this danger was making him calm instead of jacking him higher, so high he couldn't think straight. Roberts realized he was enjoying the game as much as the Kikongo, now that he knew the rules. He walked on patiently, keeping an eye on the Kikongo, in his succeeding-window-reflected self, this parody of a soldier in pink tennis shoes and a white undershirt. Roberts hoped he'd make it to the Ouzey market, that he wouldn't be jumped right here in the street, but he discounted the possibility.

Roberts relaxed when he got to the Ouzey market. There was a row of dying Royal palms that had probably been planted during colonial times, a welter of stalls and jerry-built shops, and a babble of languages that he couldn't understand, maybe Swahili, Lingala, Kikongo and French. Hundreds of Africans swarmed over sacks of yams, maize, onions and corn, boxes of tomatoes, bananas and plantains, and mounds of rice and beans. Roberts saw open-air bars, carpeter shops, racks and bolts of cloth, clothing, animals for sale. He was barely twenty meters inside the market when he was assaulted by five or six African children wanting to shine his shoes, sell him charms and trinkets, postcards, Chiclets chewing gum, wanting to dust his clothes and earn a franc. He couldn't understand a word these kids were saying, so he showered them with coins and they were gone, while he continued to drift in unselfconscious confusion. Behind him, Roberts could see that the Kikongo had parked his bike at the entrance to the market near a fruit stand, and was busy locking it, getting ready to come inside.

Roberts went down inside the narrow pathways, through the stalls, to where he thought the heat and the dust would choke him to death. There were a few acacias for shade, and some colorful awnings, but still not much coolness. Dry red dust rose above the stalls, and there were people packed closely together now, a lot of dickering. Almost inadvertantly, Roberts found the fetish sellers way in the back of the market, in a low place under a single scrawny mimosa tree, and he was stunned. Hanging on racks above him were hundreds of snake skins, rolls of them dried and nearly transparent. Huge bottles of herbs produced a smell he couldn't identify. The fetishists themselves stared at Roberts from their shaded arcades, jars of live spiders behind them, cages holding small forest deer, sacks of herb charms. You could hear vague traffic noise in the near distance, and the sound of music from a nearby saloon. Just now Roberts saw some vultures overhead, circling for a spot to land, and one commercial jet streaking away toward Europe. It wasn't hard to spot the Kikongo, about fifty meters away.

Roberts took a deep breath and plunged through one of the stalls, surprising the fetishist, brushing through a rack of snake skins, which he could feel dry against his own skin. He caught a glimpse of shock on the face of the Kikongo, a widening stare, something that made Roberts think the man might shout at him, but he didn't. Then Roberts got through the stall and found himself running across a vacant lot to where he could see the gray Peugeot parked, Mbenga standing outside the car with one arm on the roof, staring over it in anticipation. Roberts reached the Peugeot just as the Kikongo burst onto the empty lot, too far behind now.

Roberts sat down beside Mbenga and they started down the avenue. "Mzungu," Mbenga said, "I'm so glad to see you." He drove them east through the cité, where the streets were crowded with men sitting on corner curbs, drinking beer and smoking homemade cigarettes. There was a vague tension in the air, different from the ville, a slipstream of anguish and hopelessness, an environment of stares and taunts.

Roberts threw his bag in the backseat. He was tired and his shoulder and neck hurt. "I'm glad to see you, ndugu," he said. "But we need to talk, right now."

"Yes, we can do that, of course." They were stopping regularly for goats now, children playing soccer in the streets, and for the buses that seemed broken down, crowded, not moving at all.

"I need to know everything about you."

"This is the matter of trust you spoke of."

"Now it's time."

"You are concerned about Raymond. About the Kikongo who was following you just now."

"About Raymond, yes. But I'm more concerned about getting these diamonds two thousand miles upriver. I'm concerned about the doctor, saving her life. Somehow I don't think we've seen the last of our friend Raymond, and if we're going to travel together, then it's best I know. You've told me some things already. I just want to be sure."

Mbenga said, "I understand, mzungu." The man shrugged diffidently. "My father began his life as a miner and a farmer, with many cattle and goats, too. This is how my family in Katanga has always lived, from minerals and from cattle. I have lived around these things all my life. My brother and my sister and I were sent to the Catholic mission very early, where we learned to read and write, and to do sums. We were very happy then, and all lived together in our village." Mbenga bit his lower lip.

They were away from the main streets now, in an area of desolation, long gray patches of parched corn, some shambas. "And I've told you about the civil war. And I've told you about my years with the company, warehousing first, then some assaying, then my position in Kinshasa." Roberts knew they were off-track. He was sure of the man, but he was talking, with a faraway look in his eye. "My father and my brother went into the civil war because of their tribal allegiances. My father and brother were killed by Simbas. Of this I'm sure."

"Not the BaLese?" Roberts asked.

"Simbas," Mbenga said. "That was during the time I was being sheltered by the Belgian missionaries. My sister and my mother escaped over the border to Uganda. When they returned the United Nations troops were in control, but the situation was still very dangerous for everybody. These Big

Men, Mobutu and Lumumba and Kasavubu were fighting among themselves for control of the country. After Mobutu won this struggle, I went to work for the company because my family had no money and no home. I do not flatter myself that my work had much importance, but still, I could speak Swahili, English and Lingala, and I was versed in the ways of matabish, of the regular margoulinage that is part of the life of this country. I served in that way the company was able to obtain for me a *laissez passer,* despite the fact that I had been declared *mort civil.* Of course, I did not stay in Kinshasa. After so many years, there were no profits left, and I went back to Kisangani to work for the doctor at the clinic compound."

"How is it you were chosen for this job?" Roberts asked, trying to get around to the point sooner or later.

"The company sent a telex from Kinshasa. I don't even know these people now. They just said they wanted someone who spoke the language to come down and escort you to Kisangani. It was not made specific who should come. I took this upon myself because of my deep love for the *docteur,* and for the clinic. The docteur had been gone for two weeks, and things were very bad at the clinic. Yes, there was no help, and no docteur. When I agreed to come, the company sent a small plane for me and took me to the N'dola Airport outside Kinshasa. And then I was called to the Sozacom Building and told to be at the quay on the Brazzaville side every afternoon. This matter of waiting until the second day was my own clever idea."

Roberts finally made his point. "It's really your sister I'm interested in. I'm sorry, but I can't take any chances in this matter. Not only can't I risk another innocent life, but I don't know if she'll be able to do the job."

"Please be patient, mzungu," Mbenga said. They had come through a row of leveled hills, bleached white from the sun, and some scattered shambas with laundry drying on lines. All the trees had been cut down years before, and the hills were guttered by erosion. Roberts recognized the shamba where Mbenga's uncle lived, one of several built away from a plaza and its drugstore and bar, a small market. The shamba had a flat tin roof shaded by a single acacia tree, a curl of charcoal smoke leaking up through the dusty leaves. It was full daylight, and the wind had begun to blow laterite dust again, and there were goats in the streets, some children in rags.

Roberts touched Mbenga's arm. "It isn't any longer a matter of trust. It's a matter of doing the job. Right now I don't trust anybody but you. And your uncle, of course." Mbenga had smiled unsurely, as if he were ready for another round of questions. "It's just that I'm tired and sick, and we've got Raymond to worry about. In my line of work, you trust only one person at a time."

"And you must trust my sister now," Mbenga said.

"Your sister is next."

"You will see," Mbenga said, brightening a little.

Mbenga turned off the engine and Roberts followed him through the shamba to the back. Somehow the old uncle had erected a raffia palm fence on three sides of the shamba, transforming a dusty lot into an intimate courtyard. The old man himself looked up from a charcoal fire and smiled, revealing his blackened teeth, then bent down to stir his sombe pot and the plantains and bananas frying in a skillet. He had set a table with wooden bowls and spoons, and had put out hammered tin plates piled with groundnuts, shaved coconut and sliced mango. Roberts could smell yams boiling, and the greens. He could smell the plantains too, frying in mafuta, the rancid cooking oil. The table was shaded by the raffia fence, and streamers of red light were pouring through the limbs of the acacia. Mbenga embraced his uncle, and they spoke together in Lingala. Mbenga went around the shamba to the Peugeot and returned with Roberts' bag. Roberts was touched at the trouble the old man had gone to, trying to honor a guest. He didn't imagine there was much money, and figured that this meal would cost the uncle dearly.

It was only after Roberts had sat down at the table, while Mbenga and his uncle laughed and talked over the boiling sombe, after Roberts had taken a few bites of peanuts and drank some warm lemonade from a pitcher, that he noticed the young woman in the shade, by the side of the shamba. Mbenga was slicing plantains, and Roberts was being annoyed by flies when he saw her sitting there quietly, dressed in a dark green *pagne,* the traditional African dress, her whole body covered by the brilliant folds of cloth, her eyes beautifully expressive. She was wearing plastic sandals, the kind he'd seen everywhere since his arrival in Africa, her head was wrapped in a white turban. Above a large crucifix on her breast, her face wore an expression of complete composure, a statement of wordless serenity, almost humility. Roberts didn't know if his shock registered, but he couldn't help staring at the young woman's terrible disfigurement, too: the entire right side of her face twisted and malformed by scars, as if burned, one ear missing nearly entirely, her jaw sunken. He looked at her carefully, trying not to stare, noticing the ends of her fingers stunted, one thumb missing too. He swallowed hard and smiled, trying to think of something to say.

Mbenga and his uncle brought the sombe and fried plantains to the table and sat down. Mbenga and his uncle bowed their heads and the uncle spoke for a few minutes in Lingala.

When he was finished, Mbenga said, "The Lord's Prayer. It has a certain beauty, no?"

"Very much beauty," Roberts said. He had lowered his

eyes, but he was thinking about the woman in the pagne, her beauty and her disfigurement.

Mbenga nodded to the woman. "This is my sister, Marie," he whispered. "She will help us." Mbenga spoke to the woman in Lingala, probably an introduction for the woman smiled at Roberts and nodded.

Roberts returned the greeting. *"Madamoiselle,"* Roberts began, trying to feel his way to something that wasn't superficial. *"Votre frère est un bonn homme, très formidable."* Mbenga looked at Roberts in surprise and touched his arm. *"Je vous en pris,"* Roberts continued, *"nous voulons que vous nous joignez à la table."*

The old man spoke a quick Lingala sentence aimed at Mbenga.

"This is terrible French," Roberts continued while Mbenga spoke to his uncle, following a quick exchange between the woman and Mbenga. Marie had dropped her eyes, probably embarrassed, and was staring at the dirt floor of the compound. It was very quiet then, and Roberts could hear the flies buzzing, the nearly palpable sound of the wind kicking through the terrible wastelands. Even the pied crows seemed louder now.

"My sister is a leper," Mbenga said.

"Please ask her to join us," Roberts said. There are imperatives of feeling, and Roberts was following one of his own right then. "Please," he said, more to the woman than Mbenga.

Mbenga exchanged a few words with his sister in Lingala. Then she came forward slowly and unsurely, sitting down with her brother, across the table from Roberts. The old man was up, getting another bowl of sombe, pouring her a cup of warm lemonade. The birds were shrill now, and it was very hot.

"One does not know, mzungu," Mbenga said. "There are many ways in which people react to this disease. For many it is very unpleasant. I am sorry if we have dishonored you in any way."

"She's welcome, no?" Roberts smiled at the woman.

"In my own country," Mbenga said, "lepers are treated just like lepers!" He laughed and repeated this to his sister and uncle in Lingala. All three laughed together, the sister making just a small titter. Marie spoke quietly with Mbenga translating. "My sister is very happy you have come to help the docteur in Kisangani. She says the docteur is very good. She also says she wishes there to be no trouble for you and that you are very good to come and help. She wishes me to tell you that she has no fear."

Roberts tasted his sombe, which was full of tiny peppers and onions. He remembered being sick in the morning, how his stomach had rebelled at the food, but he continued to eat, not wanting to appear ungrateful. He exchanged small talk with the uncle, using Mbenga as an interpreter.

Mbenga finished his sombe, and was quiet. And then he said, "Mzungu, this is what I wished to tell you about my sister when you asked. But I could not. She has been at the clinic many years, and is very close to the docteur." He went on in very deliberate English. "When we are all in Kinshasa and this matter of crossing the river from Brazzaville is over, we shall meet again. You must allow her to take the weapons. And you must allow me to carry across the diamonds. You must not risk yourself in this matter. If they catch you my friend, it will go very bad for you."

Roberts brought in his bag, and took out the weapons components wrapped in newspaper. They were all conspirators now; an overt commitment among them had been made. "Ask your sister if she understands the risks she is taking,"

Roberts told Mbenga. The man spoke in Lingala, the sister nodding her head, speaking back haltingly because of her disfigurement.

"My sister understands, mzungu," Mbenga said. "I must tell you this now. Marie has smuggled many things across the river. Rice, soap, toothpaste. This is not uncommon for her, even though the risk is greater with these weapons. She is very devoted to the *docteur* and is willing to accept this thing we ask of her." Mbenga leaned across the table on one elbow. "Do not worry, mzungu, the soldiers and customs people will not bother Marie. They are very afraid of lepers. As usual, they will make her ride on the lower deck with the animals. They will be loath to search her on the other side." Mbenga shrugged knowingly. *"C'est vrai,"* he said, smiling now.

"All right," Roberts agreed. "But I'm going to take the diamonds myself. I don't want both of you taking risks on account of me. If something goes wrong with either one of us, you must be around to deal with it. I couldn't help either one of you if you were caught."

"But please, mzungu," Mbenga pleaded.

"The diamonds, I'll take them."

The old uncle had gone inside the shamba and come back with more lemonade, and some stale cookies he'd purchased at one of the markets. Mbenga had gone too, probably back to the front of the shamba. When he came back, he was holding a large tin of tooth powder.

"The diamonds are inside this tin," Mbenga said, pushing it across the table.

"And if I'm asked about this."

"There will be no questions. Nobody smuggles diamonds into Zaire. It would be amazingly stupid, no?" Mbenga helped his uncle light his pipe, and the old man went to his hammock and sat down on the edge of it.

"When do we go?" Roberts asked.

"Very soon," Mbenga said.

"We split up on the other side. I'll be staying at the Intercontinental Hotel. I'll take a taxi there."

"I will come for you the second afternoon."

"In the lobby, as before."

"I will stay with one of my cousins," Mbenga said.

"You have many cousins," Roberts said, laughing.

"Oh yes," Mbenga replied. "And I will bring your weapons to the hotel that next day, too."

"That's fine," Roberts said.

The sun had gone down behind an acacia and dusty light was dropping through the compound. You could hear the sound of vultures scratching on the tin roof of a shamba somewhere, and a neighborhood dog barked in the distance. For the first time since he'd come to Africa, Roberts felt as if he belonged to the landscape. An easing engulfed him silently, and he took up a cup of warm lemonade and smiled at Marie, who had taken away the weapons components. Mbenga raised his tin cup and they all touched their cups together. "Kwenda nzuri," Mbenga said, solemnly.

Roberts knew the Swahili phrase. *Kwenda nzuri.*

Go well.

PART TWO

LALA NZURI

1

IN THE EARLY AFTERNOON, FINISHING his meal with Mbenga, Roberts watched the old uncle fall asleep in his hammock, Mbenga pulling the lit pipe from the old man's mouth, saying a gentle and silent goodbye. Marie had packed the weapons in a wicker market basket; Mbenga explained to Roberts that she would take them across on the ferry concealed in her clothing, that this was only her duty to the docteur, who had been so kind to the lepers, who had sheltered them for many years. She stayed behind while Mbenga and Roberts went inside the shamba to talk, and you could hear her cleaning up the dishes, sweeping the dirt floor with a palm-frond broom, and later you could hear her talking to her uncle in a soothing voice, speaking the soft Lingala of their tribe.

The two men stood in the suffocating heat of the shamba. "The ferry leaves at four o'clock," Mbenga said. He pulled back the blanket door, revealing the deserted dusty streets, a few dogs, some children hot and silent. "We should go down to the ferry separately. I will take Marie. Are you sure you won't let me take the diamonds?"

Roberts patted his overnight bag. "I'm fine. I'll be at the Intercontinental. Come see me."

"Mid afternoon," Mbenga said. "You will be amazed at

this city called Kinshasa. *Poubelleville,* the City of Garbage. And a city of thieves. Be very careful. Pay what you think you must in order to achieve what you can."

Roberts shrugged and smiled, trying to imitate the African shrug of affirmation. He was short in expressiveness, unable to compress his feelings in a gesture. "I've been instructed to go directly to the EuroCopper office at Sozacom when I get to Kinshasa. It's likely there are people there who are going to want an account of what I'm doing with their money. I don't have any idea of what they're going to ask of me. All I know is I've got seventy-five thousand pounds in diamonds packed in a tooth powder tin."

Mbenga laughed gently. "Yes mzungu, the Great Vegetable would be very surprised if he knew."

"We must meet at the hotel. It is very important." Inside his mind, Roberts had set aside the formalities of their relationship. Now Mbenga was a human being to Roberts, not some strange anomaly; a possible threat, but a man on whom he could rely.

"I do have a cousin in Kinshasa," Mbenga said. "And I will come for you tomorrow at your hotel in the afternoon. You must trust in this, mzungu. Like my sister, I owe everything to the docteur."

"Before we go upriver you have to tell me everything you can about the clinic compound. And I want you to tell me what you can about the people who may have kidnapped the doctor. I need to know the terrain. Turning over these diamonds and gaining the release of a hostage isn't a simple matter. One of us could get killed, or both of us for that matter. We might lose the diamonds and the doctor might lose her life. She might already be dead."

"You must not think this, mzungu."

"I'm sorry. It's only a possibility. And there is the matter

of Monsieur Raymond. I was very proud of myself for putting plastique in his francs, but now I think he isn't very happy
with me."

"I assure you," Mbenga began, "that I will give you all the
information you need about the clinic compound. I am sure
there will be no violence. As to all these risks, they are ones
I am glad to take with you. To share with you. You can see
that I am the logical choice to be with you."

That afternoon they made their separate ways to the ferry
quay, down along the river Zaire. Roberts shook the man's
hand, embraced him, and walked down to the end of a street
where one of many taxis picked him up for the long ride to
the ferry. He had stood for a time in the shade of an acacia
outside a bar, watching the men drinking their beers and palm
wines, smoking rolled cigarettes and singing, taking their time
in slow Lingala, while others played cards and laughed among
themselves.

Roberts found himself thinking about this social situation,
the absence of women while men drank and played cards, the
lost and forlorn children without education and health care.
There was a fundamental breach, economic life without a
relation to culture—an urban Africa where every duty had
broken free of its former site. Now the men drank, the
women bore children, and a deplorable languor and despair
situated itself on every drab street corner, beneath every dusty
acacia tree. While Roberts waited there for his taxi, dark
clouds began to bubble against the horizon in the east, toward
Zaire. He could hear the sound of music lifting through the
dust and see some soldiers and police walking down the broad
avenue before him, about two or three hundred meters away.
Four or five of them had automatic weapons and were wearing gray fatigues with black T-shirts. Roberts clutched his
bags, as if they were a security blanket from his childhood,

and he became afraid. Just then a taxi rumbled down the avenue and picked him up and saved him from his preconceptions.

The taxi drove down through the outskirts of Brazzaville cité where there were brown hills cut by erosion, plateaus with fields of maize and manioc. The wind was blowing and dust funneled down from the tops of the plateaus and obscured the ville which was higher up. All along the road there were Africans on bicycle, dozens of herds of goats laboring under the chalky red sunlight, while women and children hauled laundry. "Kinshasa," Roberts said to the taxi driver, "Kwenda Nzuri." The name of the ferry caused the driver to laugh for no reason. *"Vous aimez Afrique?"* the man asked, basking in the flow of air from a small fan on the dash of his car. In the mirror Roberts could see him, a short, black African with a scarred face and a woolen cap.

Roberts pondered this, and then told the driver he hadn't been in Africa long enough to love the place. He said he liked the people and the sky and the color of the earth, but he wished for an American hamburger, all of which pleased the driver who seemed to understand Roberts' poor French. They missed a herd of goats by two feet, bouncing into the rutted shoulder of the road. *"Ndiyo, ndiyo,"* the driver said. Yes, yes. Gleeful at his own clever driving, he launched into a torpedo of Swahili and broken French, while Roberts listened. There was a slash of the river now, beyond that the almost blue horizon of jungle, some rain clouds bulking large. Roberts tried to roll down his window to get some air, but it was stuck.

He leaned over the driver's seat and asked the man's name. "Pierre Mulele," the man said proudly, repeating it without being asked, shaking Roberts' hand spontaneously. And Roberts could tell this African was thrilled to be talking to a

Westerner, that it gave him a sense of adventure, his own window to the world. Roberts was shown a picture of the man's wife and children, Mulele shouting above the whine of the engine in third gear. Going downhill now toward the river basin, Roberts saw the children who were very beautiful with shimmering smiles and huge black eyes. *"Vous avez une famille?"* he was asked. *"Les petites?"* Roberts told the man he wasn't married, that he had no children. Just then he thought again about Amanda back in London. He wondered if she was in the back garden among the early daffodils, back from the City. He grew nostalgic for his evening whiskey and Turgenev, a few soft hours in front of telly watching soccer, and beyond that, he felt the deep pull of his homeland, the plains of southern Colorado, the Flint Hills of Kansas. He sat back in his seat while the taxi driver continued to talk, Swahili and French, an admixture Roberts could no longer even pretend to understand. Again, he was feeling ill, sick to his stomach, maybe from the mafuta or the sombe.

At the ferry Roberts left the driver a good tip. He carried his bag to the quay, and watched the crowds and the soldiers. Although he searched the crowd for Mbenga and Marie, he couldn't find them among so many people. Mbenga had already given him a ticket, so he stood in the waiting line for an hour beneath a picture of the President of the Republic while a ceiling fan stirred the superheated air. He was led into the customs shed and his bags were searched and marked with chalk, even though there was hardly any attention paid to them. Mbenga was right, these officials hardly cared what was being taken out of the country, as long as it wasn't francs. They were strictly going through the motions, and not very well at that. Roberts was gripped by fear that Mbenga and Marie would be detained, that somehow the weapons would be seized and Roberts would see them being led away by

Kikongo soldiers, both in chains. A wooden barrier was raised; Roberts was swept along in a human wave onto the ferry with the animals and other passengers.

Showing his ticket five or six times, Roberts made his way to the upper deck where there were ten or fifteen other whites, some students, German tourists and one or two businessmen, along with African diplomats—an elite of soldiers and businessmen. This all seemed another world entirely, the huge river spread out below, the opposite side perhaps two miles away, and the smudge of Kinshasa on the horizon. The river was a deep chocolate brown with current swirling strongly around the rusted hull of the steamer. The water broke in creases of brown and green where there were islands and the river banks were thick with mangungu, a dark green swatch that ran in both directions, as far as Roberts could see. High up were some umbrella trees and a few hevea with white blossoms. There was a terrifying density in the picture, and a passive beauty, the blue bowl of sky and the brown water and the rectangular plateaus above it all. Clouds had continued to build over Zaire, and Roberts thought it might rain later in the afternoon.

He walked back toward the wheelhouse, and then to the foredeck, and when they had gotten under way, he explored the other two decks. Produce and animals had been piled in every possible space, sacks of rice and buckets of stinking fish, manioc, peanuts, racks of freshly cut plantains and bananas, machine tools and heavy equipment. But what caught his attention were the smoked monkeys, racks of them hanging upside down by their tails from bamboo poles, the tiny creatures no larger than rats after being charcoaled, their velvety tails curled. Their skins gave off an acrid stink that rose through the decks, wet burned fur, charred skin. Nearby were coils of skinned snakes, the meat veinous and red from blood, water rats, small forest antelope. Now Roberts remembered the Swahili word for meat—*nyama,* which also meant "wild animal." He was struck by this entomological fact, the lack of distinction between food and wild animals. Roberts went back to the upper deck, trying to shake the image of the monkeys, the small antelope, all the captured toucans and hornbills in their cages.

The ferry was an hour going across the river. On the other side Roberts nearly lost his way in the crush of passengers and animals going down, and he never caught sight of Mbenga or Marie, something that made him nervous. He expected the customs officials to find the diamonds, but they didn't search him. Even before going ashore he had wandered the upper deck, trying to spot Raymond, or one of his men, the huge Kikongo, but there was no sign of either. It was as if he expected the worst, and when he finally walked across the wooden quay, and through the guardhouse onto Zairian soil, he was vaguely disappointed. There was a long line of taxis in front of the ticket office. He negotiated his fare to the Intercontinental Hotel.

2

FROM HIS ROOM AT THE Intercontinental Roberts counted seventeen whores on the sidewalk below. They were marching in twos and threes up and down the Avenue June 30 in full sunshine, some of them gathered in front of the lobby. Roberts rubbed his chin, thinking how good-looking these girls were too, with their lamé miniskirts that revealed shapely legs, their silk brocade see-through blouses and black bras, their brass earrings and plastic pedestal shoes. He wondered how they could stand this heat, all the glare off the concrete and glass. His air-conditioning unit was making a dull hum, and he could barely hear the bumper-to-bumper traffic outside.

That afternoon Roberts had come across Kinshasa on a taxi ride that had taken about an hour. He got out about a block from his hotel and had waged a desperate dispute with the driver over his fare, which had been agreed on before the ride began, down at the ferry quay. The argument drifted on for about fifteen minutes, and then Roberts gave up because of the heat, and paid the driver his exhorbitant price, just as he noticed they were drawing attention from some policemen across the street. Once he paid, he noticed how many soldiers and whores were out in the roadway, and police too—men with machine guns and carbines, the women in their mini-skirts and huge earrings.

Once Roberts had paid and was standing on the curb with his single piece of luggage, he noticed the overpowering heat and the glare from the steel-and-glass buildings downtown. He remembered that Mbenga had called this country a *kleptocracy,* a nation of thievery, and he regretted paying seventy-five francs for a five-mile taxi ride, thinking how stupid that feeling was because it wasn't his money. He was still trying to get used to all the whores and police when the taxi sped away in a spume of exhaust. Before he could gather himself he was among the whores, who were exhorting him in French, in playful English, Roberts trying to ignore them, smiling, walking down the sidewalk that was crowded with Africans. There were whores on motorbikes and bicycles, whores lounging in the front of the hotel lobby, and even whores in the lobby itself; slick *femme libres* from rural Zaire, women broken away from their traditional village culture, now leaning back against the fake silk wallpaper of the lobby, one leg on a thigh, pouty expressions, very big-time tough girls. Roberts admired them, their bodies and their attitudes. He thought about the virus, this retrograde being in their blood, the syphillis, too; he wondered what was driving this behavior now.

The lobby of the Intercontinental was stuffy and damp, with an air of degraded Las Vegas *chic,* spackled ceilings, dying palms in art-deco pots, a curious ragged red-gray carpet with an unrecognizable design. When Roberts checked with the desk clerk, he found that his reservation had been lost, the clerk hardly bothering to check through his files, smiling up at him benignly. Roberts closed his eyes against the surreal event, then produced a roll of francs and pushed it under the nose of the African who looked again and found the reservation. At that moment, Roberts began to understand the role-playing that was matabish—the mixture of shrugging innocence, incomprehension, and thievery.

Roberts found his room by himself, down at the end of a hall on the fourth floor, and he went to the single plate-glass window with louvered side panels and tried to use the lever to open one of the panels. He found the windows locked, the levers sawed in half and soldered closed, so that he was left with only a tiny wall-mounted air-conditioner chugging humid stink into the room. At least, he thought to himself, there is a clean toilet and shower, and the bed seemed to have clean sheets, too. He tried the faucet in the sink, and there was a flow of fresh water. He sat down on the edge of his double bed and calculated the price of the room—more than two hundred dollars a night, give or take some francs—the taxi ride at seventy-five francs, the matabish one hundred francs. Not bad considering what he'd been told about Kinshasa. *Poubelleville,* Mbenga had called this place. The City of Garbage. That was when Roberts got up and went to the window again and began to count the whores down on the sidewalk, seventeen in all, just from where he was standing. Roberts tapped a fingernail against the glass, imagining fresh air.

After an hour of aimless wandering through the glass-and-fume-infused sections of central Kinshasa, glazed gray by heat and diesel exhaust, Roberts suddenly came up with his own nickname for this African city. For God's sake, his mind told him, it's a *Disneyland Hell,* an artificial toyland of suffering and glut. Crossing the Avenue June 30, trying to avoid the cadres of paratroopers assembled everywhere, like ubiquitous ants—troopers in camouflage, wearing jumping boots and carrying automatic rifles, black berets on their heads and leaping panther patches on the shoulders of their uniforms—the thought suddenly crossed his mind like an intuition. He would walk down one side of the congested avenue trying to keep to the shade and away from the soldiers and police, the screaming taxis, and stop to look in the shop windows at expensive Swiss watches, gold jewelry, cameras and diamond necklaces, all visible through barred windows, armed guards inside the flourescence. And then he would see more paratroopers, or some evil-looking police who seemed to mill aimlessly on every corner. Then he would cross the street and run into more police, maybe two or three men in starched blue shorts, light-blue sleeveless shirts carrying billy clubs and large-caliber automatic pistols. In this way he bounced from street to street, scene to scene, like a Ping-Pong ball, a minor mirror trying to avoid the glare of authority, trying to stay out of the inhuman heat and get a taste for the real city, the city buried under an official pall. Beneath a cone of pollution, there was terrible damp heat and a fuse of red emissions.

He finally recognized the World Trade Center, a gray and black basaltic form enclosed in glass, looming up through the blazing sun, reflecting back the tropical heat in thousands of starred shapes. Retreating beneath an awning, he watched paratroops patrol its grounds, marching through the concrete gardens beneath a huge all-seeing banner of Mobutu Sese Seko streaming from about the sixteenth floor. Mobutu seemed to catch Roberts' eye and look down at him with a cruel stare.

Roberts bought some lemonade from a street vendor and watched the Africans hurrying through the streets with stunned faces. The roads were jammed with steaming automobiles and motorbikes, tiny mopeds whipping like neutrons through an electronically charged field. It all was so *controlled,* he thought, as if he had emerged in a crazy eugenic laboratory where everybody knew the experiment had gone awry, as if at any moment the lab might tear apart. Disneyland Hell, without the corporations and the fun rides through towering fake waterfalls, a jumble of symbols and metaphors, ruthlessness, passion, fear—beneath the portrait of Mobutu, the glutton himself.

Down by the Monument to the Martyrs there weren't so many whores. Roberts had been out of the hotel for about two hours, reconnoitering the city, trying to reckon his distances the way an experienced pilot reckons his altitude in fog, and monitoring his health to see how long he could walk in the heat. When he got to the World Trade Center he was already faint, and he stopped for lemonade. Here the concrete was weedy and there was little shade, just some dusty gum trees on the street corners, and a few acacias.

The Monument itself stood in a dusty field of thorn bushes and ill-kept flower beds, an iron skeleton with iron eyebrows, cracked pillars, plaques in French. This part of the city was full of foreign airline offices, banks, commercial insurance houses, places where Africans did little business. The square in front of the Monument was empty except for a few policemen and bored paratroopers. Inside the airline offices, behind smoky glass, Roberts could see Europeans sitting behind *moderne* desks of steel and plastic, more like moles than human beings.

Far behind the square and the Monument, there was the Palace of the People, the *Palais du Peuple,* a vast alabaster and tile warehouse of pain that had the look of a Hindu temple with none of the playful sexual charm. Roberts began to wonder if the Disneyland Hell image would hold up for him during the rest of the afternoon, or if he would have to invent a metaphor more diabolical, if he would have to revise his images downward.

Roberts stood across from the Monument to the Martyrs,

trying to come to terms with its overt resemblance to a spider, when he saw a line of well-behaved schoolchildren dressed in plaid outfits moving across the empty square led by an African nun. He watched the children for a long time, two rows of boys and girls, handsome kids, some holding hands, and he knew he wasn't in *hell* at all, only in a place that had been running on underground power for a time. He hoped for the children's sake that something could stop this thing from happening, whatever it was, that it could be undone and made humane. He was sweating profusely, and felt as if he might collapse at any second.

In an hour he was back at his hotel. He sat down in the lobby and tried to formulate another nickname, but nothing came immediately to mind. The Intercontinental could have been the Intergalactic, or the Demented Las Vegas, with its spackled black-and-white ceiling, tiny star lights sprinkled everywhere and five tubular brass chandeliers. There was a blood red carpet and fake-lush chairs, and plastic potted plants. Floor fans generated a false wind. The whores cooled themselves on the outside stairs and toured inside, looking for customers, saying hello to guests before going back outside to begin their vigil.

Roberts bought a French newspaper and tried to read the articles one by one, practicing his language skills, trying to estimate the political climate. In the back of his mind he kept seeing the African who had come into his Brazzaville hotel room that night, the one who had searched for his money and hit him on the forehead with a gun. In this landscape, Roberts knew he would have to be much more careful, that he couldn't afford another lapse like that. Reason told him that events in Kinshasa had their own intimate destiny, that by their very nature every collision would be more dangerous, that everyone in the city, maybe everyone in Zaire, was living on the edge of something immediately dangerous and perhaps fatal. You could taste the garbage in the air, the blood on the buildings. You could hear the vultures sleeking through the trees, and if Raymond had followed him here from Brazzaville, there would be no room for more error.

Roberts felt weak and feverish after his walk, and was suffering cold chills, too. A violent thirst overcame him, which probably meant he was dehydrated. He thought that if Raymond was on his way, there might be no physical way to resist. It was a feeling of helplessness and loss that he had never experienced. Now he knew he would surely have to carry a weapon. But he also knew that Kinshasa was the most unlikely place for self-defense. If he was caught with a gun, he would disappear.

The lobby was filling with stylishly dressed African businessmen, and a few Europeans. Roberts bought a soda and went up to his room on the fourth floor, took a shower and changed clothes, and afterwards made a telephone call to EuroCopper at the Sozacom Building. A cool professional voice told him to come along immediately, that he was expected. Sitting on the edge of his bed with the air-conditioning flooding the room with damp air, he nearly passed out. He went into the bathroom and looked in the mirror, studying his own red-and-yellow eyes, sunken cheeks, the stubble beard. He took some vitamin B capsules and a dose of chloroquine, which made him feel nauseated. His hands were clammy and he thought he needed something to eat, and maybe a long cool sleep. Just to be careful, Roberts carefully moistened a single strand of hair and smoothed it down between the closed door and jamb. Then he went downstairs and caught a taxi.

When he arrived at the Sozacom Building in downtown Kinshasa, it added another dimension to his paranoia. Rising thirty stories above the superheated streets, the place had a totemic appearance, black magnesium walls, black glass windows, eyelidded balconies, and steel shutters. A moat surrounded the perimeter, and there were prowling soldiers with guard dogs. Roberts didn't bother to argue with the taxi driver, who had overcharged him for the ride, but gave the man fifty francs, watching him speed away in the red distance, down an avenue full of soldiers. He ran a gauntlet of police getting over the moat, and took an elevator to the twelfth floor. The hallways had all the barren glamour of a spaceship. A tall, black African woman led him through two oak doors into an office in the southwest corner of the structure where sun flooded through smoky glass. He could see Kinshasa burning below. Nothing had prepared him for this experience, this chrome city, the slice of river and the mangungu swamp glowing like halogen. He could see the voids of concrete shanty and warehouses, and he could hear the muffled sounds of evening traffic far below. What surprised Roberts the most was Tom Slade, rising from behind a sleek steel desk, coming forward to shake his hand.

"Welcome to Zaire," Slade said, coolly. Roberts concealed his surprise, hoping that when they shook hands Slade wouldn't notice his damp palms. "I hope you had a decent journey. Getting around these bloody countries can be a nuisance. We've been somewhat worried about you, I must say."

"Everything went fine," Roberts said. There were rolldown steel shutters on the windows, behind that the smoky visage of modern Kinshasa. The room was spare, a few tubular chairs, an empty bookcase, a bar with gin and brandy bottles. "I didn't expect to see you here," Roberts said. He sat down in one of the tubular chairs while Slade remained standing.

"I'm in charge of this operation," Slade remarked, walking to the bar and bringing back two glasses and a bottle of brandy. Slade poured two drinks and Roberts drank off some of his, hoping that it would steady his nerves. "As you know, EuroCopper really doesn't have anything to do with this matter. It is entirely in the hands of Lloyds. This is our money, and I'm from Lloyds." Slade drank some of his brandy, letting the message sink in while Roberts remained silent. There was a lock developing between the two men, but Roberts didn't know the combination yet. "Tell me about your trip," Slade said.

Roberts dissembled, spinning an unsanguine tale that left out the plastique, the late-night Kikongo visitor in his hotel room in Brazzaville, the theft of weapons from Congo Security Forces down on the river quay. He didn't mention Raymond or the diamonds. While he talked, a calm spread over Roberts like a stain, and he began to understand his needs, his desire to keep secrets from men like Slade, how he trusted Mbenga now with an implicitness that made him happy. He wanted to appear helpless to Slade because he thought that was what the man wanted. He didn't trust Slade now. There was something about his ferret face, the pointy nose and shiny blue suit. Roberts finished, smiled, noticed the red-smoke glare rising off Kinshasa, beyond the steel shutters.

"What have you done about the money?" Slade asked, sitting down now, glaring at Roberts across the shiny metal surface of the desk. "After all, we're here about the ransom." Slade folded his hands, waiting to be told about the operation.

"I'll deliver it," Roberts said, still dissembling. "What I need is intelligence from your side."

"I must insist on the details."

"I don't want to argue with you," Roberts announced calmly. "I thought we went through all this in London. As long as I'm hired to do the job, then I'll do it my way and on my own. I don't need amateurs interfering, but I do need to know what you know. For example, have you heard from the kidnappers?"

"Be reasonable," Slade announced, barely able to contain his anger. He released a smile like poison gas.

"Look, the more people involved in this thing, the more likely it is to go wrong. Besides, I'm laying my life on the line for this. You want to control the operation, then you take the money up the bloody river and deliver it to Kisangani. Then you'll have control. Know what I mean?"

"I'm only asking you to inform me. Technically speaking, you owe the company that much."

"Maybe we can compromise."

"Perhaps," Slade said.

"Suppose we begin with conditions in Kisangani. I'd like you to give me a report on the town."

"Suppose we begin with our seventy-five thousand pounds." Slade averted his gaze, misdirecting the conversation again. Here there were two dissemblers at work, both expert. Roberts studied the man again and drank some brandy, remembering the mood of the landscape in London, the calm gray day verging onto limpid summer, contrasted to the tubular furniture and the steel shutters clawing against the blood-red African evening. "I would like to know if you have our funds," Slade said, deadpan now, void of expression.

"I've got the money," Roberts said, giving Slade this much in their present tug-of-war. "The French bank in Brazzaville was very good about all that, even though the clerks and managers were surprised as hell. They had no choice but to pay over the money, right?"

"For God's sake man, you traipsed around Brazzaville with that much bloody cash?"

"Didn't have much choice, did I, old man?" Roberts said, mocking the English accent Slade had affected.

"Well, *old stick,*" Slade said sarcastically, picking up on the tone of the conversation, driving with it, "that would have worried me. It was my assumption you'd come over to the Kinshasa side of the river and we'd make some arrangement with the government to transfer the funds from the French bank in Brazzaville to a Belgian one here."

"And pay some matabish for the privilege."

"Of course. That would have been intelligent. You have to realize that in this country the rules have changed."

"You mean the soldiers and the police."

"I mean the whole bloody country. Maybe across the river there are some rules. Not many, but quite enough that the soldiers and police won't swallow you whole all at once. Over there we could help you if you got in trouble." Slade sipped some of his brandy and leaned back, head against the chrome tube of the chair. "But over here," he said, sweeping one hand in a wide, expressive arc, "the rules have been utterly abolished, you see. This country is a nightmare. If you expect to move the money to this country, you're going to need my help."

Roberts smiled, wondering how to play his hand. "The money is already in this country," he said.

"Bloody hell," Slade remarked. He seemed to sift through his available memory for something more to say. "You mean to say you've got the cash right here in Kinshasa, in this awful country?"

"Yes," Roberts replied, now enjoying his role as harbinger.

"Then you'll bring it in to Sozacom?"

"Not right now," Roberts said.

"Look Roberts, you don't understand what you're dealing

with here. You've heard of the *Movement Populaire de la Revolution?* The MPR?"

"I've only just heard of it," Roberts admitted.

"Well, you've seen the bloody soldiers and the police and the whores. That's the MPR. You've seen the bloody portraits of Mobutu hanging from skyscrapers downtown. Well, that's the MPR. You've seen garbage burning down by the river and all the tin and cardboard shacks, and the huge rats at night and the children suffering from rickets and malaria . . . well, that's the MPR, too. It's just a crowded box of words invented by Mobutu to hide the one thing this country does best, and that's theft. Bloody stealing." By now Slade was red-faced, nearly beside himself. He had vaulted his thin face over the desk and was hissing. "You bring me that money," he said.

"I'll pass. It's still my show."

"Now see here," Slade said, lecturing, schoolboy-style. "Our good Zairian citizens have nicknamed the MPR the *Mourir Pour Rien.* To die for nothing. And that pretty much sums up the situation in this place. As for a political movement, it stands for nothing except Mobutu lining his own pockets and those of his tribe, his political hacks, certain members of his immediate family. He's for maintaining absolute control through fear and poverty. If somebody—anybody—finds you with that cash, you're done for, my friend, and all your plans will go down a swirling drain of Mobutu's own making." Slade tried to relax and control his voice. "If you were to look around this country, you'd see plenty of natural resources. Rubber, copper, oil. But what you actually have is garbage and disease."

"Controlled anarchy," Roberts said.

"Quite," Slade agreed. He looked as though he thought he was getting somewhere with Roberts. "And so you see you simply can't march around Kinshasa with all that cash, and you certainly can't go upriver alone. That would be bloody suicide."

"Then why hire me?"

"We have an obligation under the policy."

"But you don't want a serious effort?"

Slade folded his hands again, exasperated. "I simply want to know what your plans are and what you're doing. I want you to bring in that cash and let us take care of it for you while you make arrangements for the ransom. I don't have to control your actions, but I'd think you would want some assistance in this project. You'll find you can't do this alone."

"Don't worry," Roberts said. "I'm going to Kisangani and I'll do my job without too much fuss. If there is a fuss, I think you'll find it causes more trouble than it's worth. You might lose the doctor by involving too many people."

"Come now," Slade said with a twinge of anger. "Let me tell you something truthfully here. Conditions in this country are deteriorating rapidly. I don't just mean business conditions, but everything—police, power, health, finances. The workers aren't working. The police are corrupt and violent. Government and law are nonexistent. Even EuroCopper is about six months away from abandoning their entire operation in Zaire simply because there isn't profit in it anymore. After the fall in copper prices, and all the bribes and hustling, and trafficking in influence, all the siphoning of material by Mobutu and his henchmen, there isn't anything left. In another six months there won't be any clinic, and no doctor from Belgium ministering to our black brothers."

Roberts bridled at the man's words. "And no insurance policy, right? You were six months from saving this cash."

"Of course."

"Reynolds gave me this line in London."

"Then you know it's true."

"You don't give a goddamn about that doctor, do you? You don't care that another human being has been kidnapped and is being held by God-knows-who. You haven't got a single bone in your body that responds to anything except the bottom line. Christ, you're a bloody sport, you know that, Slade?"

Slade reddened, the muscle in his neck rippling. "I look after the company's money. It does belong to our shareholders, you know. Have you forgotten who's paying you? Have you forgotten that you bargained your own share of this upward?"

"I like this," Roberts said. "Now we're hitting raw nerve. You'd like me to fail, wouldn't you, Slade?"

"Of course not," the man said. "I want you to bring that cash into Sozacom and let us conduct this operation in a clearly professional manner. We keep the cash safe here and make the kidnappers an offer." Slade smiled, trying to win his point softly, make Roberts feel comfortable with the arrangement whatever it might be. Roberts watched the sun go down beyond Kinshasa. Streamers of light were flooding the river plain and the sky had turned bruised purple.

"We'll blow this whole thing if we do it your way," Roberts said.

"Nonsense."

"Have you heard from the kidnappers?"

"Nothing."

"Then they're expecting a man to show up at the Stanley Hotel this week. We've got to do as they say. You can't sit here in Sozacom and negotiate with them by fax machine. You can't make this like two lawyers in gabardine at a mahogany table, haggling over details and minutiae."

"I'm only suggesting we safeguard the cash. I have a small

plane at N'dola Airport and I'll fly you up to Kisangani tomorrow morning. The flight plan has been filed and I've paid the bloody matabish to all the civil air officials. Even with the paperwork delays and the inevitable rumpus with customs officers, we could take off from N'dola by nine or ten o'clock tomorrow morning. I'll have you in Kisangani by late afternoon, or early evening before dark."

"And the cash?"

"It stays at Sozacom, of course."

"You're going to negotiate with these kidnappers without fulfilling their first condition?"

"All right, you bring the cash and we fly up together."

"And what about Mbenga?"

"The liaison," Slade said flatly. "His job is done. He's a bloody African."

Raw bone at last, Roberts thought. He bit his tongue and finished the brandy he was holding. Slade had poured some more into his own glass and sat thinking quietly. Roberts was feeling light-headed, probably the combination of brandy and chloroquine, all the vitamins and bad food. Suddenly Roberts noticed that it had become night, as if a curtain had dropped. "I can't be ready tomorrow morning," he said.

Roberts heard the unmistakable metallic roar of a helicopter. He walked to the window and watched the bird soar through some skyscrapers, its searchlights flashing downward. Two huge floodlamps were bathing the streets in blue light, a motionless sheen of moonlit silver in which he could see soldiers patrolling and police stationed on corners. Another helicopter grazed his line of sight, far away and moving fast, a moth entering death zones. There was a momentous feeling to the streets and buildings below, as if death squads were on the march. The skin on the back of Roberts' neck stiffened and he thought he felt a chill pass through the office. He was holding on to his visions by a slender visceral thread. Disneyland is wrong, he thought to himself while he stood at the shuttered window. He turned to Slade and said, "I have things to do."

"This is bloody inconvenient, Roberts," Slade said. "I can rearrange the flight but you'll have to assure me you'll be ready to go the day after tomorrow. We can't fly commercial in this country. You can't rely on the schedules or the weather. Too much red tape, too much interference and oversight."

"The day after tomorrow then."

"All right, old chap," Slade said confidentially. "I'll be after you at your hotel at six in the morning. I assume you're staying at the Intercontinental."

"Of course, isn't everybody who's anybody?"

"Right," Slade said. "I'll fly you right up to Kisangani. We can have a nice chat. The weather is a little bit dicey this time of year, especially over the central basin." Slade was feeling relaxed now, buddy-buddy. "There are storms, you know, but we'll get around those, quite. I'll have you snug as a bug in the New Stanley before nightfall."

"What the hell, it's only two thousand miles."

Slade laughed wanly. "Right," he said. Already Roberts had cleared his field of vision about Slade, his overt racism, his narcissistic self-confidence, the condescension. This guy is a piece of work, Roberts thought to himself as his level of mistrust topped out. The helicopters were going away now in a low whining cadence.

"I may need a car once we get to Kisangani. Something with four-wheel drive. Maybe a jeep, but something with guts."

"We'll see to it, old man. I'm prepared to make all the necessary arrangements. Now, let's go to your hotel and get the cash and bring it here for safekeeping."

Roberts avoided the question. "Tell me about the clinic compound."

"You've been briefed in London."

"Just go over it again."

"The clinic is about six kilometers from Kisangani up a disused logging road. Inland a ways. I suppose there are half a dozen buildings in all, including sleeping quarters for the staff, hospital, dispensary and the doctor's hut. The hospital is in an old Belgian warehouse. The rest of the structures are wooden with tin roofs. You won't find anybody there now but patients and a few staff. Maybe two hundred people in all."

"You have any photographs?"

"None I'm afraid, old man."

"What about a weapon? Can you get me one?"

"I can't help you there at all. We couldn't get one into N'dola even if we wanted to. They're bloody paranoid about guns, these customs police are."

That was it, Roberts thought. The word *paranoid* struck at him like a piano wire. Slade had smiled slightly when he said it, as if harboring a resonance in himself, too. The word and the country were somehow delicious together.

Roberts decided to dissemble further, to adopt a pose for Slade, one that might give him time. He wanted to frame some scope for himself, become an innocent. "No further word from the kidnappers," he remarked. "Any intelligence on who they might be? Anything that might give us a clue? Something you didn't tell me in London?"

"Ah," Slade said, waving a hand, dismissing the question. "Still think they're rogue Simbas. Some tribal leftovers from the groups who ran rampant at the time of the revolution, bloody beggars squashed by the Belgians and the U.N. troops." Night had caught up to the barren office. Slade walked to the bar and touched a switch, sending the room into a synthetic bath of indirect light. "Of course," he continued, replacing the brandy bottle in its glass nook, "this gives us some hope that they want only cash, and that this isn't some unnatural political statement. No bloody martyrs we're dealing with here, just outlaws."

"They could kill her," Roberts said, just to get an effect. He was weary of the man Slade, of the indirect light, and the silicon feeling of the air in the room.

"They could indeed," Slade agreed. "They could bloody well kill you too and make off with all that company money." Slade produced some badly printed brochures from a desk drawer and shoved them across to Roberts. "That would be most unfortunate," he said.

Roberts studied some hazy aerial shots printed on cheap stock, the warehouses and workers' huts in washed-out color—a slash of tangerine earth, faded green jungle, a postcard flag blowing in the breeze. He tried to read some of the descriptions written in poor English but he gave it up as EuroCopper-type propoganda: all the happy workers, the steadily improving climate for foreign investment, the holiday spirit of capitalism. Roberts slid the brochures back and something clicked inside his head, the hum of thought.

"The Simbas," Roberts said, "they must have home villages, chieftains, supporters. Maybe the local police have a dossier. Hasn't anything been done by the authorities?"

Slade raised a knowing eyebrow. The helicopters had returned in B-line vectors of malevolence, arrows of noise between the tall buildings of Kinshasa. Roberts could hear them making their sound shadows on every citizen's fears. He thought of something he had read—the force of government authority against its citizens is the force of forgetting against the force of memory. Where had the memory of Africa got to?

"You must be bloody kidding," Slade was saying, sifting his sight through the shuttered windows now, following the sound of the rotors going away. "There isn't any authority in Kisangani, none that I know of anyway." He smiled, hanging on to his thought. "And in the good old days they were bloody corrupt and stupid as it is. Nothing around here like the good old days if you ask me. Not since Leopold began the custom of cutting off the natives' hands if they didn't fill their ivory quotas, what?"

Slade offered a car to return Roberts to the Intercontinental, an offer which Roberts politely refused. They talked for another ten minutes, just chat, and then Roberts took the elevator to the Sozacom lobby and went out the front gates, across the moat, followed by maybe twenty pairs of official eyes—police, paratroopers, building sentries. He thought he might walk back to the hotel, but the dense wall of silent Kinshasa frightened him; the big buildings with Mobutu facades, acres of empty concrete for the tanks, the police squads. Pretty soon he flagged down a black Mercedes taxi that took him around the flanking white stones of the cemetery that separated the cité from the ville, a huge colonial necropolis gleaming in the tropical moonlight. All the way back Roberts noticed the smell of diesel, river water and garbage, and watched the great stars canopied over the forest far away. He was happy to get back to the hotel noise, the disco and the whores.

He walked through the animated lobby of the hotel, tired by his decisions and the long day of walking and tension. When he got to his room the strand of hair was in place, and he relaxed and thought about eating a late meal. He decided that he was too tired and ill, that what he needed was sleep, not a noisy disco dinner of boiled goat and sombe. The bathroom door was open and he could hear water dripping from the showerhead in the bathroom. Dark sequences of thought went through him and twice more he heard helicopters droning in the far distance, back over official Kinshasa. He washed his hands and feet in the wash basin after finding the shower only a mush of warm brown water. Two tablespoons of paregoric offered him sleep and terrible dreams.

3

FORTY U.S. DOLLARS BOUGHT Roberts some orange slices, cold coffee and French bread in the hotel restaurant, all served by a surly Chadian refugee. Roberts sat where he could observe the street outside and its swirling masses of *mamas doing business,* young ladies called femme libres in the ville who had come from their rural villages and were adapting to a new environment, strutting and pecking at businessmen and diplomats, arguing among themselves for choice space in the lobby, lighting Western cigarettes and smoking them in full sunshine, one hand on a hip, eyes darting nervously from customer to customer.

These girls fascinated Roberts because they had obviously broken loose from an ancient social milieu in which their ancestors had been going about village life for centuries, and were now living dangerously in this huge city of millions where venereal disease, AIDS and cholera swept through like hot winds. All this disease and dislocation had been tormenting Uganda, Rwanda, and the entire Lualaba basin for twenty years, pushing people away from the countryside and toward this huge teeming city of poverty and garbage, and now these girls were risking those dangers along with the danger of beatings and torture, just to earn a few bucks, enough to wear

Western clothes, big earrings, drink some palm wine and dance with strangers. Roberts ate some of his French bread with jam, then ordered cornflakes, but the cornflakes didn't come.

He had found a single cool patch under an air-conditioning vent, and was enjoying the fresh air *manqué,* even though he could feel a fine, thin film of sweat all over his body, and even though his stomach ached and he had a terrible headache. There were police across the street from the hotel, watching the girls parade, and busy Africans hustled up and down the street on bicycles and mopeds. The air was dense with gray and brown soot, and far away he could make out the semblance of the grim World Trade Center. He even thought he saw some pelicans streaking away toward the river, but he wasn't sure.

Roberts had stayed in bed until noon, not sleeping exactly, just exhausted and doped, spending all night imprisoned in the grip of very bad dreams, tossing and turning on wet sheets. By dawn he was awake, and then fell asleep again just after the sun rose over the city, a deep narcotic slumber that was broken by sunshine splitting through the hotel windows, falling all over him like fire, and then he was awake and knew it was late. To his surprise, there was plenty of hot water and he took a long refreshing shower, then turned on cold water and stayed under it for about twenty minutes, until he felt completely and finally clean. He changed into fresh khakis, and took some chloroquine and vitamin B, and then went downstairs and checked his nonexistent messages. The clerk remembered him and put on a smile, expecting some more tips, but Roberts ignored him.

After his late breakfast he decided to take another walk, just to check his perceptions of the city, knowing that Mbenga wouldn't come looking for him at the hotel until later in the afternoon. He walked down the Boulevard June 30 again, toward the Sozacom building, north and west of the hotel for about fifteen blocks under the distended shade of gum trees full of pied crows and ant thrushes. There was a dull sulphuric smell in the air and the sky was permanently brown. The streets were thronged with Africans, taxis, bicycles. The Boulevard ended at the colonial cemetery and Roberts walked about two kilometers around its circumference, amazed at the vastness of the necropolis, its white stones and green grounds, and just beyond, the truly African section of Kinshasa with its miles of concrete bunker shambas, tin hovels, warehouses and bars. In the distance was smoke, a pall from burning garbage.

What had he read? There were three million Africans crammed into a few square miles of the cité, more pouring in every day from the bush, living cut off from all their traditions and values, without adequate food or employment, not even minimal public health, an ooze of Third World obscurity fogged over by alcohol, despair and poverty.

By the time he went around the third corner of the cemetery he was feeling weak and abstracted again, just like he had felt the day before, an effect of all the heat and exhaust fumes. His stomach trouble had gotten so bad that he was forced to stop two or three times, doubled over from cramps, a hidden message of diarrhea. The crowds were thick as flies and everybody seemed to be arguing, or maybe that was just the present music of urban Africa. He began to worry about Mbenga and Marie.

Back at the hotel he checked his messages again but found nothing, so he went up to his room and lay down on the bed to rest in damp sheets. At least, he thought, the room had been made up, the bathroom cleaned and fresh towels put in. It was late in the day and once or twice jets growled over the city heading for the international airport at N'dola. There were more helicopters, too, but he hardly noticed them at all. Maybe he drifted into a sleep, but maybe not; it was that vague a sensation, as if he were suspended between states of being, in a no-man's-land of consciousness.

When he woke, his room was a shade of dun brown and the air-conditioning was droning dully. He heard a faint knock on his door. When he opened the door, he saw Mbenga standing in the middle of the hallway smiling sheepishly, wearing his Nigerian skullcap, a bright print shirt, dirty polyester pants with Nike running shoes.

"I'm glad to see you, mzungu," Mbenga said.

Roberts pulled him inside. "That goes double for me," he said, really meaning it. He touched the man's face and put an arm around his shoulder. Deep inside he recognized the tyranny of his anxieties. "Your sister?" he asked, shutting the door.

"She is quite fine, mzungu."

"I'm just edgy, nervous, you know?"

"Oh yes, I know. Such a *mal adventure!*" Roberts felt so sick he had to sit on the bed, then recline with his back on the stead. "I was delayed by customs at the ferry," Mbenga continued, by way of apology. "But don't worry, my sister was let through without difficulty. These officials detained me only so they could extract their small matabish. They pretended to wish to search me, but they only required a small stipend for the government service they do. It was a simple matter, but it took some time. And then my cousin's wife was sick and he was spending some time at his brother's shamba in the cité and so this delayed me further until I could get his taxi and come to see you. It was only after lunch that I was able to find him, and by then I knew you must be worried about me. I hope this has not caused you too much suffering." Mbenga placed his hands in his pockets.

"And our secret cargo?" Roberts asked, wearily.

"My sister has charge of this secret cargo," he said, delighted at the conspiratorial argot. "She is waiting for you in the cité where your weapons are quite safe. You would be amused to see the soldiers and police on the ferry avoid her."

Roberts relaxed and made Mbenga sit down in the rattan chair beside the hotel window. There were blue-suffused clouds on the horizon, visible between the skyscrapers. Something subconscious was taking over his mind, working deep below the everydayness of his concern.

"We have a small problem," Roberts said.

"I hope it is nothing serious, mzungu," Mbenga replied, now listening intently. The air in the room was dead, as if it had been manufactured poorly.

"Nothing insurmountable I think," Roberts said. "But I want to get the weapons as soon as possible. I want to assemble them and make sure they're safe. I also want to get them away from Marie. I don't like involving her any more than necessary. She's a wonderful person and I don't want her hurt."

"She is very strong," Mbenga said. "But I must ask you something." Here Mbenga looked away shyly. "My cousin and his family are at the shamba now. I am ashamed to say that they know nothing of these weapons that Marie has on her person. This is somewhat dangerous and they are not connected to this affair. If anything were to go wrong it would go very bad for them. For myself and my sister, and even for my uncle I am willing to take these risks. But I am not willing to take these risks for my cousin and his children. In only a few hours they will leave again and my sister will be there alone. Then we can retrieve your weapons and all will be well. Is this possible, mzungu?"

Roberts had no problem with any of that and he told

Mbenga to relax. Roberts washed his face and hands while Mbenga waited by the window in the half-dark where the sun had gone behind some skyscrapers. The sky was luminescent from all the vapors and smoke.

"Have you any hunger?" Mbenga asked.

Roberts was drying himself, standing beside Mbenga in the window, watching the city burn. Experience was lifting away from him now, he was bubbling with pure phenomenal vision. There was no more between him and the burning buildings than a thin film of skin full of nerves. He could feel the steel and glass cracking from all the heat. Lightning creased over the cuvée, a slick of yellow electricity above a blue bowl. "I could try to eat again," Roberts said, aware that he was probably kidding himself.

"Let us go away from this hotel," Mbenga said. "There are too many eyes here. Too many femme libres. I do not like it here. It makes me ashamed for my people. It is like a combustible substance, too hot for me to witness."

Roberts clapped Mbenga on the shoulder, sublimating both their fears. "You worrying about our friend Raymond?" he asked Mbenga, who was studying the whores, the police across the street.

"He is something to worry about, no?"

Roberts said he was something to worry about, very worthwhile. "But we left him in the Republic, and he doesn't bother us anymore? What do you think about that?"

"I wish it was so, mzungu."

Roberts took another vitamin B and said he was ready.

"We go to the cité, no?" Roberts asked. "We can drive around this Kinshasa and discuss your problem and maybe have something good to eat. Perhaps we can see if someone is following us."

They were standing in the hallway, Mbenga just behind

Roberts, watching him paste a strand of hair against the jamb. "Maybe someone is following us. You never know," Roberts said.

Mbenga gave a worried shrug, but didn't ask any questions. Roberts had purchased another black valise, and he was carrying it, stocked with enough francs and Zaire notes to get them a good meal, enough to pay any policeman who might stop them on a lark.

They went down through the lobby and found Mbenga's taxi where he had parked it about three blocks away on the sidewalk near an alley. Driving north and west, away from the ville, Mbenga skirted the cemetery, punching through heavy evening traffic, and thousands of pedestrians and bicyclists. Once they got north of the cemetery Roberts began to see the first shambas and slums, the small tin warehouses and hovels, open sewers and empty lots. The sun was fully down now, behind the buildings, and the sky had telescoped down to an orange flare shape above them, a dark blotch full of pied crows and pelicans, some ragged vultures sitting on telephone wires. Night was closing in around them, and it wouldn't be long before it would be full dark in the cité. Roberts was riding in the front seat with Mbenga while they waded through other taxis, a dangerous and complicated game of traffic control without computer banks and directional finders. It seemed to Roberts that the flow was not uniform, and that at any moment someone would smash into them from the side, or they would hit a pedestrian and send him tumbling over the hood in a stream of broken glass and blood.

When Roberts smelled charcoal he knew he was in the cité. There were hordes of men in front of bars, drinking Primus and palm wine; at other corners children of all ages; with cigarettes and sweaty faces mingled. It was fully night and the streets had no pattern.

"This is *Matonge*," Mbenga said. "This is modern Africa."

"Spot anybody on us?" Roberts asked.

"Nobody," Mbenga said. They were in an old Chevrolet Bel Air with cracked windshield and rumpled fenders. The thing burned oil and they were leaving a trail of white smoke. "There aren't so many taxis in Matonge. I don't see anybody."

"I don't even see any police or soldiers."

"Matonge is too difficult for them, you see."

Roberts was trying to decipher Mbenga's comment. On every corner there was a bar or nightclub, and a few open-air dance halls under tents.

A grove of pepper trees covered them. "We'll eat at an *nganda*," Mbenga said, stopping. At the far end of a corridor of trees Roberts saw a pavilion tent of heavy-duty construction with a makeshift tin roof and a raffia palm border around the perimeter. The music in the shelter of the pepper trees was loud and driven. "You will maybe not very soon believe this, mzunugu. But one of my cousins is a waiter at this nganda. This is why I have brought you here."

There were only a few cars in the pepper tree grove, mostly bicycles and mopeds. Roberts could see Africans dancing under the pavilion, others sitting at small tables around the floor eating goat and chicken, boiled sombe and rice. Wild driven music poured from a band—guitar, bass, horns and drums—everyone moving to the world beat, crazy shouts of rhythm drifting through the night air. Mbenga led Roberts through the crowds and found them a table in a far corner of the pavilion where they could see the band and the dance floor. Mbenga's cousin spotted them and brought them two Primus beers without being asked. They were introduced and Mbenga ordered dinner.

"Don't worry, mzungu," Mbenga said. "Nothing is going to happen to you here, except you will eat and enjoy."

"I think I'm conspicuous," Roberts said.

Mbenga laughed. "Maybe a little." Roberts was the only white in the place. "But I think we are finished with your friend Raymond. There is nothing that this Raymond could do to you here anyway. I have many friends in this place. Not only my cousin." Mbenga picked up his beer and touched Roberts' glass. "You *comprend* this, no?"

Roberts thought that was no problem. A few Africans had stared at him, but he was fading in. Mbenga rose and went over to another table and spoke to some Africans in Lingala. He came back and said, "I have ordered us sweet potatoes and fish. Some hot rice. I hope that is all right, mzungu."

Roberts didn't know if he could eat, but he said he would try. His stomach was bothering him badly, and he had a headache just behind his eyes. He sipped cold beer and there began to formulate in his nostrils the deep acrid smell of bangi, a thick sweet drift of smoke in the rafters that hung like a curtain above all the dancers. Just smelling it made his head spin. Roberts sat and listened to Mbenga give him the story of all his cousins in Zaire—the waiters and taxi drivers, the ones who had fled Katanga province when the revolution destroyed all the mines and factories, when the farms disappeared and the animals had no place to graze. This result, Mbenga said, spreading his arms to encompass the pavilion, was the nganda where all the village people came to congregate and smoke bangi, dance and laugh, forget their urban troubles and fears. Only a few years before these same people had lived in the bush, raising families and a small herd of goats, some scrawny cattle, hauling their drinking water from a stream. Now they came to the nganda to drink and smoke themselves into oblivion, to dance to world-beat music and whirl into a glorious unknown, free of pain and filth.

Roberts surveyed the dance floors, the young women in tight jeans and halter tops, men in flared bell-bottoms and polyester slacks, faces animated and slick with sweat, a society abandoning its past, a wild moment of existential nothingness, here in Kinshasa's cité. Roberts knew that something was happening in his own country as well, that Western cultures were changing their identities, too, freedom exchanging itself for mediocrity, conformity and petty war. But a whole generation of African men, Roberts thought, is bleary-eyed, half-drunk, stunned with dope, most without work or hope—where are they going? What will they do while the West wallows in shallow materialism, while the West degenerates into its own boring box of greed and violence? Maybe the answer was in this music, its blend of hard rock, Motown and traditional drumming. And then he thought of the Lord's Prayer said in Lingala, how beautiful it had been.

The waiter brought their food, boiled fish, rice and sweet potatoes in steaming heaps on wooden plates. Roberts stirred his food while Mbenga ate hungrily.

"You said you had a small problem," Mbenga said, leaning over the table to speak quietly.

"I went to Sozacom yesterday," Roberts said. Mbenga shrugged knowingly, as if to say, what could he do? "It's a fine piece of architecture. Like a glass-and-steel Venus-fly-trap."

Mbenga laughed and drank some of his Primus beer. Roberts had tasted the beer, but it made his head ache even more. "I know what you mean," Mbenga said.

"I especially like the soldiers and the helicopters at night, and the dreamy blue floodlights all over the grounds. It has a cozy charm."

"We say in Kinshasa that the Sozacom is where the *dawa* and *mbolozi* live. Demons and witches, no?"

"Who does the architecture for Mobutu? Albert Speer?"

"This is called the architecture of necessity. Where there is fear and violence, there is building for security."

Roberts comprehended the concept, an architecture of necessity, building from fear. He remembered the wide concrete avenues all the way in from Maya Maya Airport in Brazzaville, a ribbon built for tanks so that the security forces could handle a *coup d'état*. It was the same in South Africa, architecture freezing human beings in place, a status quo in concrete, something so literal you could touch it. "Any chance that Mobutu can be overthrown in the near future? Any political movement that has enough strength to be dangerous? I mean this guy has been in power since the early '60s and he's bled the country dry."

Mbenga shrugged again, sadly. "The structure is paralyzed, mzungu. The arms and legs are not functioning, and the brain is dead. There is only the stomach feeding itself, while all the other parts are atrophied." Mbenga drank some beer, contemplating now that the band had taken a break. "There are many Big Men in Africa. Kenneth Kaunda. You have heard of Idi Amin. They rule in Ghana, Togo, Liberia and in South Africa where the Big Man is white and Afrikaaner. They have been in power for more than thirty years now and they are very rich and very powerful. Their riches are stolen from the people and from the earth. They siphon away all the riches of the labor of the people, they give to their friends and to their enemies, as well. To the members of their own tribes they offer high government office. To the heads of other tribes they offer money and enjoyment, so that there is never any animosity between tribes. This way they corrupt everyone who might rise up against them."

Mbenga drank some beer, smiled across the pavilion to a young man who had called to him in Lingala.

"And you must understand, mzungu," Mbenga continued, "there is no political philosophy in this country. And so if you even think that someday Mobutu might be overthrown, you have to think that there is nothing to take his place. There are no laws, no institutions, no traditions, nothing in our past but ten years of revolution, thirty years of bribery and corruption. And before that what is there? Two hundred years of slave taking, of foreign domination by the Belgian king during a time of exploitation and terror. There is no structure to carry this load of poverty and disease. Even the tradition of village culture you see falling apart before your very eyes, these young men and women in the cité, wild with drunkenness and loss. It is one of the reasons I brought you here, mzungu, so that you could see my country. So that somehow you can understand why we need the docteur so much. Many people would give up in the face of so much suffering. But our docteur, she does not give up. It is a struggle of this docteur in the bush outside Kisangani, against those who hide in Sozacom, behind the portraits of Mobutu, behind their sunglasses and automatic rifles, behind the Kikongo and the matabish."

When Mbenga stopped talking he looked embarrassed, as if he had given an after-dinner speech for a sleeping crowd. "My own country has a paralysis," Roberts said. "I could take you to any city in America and show you human suffering that you would recognize. And I could show you the houses of rich men high on a hill, where that suffering doesn't penetrate."

"I know, mzungu," Mbenga said. "Sometimes I feel the

suffering does not penetrate anywhere. We have an opposition to Mobutu, but these are factions and do not have the interests of the people at heart, I believe. When a place has grown used to greed and luxury, there are many standing in line to enjoy these things. There are no ideas."

"Ideas," Roberts repeated in a whisper. "America has no ideas any longer. I'm afraid all we have is hypocrisy and an overbearing nationalism. This is the same thing as greed masquerading behind emptiness."

The band had begun again, driving out a beat that was both passionate and sincere. Roberts was very impressed with Mbenga now, both for the depth of his thought and the earnestness of his feeling, his subtle intelligence and good humor, his courage. Sitting in the noisy smoke-filled pavilion, he knew that he would travel upriver with Mbenga, not fly with Slade. In his mind Roberts remembered Slade saying "He's an *African,*" his insousciant voice like filthy laundry in one's face.

"There is a hole in our hearts," Mbenga said, over the sound, after thinking for a long time. Both men were in a shared tunnel of expression now, the music far away from them. "There is a great yearning. You can see it here in the dance and the music. But there is no hope to cling to any longer." Mbenga shrugged and smiled.

"This is happening everywhere, ndugu," Roberts said. "This age is filled with surface images, smoke and mirrors, the sound bites of politicians and the crack of automatic-weapons fire. One must ask what a good man is to do in times like these. It is the question of the ages. Perhaps it has always been this way for men, for the people in a corrupt country. Not every man is fortunate enough to live in an age of Pericles."

"But to have one's heart frozen," Mbenga said, unable to

continue, merely gesturing with his hand at the dancers in the pavilion. "This is a terrible tragedy for my people."

Roberts ate some of his boiled fish. He thought about the doe-eyed clerk at the hotel in Brazzaville, the man smiling at Roberts in total awe. They had spoken briefly in the dusty, fly-ridden lobby while the fans stirred the dry air and the palms outside clicked in the wind. Showing Roberts a picture of his family, the clerk had asked him to exchange letters when he returned to London, expressing his yearning for news of the world outside the hotel lobby, the tired colonial town. To Roberts this was insufferably sad, seeing a man so anxious to use his mind, to escape the prison of his own existence. He knew it was repeated in millions of African minds and souls. He had seen it in Jamaica, Trinidad, Haiti and now in Central Africa. This was a world of fading snapshots of another life. And in the place of the fading world of tribal culture and village customs, there was only a seedy materialism, political systems of graft and mindless violence. Now, Roberts thought, the world needed a revolution of spirit, a refinement of sensibility, but he knew it was impossible to change the world, that the growing away from spirit was ongoing and eternal. Where it would end, he didn't know.

"Hey my friend," Roberts called to the distracted Mbenga. "We can't save the world, but we can save the docteur, no?"

"I know we can," Mbenga replied, brightened now. "And I think we are good men, mzungu." Mbenga shrugged again, this time in a meta-language that both men shared, an ineffable measure of how their relationship had grown. "And you are right," he continued. "What are good men to do in an evil world?"

The waiter brought more beer. Roberts felt better now,

even though his head still ached. Maybe it was the music, the world beat shuddering through this open-air tent, or maybe it was just the thought of being far away from downtown Kinshasa and its mask of glass and steel, or maybe it was just the thought of being buried in Africa, under the charcoal smoke. Between the measures of music, Roberts could hear the songs of tree frogs, traffic noise, some dogs barking at the dark night.

"Here's my problem," Roberts said, getting Mbenga's attention. "Slade from Lloyd's wants me to fly with him to Kisangani. He has a plane ready at N'dola and a flight plan cleared for the day after tomorrow, first thing in the morning. He's sending a company car for me at the hotel. It's his view that Lloyd's should control the operation because it's their money."

"This is only a problem for me, mzungu."

"It's our problem," Roberts said. "Slade sees this as purely a question of business. For him, it isn't personal."

"And for you?" Mbenga asked.

"For me this is personal now."

"I think I am glad to hear this, mzungu."

"Don't worry, Adam," Roberts said. "I'm not going to let Slade control the flow of things. I don't like him and I don't want to work with this amateur insurance man whose only concern is his investment. For someone like him, his only care is the company. He's sorry that this didn't happen six months from now when EuroCopper was gone from Zaire and his company had no responsibility. It's also partly that I almost lost the money in Brazzaville, when that African hit me on the head. So there are many reasons why this is personal for me."

"You must be very careful now."

"I know," Roberts said. "I didn't tell him that we had the

cash in diamonds, and I didn't tell him that I was going up the river with you."

"You won't fly with Slade?"

"We go up the river together, no?"

Mbenga smiled, his face bright with sweat. The pavilion was very smoky and there was no breeze. "I will do what you say and help you in any way I can."

"Can we catch a boat upriver to Kisangani tomorrow?" Roberts asked. "Can you arrange that? So when Slade comes for me at the hotel, we'll be gone? Maybe by the time he locates me we can have our business done. Maybe we can formulate our own plans, do the job. I don't mind saying that leaving Slade out of this equation doesn't bother me at all. I have my instructions, you know."

"Is it that you do not trust this man Slade?"

"That's not it exactly. He's just another bony insurance man from London trying to do his job. There's probably another bony insurance man above him, telling him what to do. In an order of things, he's part of the order. But I don't like him and I don't want him part of my operation. We go our own way for a week, maybe he catches up, maybe he doesn't. Maybe when he catches up, the docteur will be safe. He bothers me and I don't think I'd be comfortable working with him. He's too concerned with money, not enough with the docteur."

"I do not wish for trouble, mzungu."

"Don't worry about it. Can you get us tickets on the boat for Kisangani tomorrow?"

"I'm sure I can," Mbenga said, smiling. "With the right amount of matabish." He had finished his Primus and taken out a small pipe, like the one his uncle smoked. "I will make the arrangements. My sister is going upriver with us. I hope that is all right. We all go together."

"Fine," Roberts said. "You don't know of any deadline for delivery of the ransom?"

"I know nothing of their demands. But I am sure I can book passage on the boat if you give me enough francs. The officials who sell tickets love francs." Mbenga smiled again, more openly. "When one is *mort civil,* the heartbeat is measured by the franc."

"When can you know?"

"Tomorrow morning. By ten o'clock at the latest."

"When does the boat leave?"

"It is scheduled for noon. One never knows. With good luck we could be under way before night." Mbenga shrugged. "It is the way with Zaire."

"You'll come for me tomorrow morning?"

"After breakfast," Mbenga said.

Roberts was trying to eat his boiled fish and rice. He had begun to feel weak and feverish again.

"My cousin will be gone from the shamba," Mbenga said, glancing at his wristwatch.

"Your sister is there with the weapons?"

"Yes, mzungu."

Roberts paid the bill and handed over some francs to Mbenga for use as matabish. When they left the pavilion the world-beat band was playing loudly and the whole floor was covered with dancing Africans. As they drove out of the parking area and past the cemetery, Roberts could see people everywhere on the streets, milling aimlessly, drinking beer and palm wine, clots of dancers in open-air ngandas that made up most of the Matonge. Roberts realized it was Saturday night. He hadn't thought about the day of the week since his arrival in Brazzaville on the night flight from Paris. Strange, he thought, to forget the time, this utter abandonment of formal appearance. He wondered if Africa had done this to

him, if he had suffered some kind of shock to his system, his
Western sensibility, or if he was just tired and a little bit sick.
While Mbenga drove, Roberts watched the cité out the window. There were acres of endless concrete shambas with their
garish spray-painted slogans and pictographs, tethered animals
in dirt yards, laundry swinging in the breeze, garbage heaps
smoldering, and miles and miles of tin and plywood shacks—
all shapes and sizes—where all the trees and shrubs had been
cut for firewood. He was reminded of evening news broad-
casts from Soweto, the lack of trees, the dusty streets, the bars
and abandoned lots, the women keening after some deadly
political fight, a vast steaming conglomerate of misery. It was
only when you could actually see this misery that you knew
that millions of Africans suffered from some form of the illness
of poverty; what that truly meant, how it smelled and tasted
and looked, not merely how it sounded on the BBC. They
stopped in front of one of the concrete shambas and Mbenga
honked the horn of the taxi. There was nothing to differen-
tiate this shamba from any of the thousands of others Roberts
had witnessed going by on the journey.

Marie appeared in the doorway, holding back a black blanket that was nailed over the opening. Roberts recognized her
half-expectant look as she stood in the darkness wearing a
pagne and pathetic plastic sandals. They greeted her and went
inside where Roberts took his time reassembling the Fusil
Automatic, the M1950 machine pistol. He didn't know the
weapons well at all, and the job took him about thirty minutes
of work inside the insufferably close air of the bunker.
Mbenga and his sister talked together in Lingala while he
labored. When he was finished he wrapped both weapons in
newspaper and put them in his new traveling case. Marie had
kept to the shadows in one corner of the shamba near a single
folding cot, some collections of utensils, an old double bed

without a box spring. By his reckoning of clothes and the few toys, Roberts decided that four or five people shared this space that was probably ten-by-ten, with no privacy, no indoor plumbing or running water of any kind. Mats had been placed on the floor where children probably slept and there was a wooden crucifix on the wall.

Marie offered Roberts some lemonade, which he refused, because of his sick stomach. He didn't think he could keep anything down, not even lemonade. His skin felt dry and warm, and he thought his fever had probably increased. It was all he could do at this point to assemble the weapons, say a polite goodnight to Marie and get himself out the door. He was tired and needed to get some sleep in order to be ready for the boat trip, which he knew would be exhausting and difficult. In his mind, he was already on the boat going upriver through the cuvée, across the equator in the dark green bowl of jungle and forest, heading for the New Stanley Hotel in Kisangani. Then a shudder of misanthropic delight went through him just thinking about Slade, the guy showing up bright and early at the Intercontinental in a showy American car, finding the room empty.

It was only a little after nine o'clock when Mbenga dropped Roberts at the Intercontinental. They stopped down the street from the lobby, where there were fewer whores and police, where they could be away from the pounding disco sounds erupting from the hotel lobby and where Roberts could see hundreds of people milling around, coming in and out like ants.

"Tomorrow after breakfast then," Mbenga said hopefully.

"We'll get this thing done," Roberts replied. They were sharing confidences now, in both senses, in the true meaning of the word. Roberts got out, stood on the curb and watched

Mbenga chart a course down the avenue, between the whores and drunken policemen.

Roberts rode the elevator to the fourth floor. Even this far up in the glass-and-steel cocoon of the hotel he could hear disco music pounding through the thin walls. He stopped in front of his room, listening, every nerve alive because the tiny strand of hair between the jamb and door was missing. Taking deep breaths, nearly hyperventilating, his mind ran ice cold and clear. With one ear to the door, he took out the M1950 machine pistol and pushed inside his room.

A slice of light dropped on the foot of the bed. The musty aroma of air-conditioning swept past, and in seconds his eyes adjusted to the half-light. He moved inside the room where he stood in shadow.

Roberts detected a sweeping silver arc of motion, then a flash when something hard struck him on the shoulder. There was an African only a few feet away from him now and Roberts' reflexes made him crouch to avoid another blow. Miles of electrical connections clicked open and shut, open and shut, and instinctively Roberts fired the pistol once, hearing a dull thud as the weapon popped, and then a rush of breath and a gasp. The African fell down on top of Roberts, pinning him against the carpet, against the half-open door. Roberts pushed the door shut and it snapped behind him. Roberts lay trapped that way as silence tickled through his head. Far away there was disco music.

Goddamn that Raymond, he thought. Goddamn that guy Raymond. Goddamn.

4

SOMETHING BRIGHT AND INTEGRATED SNAPPED on glass, just behind Roberts' right ear. Focusing, he realized that the sensation was heat streaming onto the hotel window, a wild molecular blooming of tropical day. Sitting there on the window ledge with his knees under his chin, Roberts knew that once again he had lost his sense of time, that he may have been perched that way for hours, perhaps all night, while the room air-conditioning stirred and restirred the air. He remembered the night sounds. Tree frogs, helicopters, faint and awesome Kinshasa at night while Roberts suffered wavelike fevers from incalculable causes, experiences which overwhelmed him one by one. Now he knew it was morning, that he had passed the entire night without sleep, without even shutting his eyes, even though he had shut down his consciousness. He felt like a stick-figure doll, a barely functioning anatomical model of himself. When he placed his cheek against the glass it came away warm and wet.

His fear had levels like the rooms in a dark old house, a dream house of pain and frustration. He reconstructed the feel of steel against his shoulder, what had turned out to be a short machete made of hammered steel, about sixteen inches long, a homemade weapon honed to razor sharpness. As if from another life, Roberts saw the weapon jump under his tender pressure; he heard a huge explosion of gas and cordite as the bullet left its chamber achieving a tight spiral convulsion, ejaculating into flight, its buzz and rasp, and the final dull thud. In that single instant, Roberts transferred his fears and pointed himself into another realm—a nerveless environment that translated itself neuron to neuron, molecule to molecule—until he had arrived at himself sitting in the hotel window, chin to knee, while the hot African morning coagulated against glass.

That night he had felt himself falling with the African on top, both men against the door as it clicked shut. For a moment, Roberts thought he might have to fire again, but then he knew it was his panic speaking, that if he fired again he wouldn't stop, but would fire again and again, until the whole hotel room shuddered with noise. Even then he would only be scattering his fears; there would be no purpose in it. He had sat with his back against the hotel door, with the African across his feet, this huge bulk connected to him that he could see in outline only, one forearm stretched out across the carpet, torso on Roberts' legs, face upturned until Roberts thought he could see the man staring openly, or in supplication. Roberts had touched the face, the eyelids, and had recognized the beginning blankness of death.

There had been a slick of drool on the African's mouth. Roberts studied the face then, the lips that looked as if they were forming syllables, as if the syllables would coalesce and make words, would begin a supplication, an argument, a vague pleading for life. Roberts placed a finger on the man's neck and knew that the spindle of existence had turned away forever.

Roberts sat that way for a long time, listening for sounds in the hallway. All he could hear was the pounding of the disco on the mezzanine far below, the barely audible drip of water in the shower, the creaking of insects outside the window. A blip of sweat leaked down from Roberts' face, dropping onto the face of the African. Right then Roberts tried to think of some exemplar for his fear, shifting perspectives inside himself while he tried to achieve some kind of rational lock, a radar that would allow him to place the fear, master it, put it behind him so that he could have some more useful emotion. Maybe, he thought, he had five minutes or so before someone came to the room because of the gunshot. Not time enough to move the African, check for blood, casually go down to the disco, get drunk on Primus beer and listen to some Western rock and roll, which is what he thought he would like to do just then. Breathing deeply, trying to control his mind, Roberts listened to the enormity of silence behind the door, the blank hallway whispering to him under its curtain of fluorescence. Moths were fluttering at the window and the lights of the city spoke to him, but even so, he began to calm himself.

If someone heard the shot, events would guide themselves along a smooth path. There would be a commotion in the hall as guests gathered. There would be the Kinshasa police, the hotel manager, and maybe even a soldier or two. Then the pounding on the door would begin. Roberts remembered something Mbenga had told him. If he were found with weapons in Zaire, he would face the prospect of torture. He imagined the long days in a dark cell, the nights and days waiting, the slogans, the trial, the uncertainty and pain. He closed his eyes and sat quite still.

For about twenty minutes he sat that way with the African across his knees and his back to the closed door of his hotel room. Finally he moved the African and flipped on a desk lamp. His room was in disarray, drawers opened, bed overturned, his bag rifled. Roberts shut down his fear and went through the African's pockets, finding only some Zaire notes, gum, and a few bangi cigarettes. The M1950 had put a small blue hole in the man's sternum, just beside the heart, and there was a bloom of blood on the man's chest, but no flow, and no exit wound in the back. The African had a large head of matted black hair, a black T-shirt, fatigue pants, torn sneakers with pink shoelaces. His black skin had the cold halosheen of death.

And now that it was early morning Roberts opened his eyes to see no whores on the avenue below his hotel room, only a few police walking tired circles, some taxis and scattered bicycle riders in the heat. A green mist hovered above the river valley and the buildings of Kinshasa were lit by an early morning orange glow from the low sun. To his surprise, Roberts found that he was clutching the pistol in his right hand. He knew he must have sat that way all night, cradling the gun in his lap, one finger caressing the trigger, his palm on the plastic grips, an elemental bulk in his hand now, an object born of trauma. The night was reconstructing itself in his head now, painful awarenesses that dripped into his consciousness like dope. Roberts looked at the African lying in the middle of his hotel room floor, his upturned face smooth of all remorse or anger, the slightly thyroid eyes, the muscular neck nearly hidden in the folds of the T-shirt which had creased upward in the fall. The machete was lying where it had fallen, a shiny half-moon of metal near the door.

Roberts was waiting now for the knock of the chambermaid come to fix his bed, for Mbenga, for the police and soldiers to take him away. He looked down at the streets of Kinshasa which webbed away to the World Trade Center. Off to the left was Sozacom with its hideous metal eyebrows and dark moat, the ideographic slogans Roberts couldn't understand, the white graffiti-marred walls of the old colonial cemetery that divided modern Kinshasa from the shantytown of the cité. Halfway up Sozacom, fluttering in the light morning breeze, was a propaganda portrait of Mobutu, President-For-Life, his dark leopard skin hat cock-strait, faintly wrinkled blue serge suit, marble black eyes piercing through to nothingness, dishonoring the citizens. Roberts drank in the bleakness of Kinshasa, its cracked concrete pavements and the mildewed shop-awnings over iron-barred windows, and beyond, in the hazy distance, the Palace of the People, a huge cosmic joke. *It's Sunday morning,* Roberts thought to himself as the window sun grew warmer; somewhere Amanda is opening the *Observer,* waiting for the toast to brown, for the oatmeal to heat, and somewhere there are cottonwoods greening, streams releasing down mountainsides. He closed and opened his eyes.

Down in the street a parade appeared, men and women, a few squadrons of paratroopers, men in dark blue suits, even a few children in white shirts, the little girls in pink and blue pagnes and dark green slacks carrying banners in Lingala and Swahili, proclamations and protocols of the MPR, the popular movement which was always stage-managed by the secret police. Behind the parade some tanks and armored vehicles rumbled, dark gray metal under steaming white sunshine. Roberts tried to convince himself that there was nothing surreal about the Mobutu portrait suspended six stories above the Sozacom, the children in gay uniforms, and the tanks, the perversion of angles and meaning it signified. Just then his cheek touched the hot glass again, and he saw the first whores appear on the street now that the day was heating up and the business of life beginning. Cars began to spit around the streets like waterbugs. Roberts put down the gun and thought about Mbenga again.

He cleaned up and took a dose of chloroquine and a few vitamin B tablets. Looking at himself in the mirror he was shocked for a moment by the thin visage in the glass, its lean yellow face like a hungry dog, the look of someone Roberts didn't know or recognize, someone desperate. It took some effort, but Roberts managed to move the dead body into the shower stall after he gained some new composure. He hoped the chambermaid wouldn't come to clean until afternoon, and that by then he would be gone upriver. He lay down on the bed and tried to rest.

A telephone woke him somewhere in time. Mbenga spoke on the other end of a fuzzy connection.

"Mzungu," he said cheerfully. "May I come up?"

"Come alone Adam, please," Roberts said.

"Are you all right, no?" Mbenga asked. "It is *adhuhuri,* nearly noon, and I thought I would let you sleep. There is no hurry for the river station. Have you had some delay or illness? I was expecting to see you in the lobby for checkout."

"Just come up Adam," Roberts said. "Please don't say or do anything right now. Just please come up."

The line clicked and five minutes later Roberts heard a tap at the door. He opened it and whisked Mbenga inside quickly. The man was wearing khaki shorts and a white cotton shirt, traveling clothes that revealed the whole metal brace on his left leg. Mbenga moved past Roberts, who sneaked a glance down the empty hallway. Roberts felt nauseated, probably the effects of the chloroquine and vitamin B on an empty stomach.

"It is a good morning, no?" Mbenga said, trying to lighten the atmosphere in the hotel room. "You are ready to go up the mighty Zaire river? This great river the west calls the Congo for no good reason!" Roberts lay down on the bed and Mbenga crouched over him. "You look ill, mzungu. Is that the problem?"

"I just need a shave and some food. I'll be all right."

"But you are very tired, no?"

"I haven't slept all night."

"Are you with a fever?"

Roberts said he thought his temperature was a little above normal, but that he had taken some medicine. Mbenga placed a hand on Robert's forehead. "I would blame it on this terrible sombe," he joked, "or on the condition of this mattress, or on the food at the nganda, but it could be any combination of life in Africa that does not suit you. It is certain that you are growing hot."

Roberts pushed himself against the bedstead, trying to stay upright to staunch the nausea. And then something happened that surprised Roberts, something that he couldn't explain, except that it felt natural. Mbenga touched him under the ear, near the cartoid, and then leaned down and placed an ear on his heart. It was done so calmly, with such firmness, that Roberts found himself deeply impressed, as if he had suddenly become a patient.

Mbenga balanced himself against Robert's chest, listening. "If you don't mind me saying this, mzungu, I am worried about your health. I think it would be very good if I took you to the consular doctor here in Kinshasa, an American of good reputation. He treats many of the diplomats and businessmen in the ville. He is well known among the many oil companies and others of the colonial colony. This man would examine you this afternoon if he was made to know that the matter was of some urgency."

"Is this a matter of some urgency?"

"I do not know, honestly. Perhaps that makes it urgent."

"You said the ferry leaves at noon."

"Very soon. But there will be inevitable delays. We have many hours to wait. There is time. And there is every reason to be cautious before going up the river. The climate is very bad and above the equator it is the rainy season. Many fevers and illnesses exist on the river." Mbenga nodded slightly to indicate a return of serve, reminding Roberts that the locus of experience tilted significantly toward the African. "And your health is more important than the ferry."

Roberts leaned up from the bed and took hold of Mbenga's shoulder for support. Sunlight was streaming through the hotel room and it was very hot. Outside, vultures were clinging to telephone wires in the near distance. "What do you think, ndugu? Do you think I've got malaria?"

"You have a fever, *ndiyo*. Yes." Mbenga put his hand on Robert's forehead again. "Tell me honestly what other problems you are having with your body. Please."

"Vomiting. Some diarrhea."

"And I know you are not eating. You didn't touch your fish and rice last night."

Roberts pushed to his feet and sat planted on the edge of the bed, expecting at any moment to be quite sick. He balanced that way, looking at the closed door to the bath, letting his imagination turn him through a kaleidoscope of emotions—fear, anger, pride—a lunacy rich with fantasy. The room had been straightened, the bed repositioned and made, all his clothes packed, the weapons cleaned and stored in the bottom of his traveling case. During the night, he had wrapped the plastique again, and had checked all the detonators and his radio transmitter device. Even the tooth powder tin full of diamonds was still on the medicine cabinet shelf where he had left it.

"I don't keep much down," Roberts admitted.

Mbenga sat down on the bed next to Roberts. "Did you eat some breakfast this morning?" he asked.

"I couldn't," Roberts said.

"You did not feel well enough?"

"In some ways. Not exactly."

Roberts got to his feet, feeling steadier now. He led Mbenga to the bath and opened the door, both men standing in the open door hearing the steady drip of the showerhead. Some cockroaches skuttled in corners, under cracks in the tile. Mbenga followed Roberts into the bathroom. The dead man was in one corner of the shower stall, leaning up against the pale blue tile, hands in his lap. The dead lips had turned purple and the face had taken on an ashy glaze. It looked as if the corpse was made of wax, a piece of fake fruit. Dripping water had made a dark circle around the blue-caked blood just above the sternum. In death, the African had a pleasant relaxed face, as if he had been frozen on the outskirts of paradise. The machete lay across his legs.

Roberts heard Mbenga's brace catch a piece of tile, a clink as the man staggered backward just a little, recoiling.

"Raymond?" Mbenga whispered, almost out of breath.

"Why not?" Roberts replied. "They tried for their diamonds once in Brazzaville. There's a lot of money at stake."

"Raymond would know you were staying here. Every Westerner who comes to Kinshasa stays at the Intercontinental. And it would not be difficult to bribe one of the porters, or the desk clerk, or a maid."

"The man didn't have a key on him. He was probably let into the room just as you say."

"It would not be difficult," Mbenga said, walking out of the bathroom, taking a seat in the rattan chair near the hotel window. "Are the diamonds safe?" he asked, when Roberts had come out of the room.

"Yes, don't worry." Roberts sat back down on the bed, feeling sick as hell. "The whole room had been searched, things torn up. But the diamonds are in the tin. Yesterday I bought an extra tin and left it in the medicine cabinet. The tin with the diamonds I hid in the air-conditioner vent."

"The room is very clean," Mbenga said.

"I was lucky. When I left last night I put a single strand of hair on the outside of the door as an early warning system. So when I returned, I knew someone had been here. I couldn't hear anyone inside, so I wasn't too worried. I thought someone had come in and had gone away. But when I opened the door this guy came at me with a machete, hit me on the shoulder with the flat part of the blade. I was lucky, it could have been much worse than it was. But I had to shoot him. It was dark, but I hit him under the chin near the center of the chest. He went down and I went down under him. We stayed that way for about twenty minutes and nobody came. The disco was making plenty of noise and I don't think there was anybody in the hallway at the time. I kept thinking about that Kinshasa *jela* you told me about, the one where they lock you up and throw away the key, and come around once a day to wire your testicles to a generator."

"I am glad for you, mzungu," Mbenga said. He crossed himself once. "But this is very bad. I see why you would not want to go to the American doctor."

"We have to move."

"What do we do?"

"I thought you might have a suggestion," Roberts said, smiling. "Slade and his chauffeur are going to be here tomorrow morning at six. I think we should leave for the terminal now." Roberts had pulled on a pair of long khaki pants, some hiking boots he had brought with him, and a white cotton shirt. "Suppose we drag this dead African down to the end of the hall and install him on the fire escape outside. I'll leave some money for the bill. What do you think would happen then?"

"There is no blood?"

"Very little. The wound was clean and he landed on his back. There wasn't an exit wound either."

"I tell you, mzungu," Mbenga said. "When the local police find this corpse on the fire escape of the Intercontinental Hotel they will not know what to do. Maybe they take his body to their headquarters and begin a large debate. There will be a captain who will shout some orders, but then the police will go to an nganda and begin to drink palm wine. In two days they will have forgotten about this dead African. He will not be spoken about at all."

Roberts shrugged now, admiring the practicality of Mbenga's mind, his astute use of the landscape. "This assumes nobody sees us moving this body."

"You don't recognize the man?" Roberts asked.

"No, I do not recognize him. He is not a Kikongo, but I don't know what tribe he is. I am sorry."

The two men lifted the dead African out of the shower stall and dragged him to the door of the hotel room, then quickly down the hall about fifteen meters and through the fire escape door. Luckily, there was nobody in the hall—no porters or chambermaids. Once out in the heat of the day, they sat the dead body on the step of the fire escape, balancing him against the wall of the hotel building. Even though they were four floors up and to one side of the facade, they could still see the whores on the sidewalk and one or two police squads. Roberts was tired and dizzy, and so he sat down next to the dead

African. Far away there was an outline of the Pool Malebo, the river running into red laterite gorges, the humped curve of the cuvée, a forest almost as large as America. In the east, storm clouds bunched on the horizon in purple fists. Roberts thought he could smell rain in the air, even though it was terribly hot.

"*Kwaheri, kwaheri,*" Mbenga said, standing above Roberts. He was looking down sadly at the dead African. "I am saying goodbye to this brother," he said. "This is no way for the soul to depart. Here in the heat, looking down at the femmes."

"Better him than us," Roberts said.

"In this you are correct, mzungu."

Roberts took a last look at the African, propped up against the stucco like a puppet, sunshine flooding his waxen face, his features swollen rigid in death. Roberts was thinking back to that day in Brazzaville when he had met Raymond under the dusty pepper trees of the central square, the thrushes chittering wildly and feral dogs prowling the garbage cans. He couldn't remember the face of the man who had driven the white Mercedes, nor could he remember the face of the man who had followed him down to the Ouzey market later, the man on the motor scooter. In the same way, he thought back to that night in his Brazzaville hotel room when a dark face had lunged at him through the night, had driven him to the floor and delivered a blow to his temple. He wondered if this were the same African, a man working for Raymond, if the man had followed him across the river, then to the Intercontinental. All Roberts could remember was the dissipated pasty expression on Raymond's face, his surfer hair and the rumpled linen suit. He also remembered the vultures perched on columns, the sound of their wings rustling through the heavy humid air.

Roberts paid his hotel bill and checked out. Mbenga drove

them across the cité, around the colonial cemetery and through miles of shantytown slum. In the daylight, Roberts was astounded by all the poverty, the tin and plasterboard shacks, miles of open sewer, children splashing and playing in fetid water—the same water in which women washed clothes and animals drank. Everywhere chickens and goats roamed at will, and under groves of pepper trees and stunted acacias there were clots of drunken African men, soldiers on the prowl. Mbenga left the taxi at his cousin's shamba. They picked up Marie, and continued in a rented taxi, going farther and farther away from the center of official Kinshasa, down to the flatlands of the river plain.

Several hundred Africans had gathered in front of the ticket office on the waterfront. About fifty meters out in the river, connected to shore by a pier and gangplank, there was a rustbucket steamer with three decks riding low in the water, probably already full of cargo. Stevedores and dockers were climbing over it like ants, and Roberts could see that two tug vessels were cabled behind it in tandem, with makeshift canvas awnings, some deck chairs and hammocks. Mbenga told Roberts that there was a first-class cabin reserved for him on the lead vessel, and that he and his sister would be riding on the first tug. Roberts said goodbye to Mbenga and Marie, and went to look for his cabin.

He made his way through the crowds on the edge of the riverbank, down through the turnstiles of the ticket office and out onto the pier where there were customs officials and police. He showed his ticket, and an official checked his passport but didn't look through his bags. Dockside was a warren of sights and smells: racks of smoked monkey, bales of yams and sweet potatoes, bushel baskets full of rice, manioc, casks of iced fish, buckets of carp and river catfish, crates full of machine parts, farm implements, wild birds in cages, even tennis shoes and dried roots. A tiny African porter took him up the gangplank and across the quarterdeck, where they took a flight of stairs through two decks to a place just behind the wheelhouse, a single-story row of iron boxes that extended from fore to aft. Heat seemed to ripple off the surface of the river. Roberts tipped the porter some francs and opened the door to his cabin.

It was a cramped square of dark, rusted iron, with a bed in one corner, an open-crapper toilet leaking on the floor and one shuttered slit window in the door. Inside it was unbearably hot and Roberts thought he would have to sit outside all day in a deck chair just to be able to breathe. Sleep was probably out of the question, but he tried the bed anyway, which was lumpy and hard. He put his two bags in the room and sat down outside on an upturned bucket and studied the docksides of Kinshasa, hundreds of Africans, their animals and produce. He was feeling light-headed and abstract, part of something vague at the center of his being. Things were eroding him now, and he thought about the dead African sitting still on the fire escape with his wax eyes fixed on the horizon. He watched the police harass an African man for no reason.

A vendor came by and Roberts bought a lemonade. The cabin wall provided him some shade from the fierce sun, and he sat there drinking his lemonade, thinking about Amanda. He was about to go inside and unpack when he saw Mbenga coming up one of the deck ladders.

"You are feeling well?" Mbenga asked once he'd come up on deck. "There is no problem?"

"Better," Roberts lied.

"We will be under way—" Mbenga smiled. "When the captain deems it necessary!"

"What about you and Marie?"

"We have a square space with two hammocks. Very lucky. It is nothing special, but it will keep us for two or three days."

"I keep thinking about Slade," Roberts said. "He's going to be surprised tomorrow morning."

"And what about Monsieur Raymond?"

"Well, he's persistent, I'll give him that."

Mbenga looked inside the cabin. "You are disappointed with your quarters?"

"It will do," Roberts said.

"I must go now," Mbenga said. "But I will come back early this evening. There is a bar and restaurant in front of the wheelhouse, no?"

Roberts said that would be fine. They'd have something to eat, maybe take a stroll around the deck when the sun went down. By then they would be in the river gorges, maybe even into the forest if they got under way anytime soon. Now all Roberts wanted to do was rid himself of Kinshasa. The city felt like a film of oil on his skin. He didn't know what the river would be like, but he knew it couldn't be any worse than the Sozacom Building, the police and MPR rallies in the early morning sun. Whatever the river would be, it wouldn't be worse than that.

5

HALFWAY ACROSS POOL MALEBO THEY passed through a diaphanous blue cloud of butterflies. Roberts had been sitting
on a paint bucket chair, drinking glass after glass of lemonade,
waiting for the boat to cast off, which finally happened about
six o'clock that night after endless delays for passengers and
cargo. It took about twenty or thirty minutes for them to
maneuver through the wharfs and piers of Kinshasa quay, and
then out into open water, away from the city. It was another
thirty minutes before they reached the pool, a widening of
the river into a lake choked with lilies. The sun had gone
down behind the forest and cliffs, and there was a pale fire
haze racing up the sky as night fell, the pool about two miles
wide with a sputter of current running down the middle of
it, barely noticeable.

Roberts had gone to the bar and gotten himself more
lemonade, and then he had gone aft to where he could see the
two trailing tugs, and the African passengers packed into their
spaces with hammocks and all their belongings. Down in the
water were a few pirogues and dugout canoes, and some small
motor craft filled with men moving slowly downriver toward
Kinshasa. There were children wading in the water on the far
bank and red laterite cliffs etched against the dusky gray sky

of evening. As the sun dropped a breeze began to sift through the mangungu groves along the shore and he felt somewhat cooler, although he was sweating and uncomfortable.

Just then, as he stood on the aft deck, looking down at the two tugs jammed with Africans, he felt a touch against his skin, and then a ruffle along the sides of his arms, and he realized they were passing through an amazing blue cloud of butterflies, all the butterflies whipping up and down in dervish fashion, tonelessly, as if in a dream. Below him the children in one of the tugs were shouting, *"Kipepeo, kipepeo,"* laughing and brushing the butterflies out of their hair. The insects were royal blue with black bodies, and the boat passed through in about four or five minutes, drifting downriver as the sun set.

Roberts had been prepared for the wait on the quay while officials and sailors bustled around. While they were still tied up, he had gone into his cabin and tried to rearrange some of the furniture by pushing his bed away from the wall, toward the door, so maybe he could get some air if he left the door open all night, pushing his chest of drawers around too, and taking the one rattan chair outside. His eyes were burning and his head ached, and there was a terrible knot just under his right ear, probably the result of being struck by a gun butt. He unpacked the diamonds and put them in a drawer and just then he felt the boat moving underneath him and he knew they were under way, circling around away from the dock, past the oil tankers and fishing boats, getting into the main part of the current, which just outside Kinshasa was swift and muddy. When he went out on deck again, Kinshasa was disappearing in a dusty haze and a tug was shoving them upstream to where he could see the entire outline of the city gleaming under a bloom of orange exhaust. White and silver skyscrapers, like needles, angled sharply against a sky filled with white cumulus thunderheads. And then he was violently ill.

He tried to clean himself at the wash basin, washing his hair and face, drying with a towel, changing his khaki shirt which he had soiled with some vomit. When he switched on the single electric bulb in his cabin he examined himself. There was no way he was happy with the sunken cheeks, the pale gray skin which seemed to be peeling away from his skeleton, and for a moment he was gripped by panic. When he took his temperature, he found it elevated by two degrees. Fine, he thought, along with diarrhea and vomiting, I'm burning to death. *Just let me get to Kisangani,* he prayed to himself, where he might find a doctor, eat some decent food, maybe take a couple of days to rest before he headed out to the clinic compound to look for the Belgian doctor. There was no way he was going to be strong enough to go to work right away, and so he hoped the kidnappers would take their time finding him at the New Stanley Hotel. He thought that if he could get some rest, gain a few pounds and get back his color, then he could take on these Simba tribesmen.

Roberts had never been really sick, nothing more than a cold, a vicious Schnapps hangover and one or two sprained joints. But this illness was something else; the permanent headache, swollen fingers and toes, inflammation of his neck, a feeling of suffocation that he couldn't shake, as if he could not get his breath. He looked back into the mirror and noticed an edge of yellow in his eyes, which had sunk back into his skull like a cadaver. It was scaring the shit out of him, the way he was looking. He dosed himself with chloroquine, took some Lomotil to combat the diarrhea and went out onto the deck. That was when they passed through the cloud of blue butterflies.

After that Roberts felt well enough to walk around the

vessel where he found every deck jammed with African men and women, trade goods, animals and baggage. They had erected their own tent cities and were busy putting up hammocks, laying down bedrolls, constructing entire canvas rooms. Goats and chickens wandered everywhere, and there were more strings of smoked monkey—the tiny red colobus with its human face, huge blue monkeys that looked like wrestlers locked in combat, their tails wrapped over bamboo poles. He wandered from deck to deck, followed at times by gangs of curious children; later by a man who looked like he might be customs or police, a guy Roberts put into his memory bank just in case it turned out Raymond was along for the ride upriver. He stayed below decks for about twenty minutes because it seemed cooler nearer the water, and because he enjoyed hearing these Africans talk and argue, he enjoyed the smell of yams and manioc being boiled. On the way back to his cabin, he stopped to help two African nuns carry their steamer trunk up to the third deck where they had a cabin two doors down from his own.

And then about an hour later they went into the cliffs and the sky closed down. On the far shore there was tableland with knee-high grass, and beyond the plateaus, hills covered with thick forest. On the near shore was mangungu swamp and a fringe of palm, and then sharp red cliffs that rose up about two hundred feet as the river narrowed. Islands began to appear in the current. Roberts relaxed and tried to enjoy the journey, and he wished he had one of Mbenga's cigars. The air was thick and swampy, and he could hear children laughing in the tugs behind. There were arrows of dark cresting above the current, and he thought the forms were probably fruit bats coming out to feed now that the sun was setting. He went back to his cabin and pulled the rattan chair out, and sat down in it on the deck, waiting for Mbenga.

He closed his eyes and substituted memory for the hallucinations of his present life. Never in his wildest dreams had he thought he would witness such vividness of detail—the deep green mangungu on the river's edge, the deer-brown grass on the plateaus near Brazzaville and the blood-red laterite cliffs. When he opened his eyes again, night had become deep and he was sure he could hear bats skimming above the water, black commas of shade and a draft of sound. He moved his chair near the deck's railing, and retched pink and yellow vomit into the river. Jesus, he thought, there goes the Lomotil and chloroquine, his head spinning.

A hand touched his back. *"Wewe sawa sawa,"* Mbenga said. "Are you going to be all right, mzungu?" The man helped Roberts lean back in the chair.

Roberts told him about the headache, the vomiting and the brief attack of diarrhea that had plagued him back in Kinshasa. Mbenga squatted beside the chair and Roberts allowed the man to take his pulse and look into his eyes in the half-light from his cabin bulb. In his own mind, Roberts ran through some possibilities, from the hotel food, the boiled sombe, to the water and the insects. He had given up the idea that he might transcend these illnesses, or that it was a matter of adjustment to a new environment that was hot and dusty. He had given up the idea that the food didn't agree with him, and that in a few days he'd feel better. He knew that something was terribly wrong with his system, that it was more than just a bad piece of fish at the Matonge nightclub.

"I'm not well," he told Mbenga, managing to keep his breath, fighting down the nausea. A drunken soldier walked by just then and peered at them as if he was seeing double, then staggered away. Behind them there were a few strands of gold, all that was left of the day, but it was night-dark in the gorge. The boat was aglow with deck fires, candles and kerosene stoves. There were evening sounds: frogs gulping, fish jumping and a few fish eagles screaming far away. "I've dosed myself with chloroquine and Lomotil, but I've just lost both over the side. The Lomotil seems to be working, but I'm dry heaving now. I tell you it has me worried."

"This is not good, mzungu," Mbenga said. "We should go up to the bar and get you some cold lemonade. There is perhaps some chicken broth that could be prepared if we ask. This matter of losing fluid is very serious."

They walked to the forequarter of the third deck where there was a makeshift bar and restaurant, a slanting zinc roof, some tables and chairs, an African bartender lounging at a softwood counter behind which there were a few bottles and glasses. One drunken soldier had passed out at a table and was snoring loudly, his red eyes stretched into vacancy. Now the cliffs were high above them and the night was jet-black and noisy. They were passing through a swift current that bumped under the boat. Roberts was beginning to get a sore throat now from all the vomiting. Mbenga ordered beer and lemonade, and brought the drinks to a table near the rail, starboard.

"How far are we from Mbandaka?" Roberts asked. This was the first large town upriver from Kinshasa.

"Maybe tomorrow afternoon. This ferry stops at every village along the way and it is somewhat slow. But we could get off there and try to find an English or Belgian doctor. Perhaps it could be arranged to fly you to Kisangani. Your condition is a subject of much worry to me."

Even though the passage of the boat was creating a small breeze, the mosquitoes were terrible, swarms of them heaving up and down the decks, the boat passing through veils of them. Here between the steep gorges of the cliffs the air was heavy, almost without qualities. "Beyond Mbandaka, how far to Kisangani?" Roberts asked, trying to catch his breath.

"The next afternoon," Mbenga said. "Can you try to eat something now? It is very important to keep something in your stomach, even if it means that you will vomit it. There must be something to nourish your muscles."

"You're talking as if you expect me to keep vomiting."

"It is the diarrhea that worries me."

"I doubt it, but I can try," Roberts said. They were quiet while Roberts tried to sip some of his lemonade and eat a few of the groundnuts Mbenga had brought to the table. Mbenga had taken out his pipe and was filling it with roughcut tobacco. Below them the river was an invisible glass highway, foamy with bats skipping over the surface and the sounds of jungle logs bumping against the hull with their passage. Roberts thought about the blue butterflies, the softness of the bodies, the furry surface of their wings. Some German tourists had come out of their cabins and were loudly ordering dinner. Roberts wondered how they had managed to stay inside those hot boxes all afternoon. The sound of music filtered between decks, a hard-driving world-beat sound that was probably coming from somebody's cheap cassette deck or jambox. The music engaged him, wound around inside his head and created a *lacunae,* something geometric. Roberts bought a cigar from the bartender and came back to the table and tried to smoke it, but it made him sick. He ordered more lemonade, even though the first glass was making him nauseated.

"Just so you'll know," he told Mbenga, "I'm not going to die on you. This is one of my personal prejudices."

"Please don't say such things, mzungu. That is very bad luck."

"You think it is bad luck?"

"This luck. This is in the head, no?"

Roberts drank down his lemonade in one gulp, hoping that

way to keep it in his stomach. His fingers had gone numb, and his lips seemed to be without sensation. Roberts took out the tooth powder tin full of diamonds and laid it on the table. "I'm not strong enough to look after this," he said to Mbenga. "If one of Raymond's men is on board, I couldn't do anything to stop him from taking this. I don't think they know about you, but even if they do you'd better take this until we get to Kisangani. Maybe I'll feel better by then, maybe not. Anyway, you can just give it back to me when I check into the New Stanley Hotel."

"Oh, mzungu," Mbenga sighed.

"No, it's okay."

"But I have a better idea." Mbenga puffed some smoke over the side. The German tourists were engaged in a loud, meaningless argument with their waiter.

"What's your idea?" Roberts asked.

"We give the diamonds to Marie. Even if Monsieur Raymond knows about both of us, he couldn't possibly know about my sister. Even if he noticed me in the taxi that day in Brazzaville, or if his man saw me pick you up behind the Ouzey market, I think I was too far away for them to recognize. But just in case, perhaps I could give this to Marie. She would be perfect. No problem, heh?" Mbenga picked up the diamonds. "Marie is devoted to the docteur. You can trust her, mzungu. Of this you can be assured, *comprenez?*"

"*Oui,*" Roberts agreed. Above the gorge, lightning flicked through the clouds. He closed his eyes and rested. *"Oui,"* he said again. "That's fine, *alors.*"

"Mzungu," Mbenga said. "We must stop at Mbandaka."

"I don't want to stop."

"But the doctor there . . ."

"We mustn't stop," Roberts insisted. "If Raymond is following us and we get off in Mbandaka we'll be at his mercy.

On this boat we have some safety because it's so small. Maybe by the time we arrive in Kisangani, I'll feel better."

"But you are very ill," Mbenga protested. "This is not to be taken lightly. I have seen these things grow serious very quickly. Already I think this is dangerous. Your skin is dry and you are becoming dehydrated. Your temperature is elevated and if it becomes more elevated, then your dehydration will increase all that much more quickly. Perhaps stopping for the doctor in Mbandaka is unavoidable." Mbenga puffed again on his pipe, releasing smoke that drifted aft. "Besides, I have become fond of you, mon ami. I do not wish anything bad to happen to you after all you have done for the docteur."

"In Kisangani," Roberts muttered, now halfway through a dense dream of himself, in another life. His head was floating through an underbrush of hallucination. "I'm told Kisangani is the garden spot of Zaire. I have to see this place. There are mimosas on the central square, and cafes that serve chocolate coffee, and frangipani as big as basketballs." Roberts laughed out loud, trying to ease the tension.

Mbenga put the powder tin into his pocket. "I will deliver this to Marie. They will be safe with her. We share your interest in the docteur. You must not worry, as I've told you why no police or customs people will bother her. Are you in agreement?"

Roberts nodded, about the only gesture he had strength enough to make now. Never in his life had he suffered through such a tremendous headache, something that lifted off the top of his head and poured in boiling water. He wanted to lie down someplace cool and quiet, but he remembered the heated cabin and its urine smell, the cockroaches scurrying around the hole-toilet, the metal walls seeping water. Now the night was happening without Roberts, an object outside himself that was passing through in screams and music, the ghostly whisper of the bats skimming water. When the feeling eased a little, he took out his map of the Kisangani area, spreading it out on the table in front of them. He ordered more lemonade and chuckled to himself giddily. On the map he traced the location of the timber road out of Kisangani, the old warehouse and mining complex that was now the clinic, the northeast tilt of land that evolved into hills above the river. "This area heavily wooded?" he asked Mbenga.

"Do you feel well enough to do this?"

"Adam," Roberts said, "before I get completely crazy with fever or whatever the hell I've got, we've got to talk about our plans for the docteur. If I'm not any good, you're going to have to do the whole thing yourself. Otherwise we could waste weeks while I get well. And I'm not sure the docteur will have weeks once we're contacted in Kisangani by the kidnappers."

Mbenga showed Roberts the timber road, its intersection with hills near the river, the huge vacant cuvée beyond. On the map, the African plotted all the clinic buildings. Then he drew Roberts sketches of each and plotted the interiors of the buildings. Roberts asked the man to make a topographical plot of the surrounding terrain, which he did carefully, outlining the hills and waterways. No roads led beyond the compound, and there were only two villages nearby, about fifty kilometers out into the forest, no airstrips, just trails and animals' routes. The waiter brought Roberts another lemonade, and he tried to drink it while talking. Deployed running lights of the boat and the trailing tugs cast a faint patina on the river, an ethereal glow that blended with the music from below deck. Roberts noticed that the third deck was filling with women and children looking for places to sleep, spreading their blankets, taking care of their animals—a few goats, some black bush pigs, even a few dogs and cats. There were Zairian paratroopers, men probably on leave from the Army, wandering the decks drunkenly, singing together, shouting out at the night. Roberts estimated the width of the river at maybe two miles, and they had come through the cliffs and were deep in forest, trees at least a hundred feet tall. You could hear monkeys chattering there and now Roberts could smell the sharp cheese-rot smell of bangi hovering over the vessel.

"What do we do?" Mbenga asked, when he had finished sketching the terrain, the clinic buildings.

Roberts told Mbenga he had two pounds of plastique in his travel bag. "There is a transmitter," he said, "and detonators buried in the plastique explode the charges when timed properly. Essentially we're going to play the same game with the kidnappers that we played with Raymond. I know you don't know how to set the charges, but I'll do it for you. Surely, I'll be well enough to do that. I'll show you how later, just in case. We're going to arrange a meeting with the kidnappers somewhere near the clinic compound, somewhere open. And then we'll trade the diamonds for the docteur, but we'll have the plastique and the weapons as insurance. If I'm sick, you'll have to handle this yourself."

Mbenga remained quiet. Roberts could tell he was upset by the conversation and he didn't blame him. It was a terrible thing out here on the dark river, this talk about danger and death while paratroopers on leave smoked bangi. "I think I can do this thing," Mbenga said quietly. "But I will pray for your recovery."

"Whatever happens," Roberts said. "When we get to Kisangani you have to check me into the New Stanley Hotel. Everybody in town will see the white Westerner and that's what I want to happen. Even if Raymond and Slade are there to greet me, I have to check into the hotel. You stay away from me for a few days. Let Marie hide the diamonds. I'll contact you when the time comes. If I'm ill, you'll have to do it yourself when we've been contacted." Roberts fought to breathe. "It might help if we had a vehicle in Kisangani."

"I have a cousin!" Mbenga said.

Roberts laughed and clapped the African on the shoulder. "I should have known," he said.

The boat angled into shore where a series of lights had appeared in the bush. Roberts knew they were offshore from a village and that they were surrounded by canoes and barges, villagers clamboring on board to trade and gossip. The drunken paratroopers had found some femme libres going upriver and had surrounded them to talk, share palm wine and smoke bangi. The village itself had neither shape nor tone. There were just a few fires, some lights, the smell of charcoal.

"You will be fine," Mbenga said encouragingly.

"No matter what," Roberts replied, "we have to be in control of the situation in Kisangani. We have to dictate where the meeting is to take place and be in charge of the terrain and timing. That's vital to our success in getting back the doctor. This meeting has to be in a place we know, in a place where we've been before. So, we have to scout the area. Even if I can't do this myself, you'll have to do it. And another thing. Slade won't be involved, even if that means we keep him uninformed. He's a man concerned only about his insurance money. This is between you and me and the doctor, nobody else. When the Simbas contact me, I'll rig the explosive and teach you how to detonate it. It's quite simple. Then you and I, or you alone, can scout the territory and pick our meeting place. Then all you have to do is show up early and arrange for the exchange. If something goes wrong, which I doubt, you blow the plastique and we start shooting. This depends on how many Simbas show up at the meet." Roberts was short of breath again and very dizzy. "This is just like the meet with Raymond, *comprenez?* You have to maintain a certain psychological distance from your work. Do you think you can do this?"

"I can do this, mzungu," Mbenga replied.

"The vehicle," Roberts said.

"There is a jeep that belongs to the docteur," Mbenga said. "Or my cousin has an Opel, very old but reliable."

"You must survey the meeting area. Bring me the sketch if I'm too sick to go."

"I will do this."

"The doctor has to be exchanged where we say. We must be firm on this point."

"It will be done, mzungu."

"I've asked this before, but you don't have any idea where these Simbas come from, how many there are? Do they have a local village we could scout, maybe intercept them?"

"I don't think so, mzungu," Mbenga replied.

"Now, about the local police," Roberts said. "Any of them reliable, not corrupt or stupid or cowardly?"

Mbenga laughed primly. "They are all corrupt," he said. "There is nobody reliable in a position of power. These are contradictory elements in Zaire."

Roberts put his head down on the table. He felt light-headed, vague, as if suffering from déjà vu, an extraordinary vision of another world, another time floating in front of his head, just now that the boat moved away from shore and he could hear shouts from children. The German tourists had left their table and were replaced by drunken paratroopers who began to play cards. Roberts felt as if he might vomit over the side again, but he fought down the feeling, allowed it to pass through him. Mbenga circled the table and caught Roberts under the armpits, lifting him from his seat, whispering something in his ear Roberts didn't understand. Together the men hobbled aft to Roberts' cabin where it was hot and dark inside. Mbenga held Roberts around the waist while he vomited into the sink, then helped him down onto the bed. Mbenga pulled up a chair and sat down.

"Do I have malaria?" Roberts asked.

Mbenga put a thermometer in Roberts' mouth. In a few minutes he took it out and studied the glass tube. "Your temperature is elevated by two degrees Fahrenheit." Mbenga covered Roberts with a sheet. "But this is not malaria. You would have terrible chills. And I think you have been taking your chloroquine, so there should be no numbness either. There are strains of malaria that are resistant to the drug. It is no guarantee. But still, I think you do not have malaria."

"You could be wrong?" Roberts asked.

"If you have malaria you will be ill for several days at least. We'll know tomorrow morning." Mbenga took a room towel and soaked it in water and placed it on Roberts' forehead. "I'm more worried about your dehydration. Do you think you can sleep a little?"

"What about dysentery?" Roberts asked.

"This isn't dysentery," Mbenga said knowingly. "You have a bad headache now. *Mal de tête?*"

"Very bad, yes."

Mbenga bit his lip. "Will you let me take you to a doctor in Mbandaka when we arrive there tomorrow afternoon? This would be very wise, I think."

"We try for Kisangani," Roberts said. "If I can't make it I'll let you know tomorrow." Roberts tried a smile. His throat felt as if it had closed tight, as if he might suffocate. "Maybe I need an *mbolozi,*" he laughed.

"There will be no witch doctor," Mbenga said.

Mbenga searched until he found Roberts' medicine case. He made Roberts swallow Lomotil directly from the bottle, and dosed him with paregoric. Lying in a dazed stupor, covered to his chin with a sheet, Roberts studied his hands as if they were specimens, the untrimmed nails turning pale blue, as if he was rotting from the inside out. Down the deck, all the soldiers were laughing. Roberts didn't know it then, he had no ken of it at all, but in the morning Mbenga would be at his side, along with Marie and one of the African nuns. The cabin door would stand open to the rich green African morning, an air heavy with scents. His thoughts would be diaphanous, as fleeting as *kipepeo*.

6

ROBERTS WAS AWARE THAT HIS cabin had been rearranged, the bed moved nearer the door, somehow tilted slightly so that his feet were lower than his head, and that the chest and chair had been whisked back into the dark recesses. In this way Mbenga had connected him to something other than his illness, to the sheer luminous morning hovering in the forest, to the great green canopy of sky, the thick motionless water. He could hear toucans screeching in the trees and genou monkeys chattering, and an invisible breeze moaning through the lianas and strangler figs.

For a long time these impressions descended upon him in the form of memory, clouds of thought that fixed inside his existence in a locus of forgotten griefs, jealousies, half-fantasies of another time and place, his misbegotten childhood, the dark angry flashes of adolescence. But most of the time Roberts was simply delirious, fighting out and up from his fever.

At times he could prop himself on one elbow and engage in sensible conversations with Mbenga, study the immense sky strangled by forest. Once he thought he saw the blue butterflies again, a crazy apparition that he failed to fix and which was gone like a flash of lightning or a dream, something so tenuous that he'd mistaken it for something real.

Later the sun came up, the air heated again and swarms of insects lifted off the surface of the river and went careening through the forest. Roberts realized that there was a sharp edge to his reality, that it didn't cut through things deliniated—only through his consciousness, his dreams, fantasies, reveries—that he'd embraced another world that was as directionless as empty space. He factored himself away from reality and only then began to understand what was real and what was not, taking for granted that he might be wrong about anything. He was bound to his illusions by his temperature, and his illness, whatever it might be.

Shading his eyes, he looked at the mighty forest. It was so green it hurt him to see it. And then he faced the fact that he had soiled himself, that he had shit involuntarily all over the bed, and that the African nun had taken off his clothes during the night and taken them away, perhaps to have them laundered. Someone had bathed him and had covered him with a clean white sheet and as he lay quietly in that brief bright morning awareness, with insects lifting off the river's surface where dots of light played. He thought he remembered her face gazing down at him, a small black oval with a bony structure. He remembered feeling ashamed and hopeful, and that the smile of the nun had offered him such hope that he drifted into another of his sleeps, comforted beyond measure.

But soon he was awake again and terribly sick and he could feel sets of arms wrapped around him, anchoring him it seemed, as he retched into the toilet bowl. Isolated conversation surrounded him and he realized it was morning. Mbenga was beside him, kneeling at the foot of the bed, just outside the cabin door, and Marie had come inside and was sitting in a chair near his side. He had shit himself again, and he had vomited violently. He was dying inside, destroying his own tissue, and he felt helpless against it. Mbenga offered him a glass of lemonade and in a fit he drank off the entire glass in one gulp, feeling nauseated almost immediately. For a moment he thought he could sit up.

Mbenga leaned over the bed, tested his pulse. "Mzungu, you are awake?" Roberts nodded and allowed his wrist to be handled. He felt like a child. "Now we are coming to Mbandaka, *comprenez?*" Marie touched Roberts with a wet washcloth. "These worthy Catholic sisters must leave the boat at the town. There is a parish here and an old priest who runs a dispensary for the villagers on the outskirts of the city. He knows some medicine and there is a place where you can rest. Without intravenous injections, I don't know what will happen with your condition. You are being consumed by diarrhea and fever. Please let them take you there."

Roberts felt clear and amazingly light. "I want to make it all the way to Kisangani," he said. Without the guide of his health, he felt directionless.

"But my dear friend," Mbenga said, more firmly. "It is nearly another day's journey to Kisangani and you are very dehydrated. I have tried to get you to drink, but it is not easy."

Roberts picked up the glass and gestured for more lemonade. Mbenga filled the glass and Roberts drank, trying to show the man how capable he was, smiling up at him for fatherly approval. Marie wiped his face shyly with the cloth, then wetted his arms and neck. Even in the early morning it was terribly hot and the boat was moving slowly, coming into the city docks, surrounded by hordes of canoes and pirogues, people shouting, dogs barking.

"What the hell have I got?" Roberts asked.

"I don't know. It is very bad. Please let us take you off the boat. This town is not much of a town at all, but I know the old priest and the sisters can care for you better than anyone can care for you on this boat. I don't think you understand how serious your illness is becoming. Listen to me. You have diarrhea. You vomit everything that is put inside you. Just last night I tried to make you eat an orange and it came up in twenty or thirty minutes. I know you haven't eaten properly in two or three days before now, and your temperature is very high."

"How high?" Roberts asked.

"Four degrees elevated." Mbenga shook his finger at Roberts. "This matter of being dehydrated is the most serious thing that can happen to you in the forest. You can die. I am not trying to frighten you or to manipulate you, to make you do something you think is wrong, but you require fluids inside your body and I can't keep anything inside. This is a matter of a doctor and an infirmary. Even the poor parish clinic of Mbandaka is better than the boat. We go on up the river through a long stretch of hot jungle and there are many village stops along the way. If you can't make it that far there will be no turning back." Mbenga touched Roberts on the throat, taking his pulse. *"Please, my friend,"* he pleaded.

"You want the diamonds," Roberts said angrily. He knew he was going crazy. He could feel something slip away from him.

"Oh please, mzungu, you don't believe that?"

"All this trouble. My old friend Adam."

Mbenga looked away. He spoke to Marie in Lingala and she left the cabin.

"I am your friend," Mbenga said. "You are delirious."

"Damn you," Roberts said, feeling himself fall further and further away from what he knew. He was mixing up the real and the unreal again. In his memory he was plunging through a steep mountain stream, showered in cool air. He didn't know if he lost consciousness, but when he became aware of himself again he could see African children looking at him through the cabin door. Some passengers had leaned on the railings outside, smoking hand-rolled cigarettes, casting casual glances at the sick man inside his cabin. Sun sifted through clouds above the docks. The air smelled of garbage and boiled cabbage, fish blood, charcoal, shit, diamond dust.

Marie had come back inside the cabin and was trying to make Roberts eat honey from a spoon. Mbenga put pillows behind his head and for a while, Roberts felt almost normal.

"I'm back," he said.

"Yes, that is good," Mbenga replied, smiling warmly. "Do you remember your suspicions?"

"Not exactly."

"Good," Mbenga said. "The boat is docked in Mbandaka quay. We will be here only another two hours or so. Now is the time to leave."

"I'm going on."

"But why, mzungu?"

There was a crowd outside the cabin now. They were peering inside at Roberts.

"Think about it this way," Roberts said. He ate some honey and took another drink of lemonade. He could feel his tongue in his throat, like something lodged there unnaturally. "Slade probably flew up to the New Stanley Hotel yesterday without me. He's wondering where the hell I am. He's likely to make a fuss, try to go to the police. He may even think I've gone off with the money and have no intention of delivering it to the kidnappers and getting back the docteur. If he does go to the police and if he succeeds in making very much of a fuss, then I've got to be there to explain everything. If I show up in Kisangani tomorrow then he'll quiet down and go away, I hope. If I don't show up then he's likely to make a mess of everything. I came on this boat because I didn't like

Slade and I didn't want him to get the idea he could run the
show by himself, order me around. Kind of childish I admit,
but that's the way it is with me. The more you push me
around, the less I'll cooperate."

"You are like a donkey my family once owned."

"That's it," Roberts said. "But it's more practical than that,
too. I thought I could slip into town, get back the doctor, all
without too much interference from Slade." Roberts
watched the African faces watching him. There were even a
few soldiers outside now, gaunt men in camouflage. "Now,
I'm not too sure."

"But is this risk worth your life?"

"Surely I can make it twelve or fifteen hours."

Mbenga nodded, shrugged his gesture. Now African children had crowded around the cabin door, making quiet intense faces at the sick Westerner. Behind them cranes picked
up lugs of fruit and grain, even a few foreign automobiles.
Roberts couldn't see the town; it was too far away in the
trees.

"We can try," Mbenga said sadly. "But you must drink as
much lemonade as you can, even if you feel too sick to drink,
you must try. You must try to eat honey and take some salt."

There was a pitcher of lemonade and Mbenga filled Roberts' glass, making him drink by taking his head and tilting it
backward. Marie spoke a quick Lingala phrase and Mbenga
returned it. Marie continued to wipe Roberts with a wet
cloth and hum slightly.

"There is something else," Roberts said.

"Anything my friend."

Roberts sat up and looked around for his black bag. "What
about the guns and diamonds?" he asked quietly.

"Marie has the diamonds," Mbenga said.

"Of course. They are safe? She has the tooth powder tin?"

"Yes. There is no problem, *comprenez?*"

"The guns?"

"In your bag, under this bed."

Roberts reached for Mbenga and felt immediately weak. He was trying to make some contact but he could feel himself drifting away, as though he was rising up through the forest canopy, attached to a green umbrella. For a moment he felt as if his soul had detached itself and was being carried aloft without him. He recognized his own delirium and became a participant in his own illness. There were two separate beings now, Roberts alive, thoughtful, active, and Roberts inert—soulless.

"And I'm worried about Raymond," Roberts said finally.

"Of course, this bad man."

"Please find another tin of powder and put some of Marie's rhinestones in it."

"You create a diversion?"

"I'm giving Raymond something to steal. If he has a man on this boat then I want that man to have something he can take. He may take the black bag and leave us alone for a short time. I'm too weak and sick to do anything about it now, and you're too busy. Besides, I don't want either you or Marie to come to any harm because of some dirty trick I played on a French scoundrel back in Brazzaville."

"I will do this, mzungu."

"And if anyone comes into the cabin, just let him look around. It isn't worth trying to stop him now. Besides, anybody that Raymond sends after us is going to have a weapon."

"I will not bother the man if he comes."

"And another thing. Give Marie the guns. Wrap them in newsprint and have her hide them in her wicker bags, like she did before. When we get to Kisangani she can give this all back to me, the diamonds and the guns."

Mbenga spoke to Marie in Lingala. The woman took the powder tin from under the bed and hurriedly left the cabin. "She understands what to do," Mbenga said as she went away. "Please try to get some sleep now, and I will arrange to put another tin of tooth powder in the black bag. Marie will do this."

"Remember," Roberts said, closing his eyes. "If anyone comes to the cabin, don't bother them. Let them look around and take what they want to take. They'll figure out there aren't any diamonds in the tin sooner or later, but maybe by then we can organize a way to fuck them up." Roberts smiled. "I'm probably going to have to blow the shit out of Raymond one day as it is."

"If only I had a syringe, a rubber tube."

Roberts lay still, listening to the boat creak against the wharf pilings. He could hear goats bawling, chickens and pigs. He felt a semblance of motion and wondered if the boat had pulled away from the wharf quay. The crowd outside his door disappeared, and he could tell the boat had moved because he could see islands, downed trees streaming by in the river current. Somewhere upriver there had been a violent storm and flotsam was sailing past. Again, Roberts studied his skin, the yellow cast on his arms. He couldn't go to the mirror and look at himself, and he wondered if it would frighten him if he did. His stomach contracted, and he felt the surge of diarrhea again, something painful.

"Let us be careful," he heard Mbenga say. The man had lifted him from under the arms. Roberts felt himself begin to vomit. He was burning up with fever. He knew he would be utterly helpless if one of Raymond's men were to come after him. Somehow Mbenga managed to get Roberts to the toilet and back to the bed.

"If something happens to me," Roberts began.

"Don't talk now, mzungu. Please."

Roberts could smell diesel again and he knew they were out on the river, drifting in the swell of the current. The sun was hidden in the trees and the air had a dank smell.

"If something happens to me you'll have to free the doctor. You'll have to free the doctor."

"Nothing will happen to you," Mbenga said.

"No, I don't know. Can you do it?"

"Whatever you say, my friend. But you must not talk right now. You are losing your strength and you will need all of it."

Roberts struggled himself upright. The city of Mbandaka appeared through thick trees: some warehouses, shacks, a long red incline of barren hill, and then concrete bunkers lining a sewage canal. It was gray in the morning fog. "Here's what to do if I can't make it."

"You will make it, please."

"Just in case, now," Roberts said. "Don't get tied up with Slade. I've explained that he's a company man down the line. I mean that if the going becomes difficult, he's likely to be no good to you or the doctor. If I can't help you, do it on your own. I think you'll have only a few days, nothing more, before the kidnappers contact us. They'll probably know when we get into Kisangani. If I'm too sick to move, just get me to the hotel. You can stay close by so that when the kidnappers contact me, I'll be able to tell you about it. Marie can keep the diamonds. She can keep the guns. But you have to get me into the city. I have to show up at the New Stanley Hotel."

"I understand, mzungu." Mbenga was trying to make Roberts lie still.

"Get me a room at the New Stanley. Send Marie back to the clinic with the diamonds."

"You can rely upon me."

Roberts became momentarily lost in nausea. He was ill for a time, too sick to speak, and then his head cleared. There was scattered sound on the riverbank, probably a village on the outskirts of Mbandaka. Sounds filtered through the forest, something with the force of an echo. The boat was being followed by canoes full of children, men selling snacks and trinkets. Some of the soldiers were standing on the deck, shouting down at the canoes and their passengers in a language Roberts couldn't understand.

"There is a chance," Roberts said, "that either I won't make it to Kisangani, or when I get there I'll be too sick to handle any of this. If that happens, then you'll have to be responsible for the doctor."

"You will make it to Kisangani," Mbenga said.

"If I don't, then you'll have to choose a place to meet with these abductors. It will have to be someplace you're quite familiar with, someplace open and with a good view."

"I know such a place," Mbenga said, touching Roberts again on the throat, below his ear. He shook down the thermometer and swabbed it with alcohol. Marie had come back into the cabin and was saying something soothing in Lingala, speaking directly to Roberts from across the room. "My sister is saying a Christian prayer for you, my friend," Mbenga said. "This is a prayer for your recovery and good health."

Roberts thanked Marie in French. "When you go to meet them," Roberts said to Mbenga, "make sure to place the detonators in the plastique and take the transmitter with you. You've seen me set this explosive in Brazzaville. Dictate the terms of the meeting in the same way I did it with Raymond.

There is a certain risk in doing this, but more risk if you have no security. Under no circumstances should you give up the diamonds until you have possession of the doctor. Even if this means refusing to surrender the bag. If you are tempted to surrender the bag before you have the doctor, then think of this. You will die yourself, and the doctor will die, and the kidnappers will have the diamonds."

"You are very wise in these matters," Mbenga said, trying to sound positive.

"Can you fire a gun?"

Mbenga looked away again at Marie. "I think so," he said.

"Don't hesitate to do it. Protect yourself at all costs. You are the doctor's only hope. If they kill you, or take away your ransom, then she is dead. There is no use being coy or compliant about this. The people you're dealing with are probably without morals. Shoot anyone who tries to take away the diamonds. And if they don't show the doctor immediately, go away. Try again some other time, some other place. You give them one chance and one chance only."

Marie had taken up a wicker basket and busied herself with a necklace of cheap jewelry. She spoke to her brother for a long time while Roberts rested. His speech had tired him immeasurably. The fever hammered him, as did the thought that Mbenga and his sister would be alone against the kidnappers.

Mbenga leaned over Roberts to whisper. "My sister has a string of costume jewelry. Cheap paste. We will put this in a powder tin and place the tin in your black bag. This is a very smart thing, no?"

Roberts agreed that it might give them even more time if Raymond showed up.

"What about the guns?" Roberts asked.

"My sister has put them with our things back in the second-class boat. I don't think there is any need to worry. Already the soldiers know she is a leper, and they leave her alone. They will not touch her things because they have a great superstitious fear of her disease." Marie had gone back to wiping Roberts with a wet cloth. Mbenga put the thermometer in Robert's mouth. "Now you mustn't worry any more. We are out in the river and will make good time toward Kisangani. The customs people in Kisangani know my sister very well. They believe she brings back some cloth and soap from Brazzaville, and they too are frightened of her leprosy. They will never suspect she is carrying guns for the white American. She will pass through the city very easily. I have already told her she must go directly to the clinic with these things. In the leper compound nobody will bother her. You must rest your mind on this account. Now we are all in the hands of God, no?"

"Good, good," Roberts said weakly. He was dreaming again, caught in the heat and languor of the day. It seemed to him that the brief cool of the morning had lasted only a second, that it had been an illusion. He felt utterly exhausted, his muscles like loose strands of rancid meat hanging from his bones. A huge liquid hole had opened in the middle of his stomach and his life was pouring through it. He closed his eyes and let himself go, until suddenly he wasn't afraid of his fever, nor of his sleep and dreams.

He must have slept, because the rain surprised him when he woke. It was a grave-dark rain that sheeted the river and hammered on the metal cabin roof, making a huge noise. Roberts realized after a time that his bed had been moved again, this time away from the door because of the rain. Instead of on a mattress he was lying on a sheet of plywood, which was slightly tilted toward his feet so that his head was

elevated. When he opened his eyes, he could see outside
where the rain bored down on the surface of the river. He
could barely discern the outline of the thick forest, about a
mile away across the rippled surface of the river, which was
obscured by smoke and sheets of blowing rain. Black clouds
boiled through the trees, at almost ground level, and even
though he knew it was stiflingly hot, he was not uncomfortable. He felt light again, almost weightless, and he had a
picture in his mind of the astronauts floating through metal-
sheeted rooms, bouncing off dials, smiles on their faces, and
he could almost relate to their boundless joy at shedding the
drag of gravity. There was no pain now, not in his stomach
or his limbs, and his headache was gone. In place of it there
was a supreme acuteness, as if he could see through the colors
and textures of the forest. He couldn't smell the rust or the
piss, or even the shit in the toilet.

"You are awake, no?" he heard Mbenga whisper, close to
his ear. "How are you feeling?" he asked.

"Abstract," Roberts said honestly. Mbenga was trying to
make Roberts drink lemonade, but his lips were dry and his
throat seemed closed off. When he shut his eyes, the rain
roared in his ears. The storm was very violent, but somehow
it soothed Roberts. It soothed him even though he thought
he could sense every raindrop striking every leaf, every bamboo shoot, every silver-tipped *popo* branch.

"Marie is here," Mbenga said.

"How far from Kisangani?" Roberts asked. Marie inched
closer to the bed. Roberts could see her in the thin light,
smiling down at him despite her disfigurement. "I don't even
know if it's day or night," Roberts added.

"Six hours downriver from Mbandaka," Mbenga said.
"Do you remember leaving? I tried to make you get off and
go with the nuns. But you refused."

"I remember," Roberts lied.

"Marie is here, so you see you are in no danger."

A man Roberts recognized as the bartender had walked past the cabin door, and was standing by the rail in the rain, trying to see the sick Westerner. Roberts tried to touch Marie, but she moved quickly away. He drank some lemonade, finally getting it to go down his throat. "Six hours," Roberts choked.

"You've had a long sleep," Mbenga said. "But this can't happen again, no? I cannot let you sleep that long again." Mbenga looked outside the cabin and waved away the bartender. Wind was blowing rain inside the cabin at nearly right angles. Roberts was fascinated by the look of the angry rain, a blizzard of spikes. Mbenga poured some Lomotil in the lemonade glass and Roberts drank it, and swallowed some vitamin B capsules. The Lomotil was chalky white, and Roberts nearly vomited it immediately, but he kept it down. Mbenga massaged Roberts' throat and temples, while Marie adjusted the sheet over his body.

"You must continue to hydrate yourself," Mbenga said.

Now Roberts was very sick, his insides on fire and a huge weariness overcoming him. He could not distinguish his pain from the rain, and he wished he hadn't taken the Lomotil. Things had been so peaceful before.

"Is this what it's like to die?" he asked Mbenga. "I always wondered."

Marie was humming softly. Roberts could hear the Lingala, calm and langorous, like a hymn.

"You are not going to die," Mbenga said. "I want you to hear what I'm saying. Please pay attention. You must try to make it through the night. I'm going to let you sleep only a little, and then you must come awake and take your lemonade and your Lomotil. This diarrhea is your main enemy. It is draining you of your body fluids. No matter how you feel, and no matter if you must vomit immediately, you must take down the lemonade and the Lomotil. I know you probably have a headache, but there can be no more paregoric. When you are awake, just listen to the sound of my voice, or listen to Marie singing to you. I will talk and give you lemonade and you will drink. Then Marie will sing and it will be a short journey. Do you understand, mzungu? Tell me you *understand.*"

"What about the word mzungu? What does it mean?"

"It means something respectful. You must not worry now. You must only concentrate on your Lomotil and lemonade."

Suddenly Roberts was sick. He could feel himself release his bowels, and shit himself. It was horrible and he felt degraded, all the shit running out from between his legs in a sweltering torrent. His body burned and he was lying in filth and he could hear the rain smashing down on the boat. Marie was taking another towel, wiping the shit from the plywood, cleaning it from the floor of the cabin. Roberts realized why he was lying on plywood, why Mbenga had rearranged his cabin. "I'm sorry," he mumbled.

"Don't worry, mzungu," Mbenga said. Before Roberts had regained his senses, Mbenga was forcing lemonade down his throat. "Please just talk to me. We shall talk together. Marie shall sing. Tomorrow morning we shall be in Kisangani where there are groves of mimosa trees with their purple blossoms, and where there are cool groves of coffee trees, and mountains too, where there is cool air. Just talk to me."

"My head is funny," Roberts said. "I'm seeing the Rocky Mountains now, and horses splashing through streams." Roberts tried to talk some more, but it was hard. There were blue butterflies in his head too, and the dark paranoid eyes of Mobutu, his portrait on the Sozacom Building. Roberts was tortured by false soundings, his senses no longer mirroring the real world.

"You cannot talk to me?" Mbenga asked.

Roberts nodded, then realized it was a lie. He was very far gone now. "No," he said quietly.

"Do not resign yourself," Mbenga said. "I will talk to you now, only you must promise to listen."

"I promise," Roberts said.

"Comme je descendais des Fleuves impassibles," Mbenga said, his voice lithe and silky. *"Je ne me sentis plus guidé par les haleurs."* The man touched Roberts on the forehead, where his third eye was. *"Des Peaux-Rouges criards les avaient pris pour cibles, les ayant cloués nus aux poteaux de couleurs."* Marie was continuing to hum, though now without words. Mbenga stopped, listening to the rain. "Do you hear me, mzungu?" Mbenga smiled. *"La tempête a béni mes éveils maritimes."*

Roberts realized he was holding Mbenga's hand tightly. He tried to squeeze a *yes,* but his hands had no strength.

"This is Rimbaud," Mbenga said. "The great French poet. The man who was lost in Abyssinia so long ago. The man who told the world how he sailed down the impassible rivers, no longer guided, about the angry natives taking him as a target, destroying all his guides. It is a story of great courage, all in the face of hopelessness." Marie had stopped humming and was rinsing out the towels. Roberts could smell shit now. A queer turquoise light invaded the cabin, casting every object and face into halos. Now the storm had passed and there was only a light mist on the river. "And you know in the poem the storm blessed the poet's sea voyages. And so now you are the poet, my friend, and there has been a storm, and you have an impassible river before you, but yet you must pass over it."

"I hear you, Adam," Roberts said.

"Plus léger qu'un bouchon j'ai dansé sur les flots." Mbenga had poured more lemonade. "Lighter than a cork I danced on the waves," Mbenga whispered.

"Lighter than a cork," Roberts said.

And then Roberts knew he had soiled himself again, a dirty string of shit had escaped his body. Mbenga lifted his body away from the plywood, while Marie pulled the sheet from under him. Marie began to clean him again.

"I told you I went to Catholic school in Katanga," Mbenga said, ignoring the filth. "I assure you the Belgian fathers did not teach the students Rimbaud! But when I was a young man my family was very well-to-do and before the troubles and the revolution, and before Mobutu and the soldiers, I had dreams of going to Paris and studying literature. I didn't want to be a miner and merchant like my father. And so I was sent to the Belgian school where I was taught French, and where I found my first copy of the great poetry of Rimbaud."

Roberts was helpless, listening. The rain had stopped altogether but it was hot and insects were rising from the water.

Mbenga said, "This poem is called the Drunken Boat. Do you know it, my friend?"

"Yes," Roberts said.

"Late at night in my village, after my mother and father, and my sister and brother, had all gone to sleep, I would read these beautiful and horrible words. In those days we lived in a wooden house! Do you believe this, my friend? We lived in a two-story wooden house. After all my studies, and my other work was done, I would stay awake when the house was quiet and read Rimbaud and dream of Paris. The next day I would do my work, and then go to the Catholic school run by the Belgian nuns and learn to recite Racine, and then at night I would read Rimbaud and dream of Paris. Is it possible that I was ever that young and foolish and romantic?

Is it possible that there was a time before Mobutu and all this raging violence?"

Roberts groaned.

"Listen to me, mzungu," Mbenga said firmly. "As a foolish young boy in Katanga I learned this poem from memory. I know these words by heart. I will recite it for you. It is a very long poem. You will listen. You will pay strict attention to me, as the Belgian nuns would say. And in the morning we will be in Kisangani where there will be cool groves of mimosa and there you will be clean and refreshed."

"Tell Amanda . . ." Roberts said. He fell away from his own body, but he could hear Mbenga reciting the poem.

"Comme je descendais des Fleuves impassibles. . . ."

As I was going down impassible Rivers.

PART THREE

BAKIE NZURI

1

HE SLEPT AGAIN AND DREAMED again, this time that he had
been pegged into muddy earth and snakes were slithering
over his body. It startled him and he woke with a small stifled
cry, which was drowned by the sound of rain pounding on
the tin roof of his enclosure. Right then, still afraid, he began
to take an inventory of his consciousness, as if naming and
numbering the things he knew and the objects he could see,
might assure him that he was alive and well, and not on his
way to somewhere else, somewhere terrible and lost. He was
on a double bed, lying just in the middle, covered by a
mosquito net, which gave everything an unreal shine, a
patina. He judged the wooden floor to be real mahogany,
shining in the moonlight like gold, and there was a table and
chair directly across the room from where he lay, two objects
just under the moony unreality of the jalousie windows, its
slats, the moonlight dusting through. There was a chest of
drawers, some pictures on the table, and a medicine chest
with bottles and vials reflecting dully. By his side was a nightstand with another collection of bottles and vials, a syringe, a
compress. When he tried to move, he realized that his right
hand was connected to a catheter, that he was being fed
through a spike.

Five minutes later the screams began in the outside court-yard. He heard them come through the window, high ululating shouts full of pain. There was a period of silence and then more pronounced screaming, undifferentiated and obtuse, as if two voices had crashed together and had shattered into millions of pieces. Roberts wiped the sweat from his forehead and listened, lying under his white sheet like a little boy afraid of the dark, only now he was afraid of these disembodied sounds, directionless. Roberts was lying with his head under the sheet even in the huge heat of the night, while the rain advanced across the jungle and thunder roared like an ocean in his head. It was so hot he thought he might suffocate, even at night. He no longer paid attention to his own breathing, nor did he count objects in the room.

He was saved by Mbenga, who had come through the door carrying a hurricane lamp and stood just inside the room in a subdued yellow haze of light, holding a tray of food and medicine. Roberts was so happy he moved his arm in greeting. Mbenga was wearing a white hospital smock, dirty tennis shoes and patched polyester trousers underneath the smock. Roberts tried to speak, but only croaked like a frog. Mbenga began to mash bananas with a mortar and pestle.

"Oh, Adam," Roberts said finally, something stupid as a counterpoint to his enormous pain.

"Oh my friend, you're awake," Mbenga said in return. He lifted the mosquito net and folded it back over the bed. He sat on the edge of the bed and touched Roberts' forehead gently. "Yes, you are finally awake. This is very good news. This is very good news indeed."

"Get this spike out of my hand," Roberts joked. He felt sick, but he wanted some humor to bear out his notion that he was still alive. "Christ, there's been screaming all night."

Mbenga had poured water from a pitcher and was offering Roberts some in a glass. Roberts sipped, and lay back from the enormous effort. It seemed to him that this tiny action had drained him of all his energy, and that he was left helpless as a baby, there in the sweat-laced sheets, breathing hard. Even the memories of lying awake, of his dream of snakes, of the moonlight moving on the floor, seemed to make him weary and afraid, as if at any moment the night might reach out and pull him down inside its evil mouth. He tried to remember as far back in his life as he could, but he could only remember shards of seconds on the boat upriver from Kinshasa: a shower of blue butterflies just as the boat hit the cliffs, young African boys in canoes chasing the butterflies in dark currents. He remembered having some lemonade in the bar on board. After that his life was a gulp of pain, indivisible from the heat and the exhaustion of whatever illness had made him so low. "This goddamn spike is killing me," he laughed crazily.

Mbenga stripped the tape from Roberts' hand, revealing a deep blue bruise. The man quickly slipped the needle from the vein, and unhooked an overhead bottle of glucose, placing it on the tray. He dabbed iodine on the wound and held a cotton ball against the bruise. "This spike as you call it has been in your vein for three days now. It will be a little bruised, but not too bad, no?" He smiled. "I am so glad you are living and awake to complain about it. Please, mzungu, complain all you wish. It will do you much good." He smiled again and took away the cotton ball. "When the patient complains, the patient will survive. This is the first rule of good medicine. It is when the patient does not complain, when the patient is silent or morose, that the real trouble begins. An angry patient will be saying goodbye to the hospital soon."

"Sounds like a fortune cookie," Roberts said. "Where the

bloody hell am I?" Roberts choked, his throat hurting terribly. "I've been having terrible dreams. Snakes crawling all over my body."

"Not to worry, mzungu," Mbenga said softly. "You are at the clinic compound outside Kisangani. You are being taken care of very well. You will be quite good as new, yes."

"It's so damn hot."

Mbenga placed a wet cloth on Roberts' forehead. Some of the heat seemed to drain away. "You are in a director's house on the top of a hill above the compound. You are safe, and it is as cool as anyplace here. You must try to relax and not worry too much. In this way you will regain your health and strength." Mbenga touched the glass to Roberts' lips again, in an attempt to make him drink. Water ran down his mouth, his chest, some of it going down to his stomach, but not much.

"Who brought me here?" Roberts asked, gagging.

"Marie and I brought you here from the boat. You had a terrible journey of four days from Kinshasa. There were two nights when I thought you would not survive the trip, that the fever and diarrhea would take you away before we could come to the clinic safely. But you survived. You are very stubborn, and that is good. When we got to Kisangani, we hired a taxi and brought you straight here."

"How long have I been in this room?" Roberts tried to sit up, thinking he had regained some of his senses. Mbenga piled a pillow behind his head, helping him get upright. "I've lost any sense of time or place. I don't know the day of the week, or whether it is evening getting dark, or morning getting light."

"You are only two nights in bed here," Mbenga replied. "You were in terrible condition on the boat. I have to tell you, mzungu, that your temperature was over one hundred and four Fahrenheit. Then Marie and I would bring your temperature down for a few hours and you would take some lemonade. We would become hopeful. But then you would leave your senses and your temperature would elevate again, and you would become delirious." Mbenga smiled and went back to mashing bananas, grinding the fruit with an ivory pestle. "There were many times during the three days we thought you would die. This frightened us very much. It is now the morning of your third day here. Soon it will be light."

"God," Roberts said, "I don't remember anything." He leaned back and watched the first strings of morning inch inside the jalousies, a white-yellow light that was dappled. He could hear thousands of birds, and monkeys too, fighting and playing high up in the canopy of trees. The air was still now and very hot. Dogs were barking in the distance. "I do remember Kinshasa," Roberts said. "I remember standing on the boat bridge looking back at the barges of people. I remember the blue butterflies upriver where we met the cliffs, and I remember getting something to drink with you at the bar." Roberts paused as his head began to ache. "I shit myself, didn't I?" he asked suddenly.

"This is not to be worried over. You showed much courage and fighting strength. Dehydration is a part of your illness."

Roberts raised his hands in tandem and studied them, the details of his fingers, the nails, the raised bluish knuckles. "My hands have turned blue," he said to himself while Mbenga finished mashing the banana.

"Cyanosis," Mbenga said quickly.

"Cyanosis," Roberts said.

"This is the name of your coloration, mzungu." Mbenga found a wooden spoon and made Roberts eat a bite of banana. "It only means that there is no oxygen to your blood. Your lips turn blue when they are cold. Gangrene takes away the oxygen as well, and your wounded limb turns black. In your case, there is no blood to the hands and feet. They turn blue. Or black."

Roberts smiled willfully. "I'm turning black," he said.

"That could be very serious indeed!" Mbenga joked.

"And my throat is killing me."

"I am sorry, mzungu," Mbenga said. "It was necessary to place a feeding tube down your throat last night. You were not taking nourishment. For the past week you have been either asleep or delirious. Without some kind of nourishment your dehydration would have been too serious to counteract." Mbenga held up the mortar full of mashed banana. "This is your diet over the past few days and nights. The feeding tube is the reason for your bad throat."

"What's in the tube?" Roberts asked, pointing at the catheter and bottle.

"Glucose and a small amount of antibiotics."

"This is all very professional," Roberts said. "You've saved my life. You and Marie. I don't know how to thank you. Perhaps I can do that by saving the doctor when I get better."

"No, mzungu," Mbenga said. The man looked away as if he were ashamed. "You fought very hard. It is the patient who survives."

Roberts said he thought he could sit, and Mbenga helped him with more pillows, until he was upright. Mbenga walked across the room and opened all the jalousies and turned on the overhead fan so that air began to ruffle in the room, creating a kind of imitation breeze. It seemed cooler now; the rain had definitely passed, and it looked as though the day would be blue, with high puffy clouds in the sky. There were puddles of water in the courtyard outside and steam was rising from

them. Roberts saw a swarm of lemon-barred yellowtail butterflies playing in the pools of water, dots and dashes of color
against the red laterite clay, down the hill mimosas in blossom
and a slash of green that looked like coffee trees. Now Roberts could hear goats bleating, as well as the compound's dogs
barking.

Mbenga sat down in a chair beside the bed. "You will
continue to improve," he said. "Perhaps later this morning
you will get out of bed and walk around the room. The color
in your hands and feet will return, too. Part of this is from
being on your back for so long, and from losing so much body
water." Mbenga rolled away the catheter apparatus and unhooked the plastic tubing and rubber stoppers. "You have lost
much weight. You will begin to regain it quickly, and you
will find yourself very hungry. You will wish for more than
bananas and rice." Mbenga handed up the mortar with its
mashed banana residue. "You will become stronger every
day, yes?"

"How many days?" Roberts asked.

"Do not be impatient. Two, three, four. Who knows?"
Mbenga shrugged noncommittally. "Within the week you
will be mostly your old self."

"I've got to get moving sooner than that."

"Impossible," Mbenga said.

"I have work to do. We have work to do for the doctor.
She must be rescued quickly from the people who are holding
her. You said yourself that time was of the essence."

"But you are too weak. Please do not hurry this for your
own sake, and the sake of your health."

"The doctor might be killed," Roberts protested.

"But mzungu, you are still very ill."

For some inexplicable reason Roberts thought about the
diamonds and became very frustrated. He tried to look out-

side the room and see clearly downhill where there were coffee trees, as if this might clear his head and expel the anger. He took a deep breath. Down the hill there was a broad expanse of elephant grass down to a copse of mimosas, maybe twenty or thirty trees, and then a stand of coffee trees, dark green in the morning sun. Sun was highlighting the trees, too, and there were puffy white clouds. Roberts guessed that he was looking west, with the sun behind the hut. "It's very fine up here," he said finally, breaking his mood.

"The river was bad for you."

"I still feel lucky," he said.

"You are lucky, mzungu," Mbenga said. "And there is more to that than just your health. The usual river steamer is called the *Colonel Ebeya*. It is run by the government. This Colonel Ebeya is a terrible rusted boat that pulls perhaps five or six ferries behind it with five thousand passengers at a time. It takes perhaps twelve days to run upriver to Kisangani from Kinshasa, sometimes two weeks. If we had been on that boat, you would have never made it. It would have taken too long. It is lucky we made this journey on one of the private vessels, one of the last of its kind. In this way, your life was probably saved. Otherwise, the journey would have taken too long."

Roberts finished the green banana mush. Somewhere in the compound *matoke* was being cooked. He could smell it.

"What about the diamonds and guns?" Roberts asked.

"Marie has them. They are quite safe with her. They are exactly as you left them." Mbenga gestured to a corner of the room where Roberts saw his black valise. "Your clothes are here," Mbenga said. "This bag is exactly as you left it, with the rhinestones in a tooth powder tin, along with your camera and books. Marie has the weapons in the leper colony, wrapped in newspaper, along with the real diamonds. Nothing has changed. You are in quite good hands here."

"I thought I heard screaming in the night. Just outside in the courtyard."

"Ah, that," Mbenga sighed. "You heard screaming, yes."

"What the hell was it all about?"

Mbenga glanced out to the courtyard where some monkeys were playing in puddles of rainwater. "There are many children in the compound, mzungu," he said sadly. "Some of them are the *abandonées,* left alone by their parents. Some are alone because their parents have died. But many of the children here are afflicted by illnesses which are serious. When these children die, their mothers come up the hill to mourn. The screaming you heard during the night was the sound of mothers mourning their dead children. I am sorry it disturbed you, but it cannot be helped. Here is where the mothers come to cry."

"I didn't know," Roberts said. He thought he should say something else, but he didn't know what it might be.

"This is one of the reasons our docteur wishes to keep the clinic open. There is a great need to be filled here. Children are ill, villagers are without medicine. There is great suffering everywhere one looks."

Roberts drank some of the water by himself. When he took a personal inventory, he found his arms and legs quite skinny, his cheeks hollow, his skin scarred by open sores. He was surprised to find himself clean-shaven.

"I shaved you yesterday, mzungu," Mbenga said. "I hope you don't mind, but you looked quite fierce and horrible."

Roberts relaxed and enjoyed the early morning stillness. He could hear a wind whispering faintly in the mimosas. He admired the sound of the elephant grass, one great continuous moan.

"You haven't told me what my illness was," Roberts said at last. "I suppose I drank some bad water in that Matonge

nightclub you took me to. Or maybe it was the boiled fish."
Roberts smiled up at Mbenga, who was very somber.

"You've had cholera," Mbenga said.

"Cholera," Roberts said stupidly. "It couldn't be cholera.
I was vaccinated back in London."

"There are many new strains now. You've had a new kind
of cerebral fever. It is not uncommon to find that innoculation against a disease fails to protect against another strain of
the illness. The drugs once used to combat tuberculosis are
now nearly worthless, and the same thing can be said for
malaria. These creatures, the bacteria and the virus, are
stronger than we."

"Cholera," Roberts whispered to himself.

"But it is good you had the vaccination in London. It did
make a difference to your condition I believe. Perhaps without the innoculation you would not have had the immune
boost that helped you through the fever and dehydration.
This is a very dangerous illness, mzungu."

Roberts finished his mashed banana and relaxed back
against the bedstead. Mbenga took down the mosquito netting and stored it in a drawer beside the bed, then took
Roberts' temperature and made him take some vitamin tablets. Without another word, Mbenga began to give Roberts
a thorough sponge bath, washing his arms and legs, his feet,
his neck and back, all very roughly in traditional hospital
fashion, this very personal and highly generic action that both
pleased and amazed Roberts with its simplicity and homespun
devotion. There was something in the room that seemed
personal to Roberts, too. As he was being washed he looked
around at his quarters at the bright batik over the closet door,
a collection of African masks on the walls, a barometer, some
books, and personal photographs of European men and

women. Mbenga took Roberts' temperature again, then replaced the thermometer in a beaker of alcohol.

"These are the doctor's quarters, aren't they, Adam?"
Roberts asked.

Mbenga was squeezing out the sponge. "Yes, it is true. She
lives up here on the hill. It is no problem for you to come
here. This is a good place. Quiet and cool, much more so
than down in the compound where there is always noise from
children and dogs, and where the day can become very hot."

"We haven't talked about the doctor," Roberts said.
"Have there been any messages from her or about her? Is she
still alive do you think?"

Mbenga was quiet for a long time. He seemed in a different
world, then he was back, staring at Roberts with his black
sheenless eyes. The man got up without a word and closed
one of the jalousie panels because the wind had risen and was
kicking dust inside the room. Roberts sat up at the end of the
bed so that he could see farther downhill. There was a slope
of elephant grass and one huge tamarind tree in pod, and
farther away two outbuildings painted red with conical
thatched raffia roofs, and some goats grazing through the red
dirt for food. The sides of the huts were trellised with frangipani. Tufts of mimosa blossom floated through the breeze
and the sky was bright, crazy blue.

"There has been no word," Mbenga said.

"Have you been to town? Have you heard from Slade, or
have you been to the New Stanley Hotel?"

"I have not been there, no."

"What's my temp?" Roberts asked. Two women appeared
at the edge of the elephant grass, both carrying baskets on
their hips, followed by goats.

"It is very good. Only one hundred and one Fahrenheit."

"I'm almost human again."

"Later I will shave you again. Perhaps tonight you can put on some clothes and have a walk outside. Now you must try to get some more sleep. I will bring you some broth for lunch, when you wake up."

Roberts stopped Mbenga, who was preparing to leave. "You know I can't wait two or three days to see about your doctor. She's in terrible danger and every moment wasted puts her in greater danger than before. The group that kidnapped her probably expected me at the New Stanley two days ago. They'll be angry or suspicious or both. And there's Slade, who I don't trust any farther than I can spit his pinstripe suit, which isn't very far right now. He could be at the New Stanley, and he could ruin everything with his mouth. I don't want any of that to happen. So, you have to get me on my feet as soon as possible. It's that simple."

"Today is not possible, mzungu," Mbenga replied, almost before Roberts had finished. He shook his head, emphasizing the point. "You are not well enough to move yet. You will find yourself very weak when you get out of bed today. We must wait at least two or three days so that you can be fed broth and bananas, and so that the antibiotics have time to do their work. Then you will have enough strength if you wish to go down to the New Stanley. I can drive you in the Land Rover."

"But I feel much better already."

"You will weaken today. You must listen to me."

"So what if I go down to the New Stanley for a couple of hours? That isn't anything compared to what might be happening to your doctor right now."

"You have lost much weight. Your fever is still elevated by almost three degrees. This is still a dangerous illness."

"It will drop. Feed me aspirin."

"If you get out of bed for fifteen minutes, you will faint."

"I'll be sitting in the Land Rover."

"You will have terrible headaches and then you will lose consciousness."

Roberts sighed audibly, just for Mbenga's benefit. "This is ridiculous," he said. "I'm going to lose whatever medical debate I have with you." Roberts felt a sudden chill and lay down in the bed and pulled up his sheet so that he was covered. He could not swallow and his head throbbed. "Have you heard anything from Slade?" he asked weakly.

"Nothing, mzungu."

"He's somebody that concerns me. I know he's probably down at the New Stanley looking for me. I gave him the slip in Kinshasa and he's probably quite irritated. Not that it bothers me terribly, but I don't want him meddling in this kidnapping and getting the doctor killed."

"You try to sleep now," Mbenga said.

Something had made Roberts very tired. Perhaps it was the steady thump of the ceiling fan as it stirred the air, or perhaps it was the breeze slicking through the elephant grass or the high blue sky he could see through the jalousie slats. He remembered his night panic, the dream of snakes on his body and the women's screams for their children. Suddenly his heart was beating very fast, so fast he could feel his pulse on the side of his head. Swarms of butterflies played in the dirty puddles outside in the courtyard.

"How is Marie?" Roberts asked tiredly.

"Oh she is very well, mzungu," Mbenga said brightly. "She asks after you and she prays for you. During the last day of our journey on the river she was with you every moment. There were many soldiers on the boat, and with her near you they did not come to rob us. Any other time they probably would have stolen your valises, and where would we have been? You would have had no clothes. And of course the good nuns helped you, as well."

"Oh yes, I remember them now," Roberts said. He felt frail and weak, like an old man.

Roberts didn't feel himself go to sleep, nor did he remember the moment of its occurrence when he woke much later. He sat up in surprise and found a stiff breeze rattling the jalousies and sun ticking on the tin roof. The room was empty and quiet and it was very hot. The mosquito netting had been placed over his bed again. Roberts sat up further and put his feet on the floor. He was naked and when he looked at his body it seemed to belong to someone else, someone whose legs had turned thin and red, covered by insect bites that were producing pus. The joints of his arms and legs were swollen and very sore, and when he placed his feet on the floor he became instantly dizzy and he thought he might pass out and fall down. He tried to stand and then walk three or four paces away from the bed, which he accomplished after about ten minutes of effort. He wanted to stroll around the room and look at the photographs and books, maybe learn a bit more about the doctor, but he didn't have the strength. When he sat back down on the edge of the bed his head was pounding and his mouth dry. Mbenga had left a bowl of milk beside his bed, and he ate a banana and drank some of the milk, feeling nauseated when he finished.

He drifted off to sleep again and woke to find Mbenga standing beside the bed, humming to himself in Lingala. The tamarind pods were frenzied in the breeze and Roberts could see the sun angling in through the jalousies, dropping beautifully through the coffee trees and mimosas, in early evening. Dark clouds had bunched on the northwestern horizon, out over the cuvée. Mbenga took Roberts' temperature and made him finish the bowl of milk and eat another banana.

"You did sleep. You feel better?" Mbenga asked.

Roberts said he did feel better, but was still weak. His temp was one hundred and one. Without speaking, Mbenga sponged Roberts thoroughly again, and made him put on some clean underwear and a pair of pajamas. Roberts let himself be handled like an object, something foreign to himself even, but it comforted him. He found himself wondering inwardly about Marie, about all the abandonées. There were no sounds coming from the compound and he wondered about the silence as well. Now that it was technically summer in Zaire, it probably rained every day, sometimes very hard, with huge thunderstorms north of the equator. Insects and frogs were starting to make noise too, along with the rumble of distant thunder. Mbenga helped Roberts put on some plastic sandals, and then stand on the floor. For twenty minutes he manhandled Roberts around the hut, back and forth. They must have made a fine picture, Roberts thought, the small muscular African man with a metal brace on his left leg, and the skinny sick American with hollow cheeks and unkempt dirty hair. Then Mbenga placed Roberts back in bed. He made up some pillows behind his head and sat down beside the nightstand. The sky outside had turned as purple as a bruise.

"Tomorrow morning," Roberts said. He found himself short of breath. "I've got to go into Kisangani tomorrow morning. I've got to get to the New Stanley Hotel."

"I will get your broth. You slept through lunch."

They were out of sequence now, *non sequiturs* lining up one behind another. Roberts recognized an unwillingness of Mbenga to talk, which was being fostered by an obliqueness, a deflection of wills.

"Talk to me, Adam," Roberts said.

"I am sorry, mzungu. Do you wish me to shave you now?

I could go for the soap and razor if that is what you'd like."

"Is there something wrong?"

"No there is nothing wrong."

"Then what is it? You seem jumpy and nervous."

"I am only concerned for your health. You know that I could go to the New Stanley Hotel myself. I could go in your place. Because you are too weak and tired I could do this thing. You said yourself that I could receive the message and deliver the ransom. This would be rational, no?"

"You're a very Cartesian soul," Roberts joked. "But I need to do this myself. They'll have more respect for somebody from London with the money. Besides, I took on the job and I think I should go through with it. I don't want you to be in any more danger than you've already suffered through."

Mbenga took out the mosquito net and placed it on its hook above the bed, folding it down over Roberts. "You must get some sleep now," Mbenga said softly.

"What is it?" Roberts insisted, seeing how troubled Mbenga appeared. The walk had left him tired and disoriented; it was all he could do to keep his eyes open. Lizards had wandered onto the windowsill. He heard music from the compound, something on a radio. "Can't you tell me what's going on?"

"It is nothing, mzungu," Mbenga replied. "You are not as strong as you think. I also believe you are still in danger from the illness. If you refuse to recuperate you will become feverish again. It is only that you have come through so much that I do not want to lose you now. If you rest, everything will come much easier later. Without you we would never have seen the money delivered, and so you have done quite enough for now." Mbenga shrugged, a sign that he had finished something important.

Roberts shrugged back and said he'd like to go into town if it could be arranged. Mbenga poured a glass of lemonade and left it on the nightstand for Roberts. Sleep was coming now, and Roberts could feel himself folding up inside its shell, where softness and warmth were natural. He could see through the mosquito netting, the fan twirling silently above him and purple shadows on the walls. He thought for a moment about home, and then he touched his tongue to one of his front teeth and found the tooth loose.

He slept again and woke in the dark. The jalousies were wide open and there was thunder pounding the far-off horizon. A great gray waft of moonlight streaked the courtyard, and Roberts could see that it must have rained because there were pools of water in the courtyard again. Fruit bats were swooping in and out of the coffee trees. Roberts didn't know how long he lay there, but after a time the double doors of the hut opened and Mbenga came inside wearing his white smock and tennis shoes, followed by a smallish woman in a gray pleated skirt and white blouse. Mbenga's head had been bandaged and the bandages were bloody. An adhesive had been placed over his right eye, and the eye was nearly swollen shut. The woman walked around Mbenga and closed the jalousies in sequence, one by one. Mbenga brought a bowl of broth to the nightstand and set it down. Roberts was sure he had seen a picture of the woman before at the University in London.

There was only moonlight in the room, but Roberts was certain he knew the woman. *Docteur,* he wanted to say. But he closed his eyes and waited for something else to happen.

2

SOUNDS STUTTERED AGAINST A TIN roof: the ticking of the sun, a fall of dying insects that Roberts first grew to recognize in Brazzaville. The insects powdered down in their tiny deaths, brushing against hot metal, a snow of creatures. He closed his eyes, not wanting to see the bandaged face of his friend, shutting himself off from the doctor whose presence in the room he found disconcerting and vaguely threatening, as if a spirit had returned from the dead. Instead, he found images of the past dropping through his mind, as if a time-release capsule of himself had been let loose inside his body and tiny blips of forgotten things were entering his bloodstream one at a time.

In his mind he saw a necklace of razor blades against the black skin of a Kikongo soldier. Going further back he found himself making involuntary associations of thought, which unnerved him at first, until he discovered for himself that each had almost universal significance—the necklace linked to the sweet-hot smell of his hotel room in Brazzaville where he first heard the nightly powdering-down of dead insects, brief moments of tropical twilight when night held itself in pale hues against the total darkness, a smell of charcoal, strains of radio music pulsating. Finally, he saw in his mind the face of Tom

Slade, the tall, ethereal Englishman he didn't trust, the man's insouciant sneer as he uttered the word "African."

There was a sudden terrible clap of thunder. The ceiling fan ceased revolving, coming to a slow stop.

"Adam, please light a lamp," the doctor said. "We've lost the electricity again."

"Shall I start a generator?" Mbenga asked. Roberts lay back in the darkness, listening.

"No, Adam," the doctor said gently in her husky voice. "We don't have much petrol in reserve. I think it will be fine to light the hurricane lamp."

Mbenga lit the lamp, which produced a yellow circle on the floor of the hut. Roberts strained to see the doctor standing in shadow, arms folded. Her hair was short and reddish, and there were dark bags under her eyes. Her hands were chafed red from working in water, her fingernails cracked. Still, Roberts thought, her face was dignified, almost beautiful. "I'm going to give Mr. Roberts his shot," the doctor said.

The rain crashed down all at once. Its coming was so loud that Roberts lost his train of thought and he could barely hear himself breathe. Mbenga silently took out a cotton robe and reached inside the mosquito netting, and helped Roberts dress himself while the doctor secured the jalousies against the huge rain outside. Roberts put his feet on the floor and steadied himself, feeling a tingle like ice on his soles, sharp spears of unnatural pain. Now the doctor crossed the room and rubbed Roberts' upper arm with alcohol, filled a hypodermic and jabbed it into his arm. Roberts was speechless.

"This is just vitamin B," the doctor said. Roberts asked if he could possibly have some broth. Mbenga gave him the bowl and he ate two or three spoonfuls of corn broth and carrots. "The effect of high fever," the doctor said, "can be devastating on the liver and heart. I'm going to keep giving you vitamin injections to stimulate your recovery. You're doing remarkably well under the circumstances. You have Adam to thank."

"I don't understand," Roberts muttered, still sleepy. "Adam, what's happened? Is everything all right?"

"Mzungu, I am so sorry," Mbenga said. He did not come out of his corner.

Roberts closed his eyes again and began to count. He counted the sounds he could discern, tree frogs groaning, rain slipping through coffee trees, barks of thunder. "Adam," Roberts said finally, "you have to tell me what's going on."

"Please get up and try to sit in a chair," the doctor said, interrupting. She helped Roberts out of bed. He sat down in a wicker chair nearby, just out of reach of the lamp glow. Mbenga had retreated to a far corner of the room where he pretended to straighten sheets.

Without the artificial breeze of the ceiling fan, it was insufferably hot in the room, and Roberts was soaked. He ate some more broth. He noticed one leg sticking out from the cotton robe, a skinny disembodied object, studded with red pustules where insects had bitten him. "My name is Elyse Revelle," the doctor said. Her voice was tight and breathless. An aura of electricity had filled the air, simultaneously with the advent of the rain. It seemed to connect everyone in the room. "Do you feel well enough to talk?"

"Weak, but better."

"There is something terrible I must tell you. You must be prepared to forgive quite a bit."

"I gathered that," Roberts said. "What's happened to Adam? Why is his head bandaged? He has a bruise under his eye."

"We can come to that eventually."

"This will be fine," Mbenga said. "My wounds are nothing. This is no problem, yes?"

The doctor held up one hand for quiet. "Everything is not fine, sadly." She sighed audibly. Her Flemish accent was noticeable, but still delicate. He presumed she spoke French to Mbenga, and perhaps Lingala to the Africans in the compound. Suddenly, Roberts felt clearheaded, as if his fever had burned away. "I've made a terrible mess of things," the doctor said. "I don't really know where to begin."

"Begin at the beginning," Roberts said. "I presume you've escaped from your captors."

"Not exactly," she said. "You have every reason to be very angry. But I want you to hear me out."

"I don't know what you're talking about."

The doctor spoke to Mbenga in swift clear French and the man left the hut hurriedly. "I've asked Adam to help with the evening meals near the compound. We have a large number of abandonées this season, and Adam is good with them. They are very frightened and he is very gentle. It is a good mixture for the children. I think they all love him, and he is very kind to them. I don't think you'll mind talking just with me alone. It is really our business we have to do, and it has nothing to do with Adam. Not directly. I think he is very ashamed at this point, and I do not wish to increase his shame. There is no reason. Adam is a good man, this you must believe."

The doctor sat down on the edge of his bed, finally giving him a good view of her face. She smiled briefly, in embarrassment. "I'm glad you're much better. When Marie and Adam brought you here you were very near death."

Roberts must have acted surprised because the doctor looked away. "You were here when I was brought up from the boat? I thought you'd been kidnapped by BaLese tribesmen, that you were being held for ransom? What the hell is going on?"

"You have every right to be bitter."

"Am I bitter?" Roberts asked. "Why should I be bitter?"

The doctor breathed deeply, holding it in. The compound dogs had stopped barking and there was an unearthly stillness under the sound of the rain. "I wish I had a cigarette," the doctor said. "But I stopped smoking years ago. But the desire hasn't stopped. Isn't that funny?"

"What's this all about?" Roberts pressed.

"I wish to tell you how sorry I am."

"That I almost died of cholera?"

"So, Adam has told you of your illness."

"He told me. He said I had a new strain of the fever. I took innoculations in London."

"Adam told you all about it?"

"Apparently not."

"Not everything then. But about the illness. When he and Marie brought you up here your temp was over one hundred and three. You were terribly dehydrated."

"So, it's you I have to thank?"

"It doesn't matter," the doctor said.

"How long will I have these headaches?" Roberts asked, just for the moment deflecting his real thoughts.

"Days. Perhaps weeks."

"My skin turned black."

"This is quite temporary."

"Cyanosis," Roberts said.

"Mr. Roberts, please," the doctor said. "Adam is a very reliable nurse. I have taught him much, and I'm not surprised he has told you about your illness. He has also told me the terrible things you two have seen together. He thinks of you as his friend and you must not be cynical about Adam. His acts were genuine and authentic. There is no artifice in him at all, nor is there any cynicism, nor any in Marie for that matter. They are both very real, and they have only me to blame for their present predicament, for bringing them to this moral crisis." The doctor had spoken against a welling of tears. Roberts thought she might cry outright, but she didn't. "All of this is the result of a moral confusion that has its genesis in my own uncertainty and pain. Marie and Adam have me to blame for this breach of confidence."

"Breach of confidence?" Roberts said. "Is that what you call it?" He felt a surge of anger. "Doctor, you're talking riddles, leading me in circles, acting the philosopher. I think there must be a straight line through this mess. But instead I'm being led around in circles, with all this talk about moral dilemmas, personal authenticity, this drama you're concocting to keep me from the truth. I don't understand what you're doing here and I don't understand what I've been through the past two weeks. It was explained to me in London that you'd been kidnapped by BaLese tribesmen and were being held for ransom. I was told to come down here with the ransom in seventy-five thousand English pounds and make delivery and save you from your captors. Now I see you're here. You've been here since I arrived on the ferry and was carried up here by Marie and Adam in a taxi. You can imagine my confusion. Now I see that somebody has beaten Adam. I haven't even gotten to the breach of confidence part yet."

"Of course you're right," the doctor said. "I intend to tell you everything. Only this is very hard for me. I am unused to dishonesty. You nearly died, and this too is on my conscience." One tear fell from the doctor's face, a single-spaced expression of her grief. "I'm a *doctor,*" she said.

Roberts tightened his thin cotton robe. The rain had

stopped and for some inexplicable reason he was chilled. His feet felt numb against the palm matting. "These are your quarters, aren't they, doctor?" he asked.

"Yes," she said tearfully. "They're mine. For the past ten years."

"I noticed the pictures and books."

"You were brought here straightaway."

"I'm grateful for that," Roberts said, seeing that he should lighten the load for now. "I'm sorry for being rough. I just don't understand any of this right now."

"If I tell you the absolute truth, will you promise to hear me out to the end?" The doctor straightened her pleated skirt. "Please don't make any judgments until I'm entirely finished and you know the entire truth. If you can do this, I'll be happy to tell you everything. I don't wish to influence your judgment of me at all. I do know how much Adam treasures his new friendship with you, and the trust he feels for you, so I feel that I must defend him somehow. But for myself, I shall make no such defense. You may do anything to me or against me that your wisdom tells you you must. I have no concern for myself at this time. But I do want you to understand the situation at the clinic, and my motives for doing what I've done. And I want you to regain your trust and confidence in Adam. I think it would break his heart if you left here with an ill will toward him."

The rain had stopped completely and a deft silence enveloped the forest. Roberts finished his broth and began to eat a banana. He could smell the evening charcoal smoke, boiled matoke and greens. "Don't worry," he told the doctor. "Judgments are like tiny sicknesses. They linger and then they go away."

The doctor smiled. "Adam told me about your wisdom."

"Did Adam tell you I killed a man in Kinshasa?"

There was a moment of dense tension, rain dripping from the tamarind in the courtyard, frogs coming awake and beginning to croak. "No, he didn't tell me," the doctor said, swallowing hard.

"Well, it happened." Roberts spoke flatly to emphasize the facticity of his statement. "I picked up your ransom money from a French bank in Brazzaville. Adam helped me get the money across the river to Kinshasa. I was staying in the Intercontinental Hotel and one evening when I came back to my room there was an African inside with a machete. He didn't say anything, he just panicked and took a swipe at me with the knife. I shot him once in the chest. Technically, it could be called self-defense. Adam and I dragged him to an outside balcony and left town."

"Why are you telling me this?"

"You mentioned moral crisis. I wanted you to know that I've had my own moral problems in the past two weeks."

"They are attributable to me."

"That could be. I don't know. But my actions are all attributable to me. Morals tend to get lost in words, but actions come through loud and clear."

"But now you know that Adam has kept your secret."

"Of course," Roberts said.

The doctor stood and sat back down in one nervous motion. It was as though she had suffered a physical attack. She steadied her gray eyes on Roberts. "As a doctor, I know about these moral dilemmas. There is always the case of a woman in childbirth. Her labor goes poorly and it becomes obvious that she cannot give birth to the child without losing her life. It is likewise obvious that you cannot save both mother and child, though you may be able to save one or the other. Which do you choose? By what criteria are you to make this choice?"

"You could say the same about self-defense." Roberts had begun to be nauseated by the corn broth. "But I understand what you're trying to say. It happens all the time. It's the condition of good people in an evil world."

The doctor suffered a small smile again, more a gesture to replace her pain. "The beginning is ten years ago when I first came to this clinic."

"Before that you were with Doctors Without Borders."

"You've read my dossier."

"Dossier," Roberts said. "It's such a lovely word. Something you'd hear from a French policeman. Let's say I studied your records in London."

"Yes, before the clinic I was in the Sudan just at the outbreak of the civil war. And I was in Chad before the coming of Qadaffi and the drought. I was even in Eritrea before the lawlessness and famine. But then the chaos descended on all of Africa, suddenly, like a plague of grasshoppers. It seems that everywhere I've been there has been civil unrest, war and starvation, and I have been forced to leave eventually. There are limits even to Doctors Without Borders. When there is no food and medicine, no blankets, no plasma, then what is there for a doctor to do? You fold your hands and watch the children die, the old men die, the women die? When the villages are pillaged what is there for a doctor to do? And when a child steps on a land mine and loses both legs? What then? You leave these people to their fate, is what you do."

"You came here after your experiences."

"It was a chance to practice real tropical medicine. And it was a chance to be at a clinic that might have some substantial funding in the long term. I knew there wouldn't be so much money, but even the little that EuroCopper was supplying seemed like a lot to me at the time. And I thought there would be a steady supply of it, too."

"You wanted to do some permanent good."

"Yes, but there is the reality of life in Zaire."

There was another gap of profound silence in which Roberts could hear his own thoughts, the processes clicking away beyond the sparks of pain and numbness. A lizard had crawled through a broken jalousie slat and sat on the sill staring at him. Its eyes glowed in the dark and Roberts wished it would go away. Finally he asked the doctor if they could go outside and continue their talk, that he was suffering from claustrophobia after the rain, he needed to see some sky and some stars now that the thunder had gone. The doctor got out a terry robe and wrapped him in it, and together they staggered outside and sat down on a bench under the tamarind tree. Downhill there were human sounds, and some dogs were barking. Bats were sliding through the coffee trees, chasing insects. The bare red dirt was littered with shiny puddles left by the rain and the clouds were brushed with moonlight.

Roberts breathed deeply, practicing being alive. He told the doctor he understood some of Zairian reality, that he had come into contact with it before now. While he talked he moved his legs, the loose flesh like rubber.

"Don't believe that I was weary with Doctors," the doctor continued. "It was my life for many years and I made many good friends there. But I treated many nomadic peoples. They would come to camp, they would be treated, and then they would drift away following their goats or sheep, or their cattle. I never had a chance to see if my treatments were helpful. They were in camp one week and then gone the next."

"Ten years ago you came here."

"I had the chance and I took it. Ten years ago this was a workers' camp for the copper trade. There were perhaps two or three hundred families. The workers transhipped minerals, did some smelting, and handled all the barge traffic in and out of Kisangani. It was mostly dangerous hot work, and there were quite a few industrial injuries and illnesses. You could see strained backs, repetitive paralysis, burns, amputated limbs. I became a regular orthopedic specialist, despite my background and training in tropical medicine. Of course, I was to treat the families, the wives and children too. And there were many complaints from them about fevers and worms. So I was kept very busy." The doctor helped Roberts with his robe, which had become tangled. "Yes, there was a resurgence of measles and yaws, even some invidious river sickness and fever. During my first few years, even with the lack of supplies and the shortage of medicine, I think I did a very good job for the people."

"And then the country fell apart."

"Adam has told you?"

"I know about it. You can see it everywhere."

"Yes, the country disintegrated. Already, after my few years here, there was a tremendous upsurge in violence. More and more I found myself treating women and children, and less and less the workers. Then the whole infrastructure of the country crumbled. The roads weeded over or filled with ruts. Truckers couldn't get parts. Air service ground to a halt. Schools closed and fields went untended. And of course the police became more corrupt, and then almost ceased to exist at all. So, it made no sense for a farmer to work his fields, or a shepherd to tend his flocks. If a farmer raised a crop, the Army would come and take it from him. If a Zairian raised his coffee or his manioc, it would be stolen before he could sell it. And if he managed to raise it without it being stolen, there was no market and no money, no trucks to ship it to town, no boats to carry it downriver. The politicians, who were always venal, became more so. Teachers were unpaid. Banks closed and soldiers vandalized and raped. Soon, there was only a black market for pilfered or stolen goods."

"I've seen all this at work," Roberts said.

"The whole system collapsed all at once. And along with it collapsed the system I had set up to service the clinic."

"What system? What are you saying?"

"Let me explain," the doctor said calmly. "When I first came here I relied on the goodwill and protection of Euro-Copper. My first duty was to the workers and their families. When there was an industrial accident, it would be reported to the company, who would make a claim against their insurance carrier. I would make my reports to the company about my supply needs, and in would come the supplies from Europe on Air Zaire. But even in the best of times, before the chaos, if I ordered ten cases of tetracycline or penicillin, perhaps six or seven would arrive. If I ordered five or six gross of surgical bandages, perhaps three would be on the airplane. But we made do with what we got. The people in the compound grew corn and manioc. We raised some goats and a cow or two. We washed our own clothes, tilled the soil and repaired our own facilities. We scrounged petrol. And with what supplies that came in from Europe, and with the insurance claims, we were reasonably well taken care of. At first. And then when the clinic became imperiled by shortages, I turned to some of my contacts in Switzerland and France." The doctor made a grim little frown. "Or to the insurance company."

"The insurance company?" Roberts asked, puzzled.

"Yes, of course." The doctor had brought out a wet cloth, and she wiped her face. "I told you before that we had some industrial accident cases. When that happened, I would make a report to the insurance company which had an office in Kinshasa. They would pay the claim, or send us supplies of medicine. As time went by, EuroCopper supplied this clinic with fewer and fewer staff and supplies, and I'm afraid I began to produce false insurance reports to make up the difference. At first I did it with a very bad conscience. I reasoned that the company was ignoring its people here, and had for years, and that both EuroCopper and the insurance company could afford a few extra crates of bandages, or a few extra cartons of penicillin. For whatever reason, I began to make false claims in order to increase the money coming into the clinic. We were desperate. I co-opted my own desperation into a moral ambiguity. I reasoned away my guilt by thinking only of my patients."

"I gather this all leads up to what happened here tonight."

"Yes, certainly," the doctor said. She cleared her throat and folded her hands. "During those middle years there became fewer and fewer workers and their families, and more and more people from the bush, rural people fleeing their traditional villages, abandoning their traditional roles, because there was chaos out there, and no money or work. This compound began to fill with women and children, abandonées, sick people in great and terrible need. So, I began to claim more from the insurance company and press EuroCopper for more money." The doctor shrugged and smiled. "It did little good to press the company for money. But I began to see more and more of Tom Slade."

"Tom Slade," Roberts said, surprised.

"Yes, Tom Slade," the doctor said, with obvious distaste. "He represents the insurance company. He would come out to the clinic and investigate some of my claims. I'm afraid he knew what I was up to, but he didn't say much about it. And then later I began to understand why. When I made a claim he would authorize its payment, and then he would hijack some of the supplies and sell them on the black market. Of course, it was impossible for me to say anything, since I was, myself, implicated in the fraud."

"Tom Slade began to steal."

"Yes, of course. I was stealing myself."

"I've met Slade," Roberts said. "In London and Kinshasa."

"Yes, Mr. Slade," the doctor said sadly. "He's a constant reminder that I've done something illegal. At first, it wasn't so bad, just a few boxes here and there, and he would take one of them and go away. But toward the end, Slade began to take more and more, especially as it became obvious that the country was sliding into utter anarchy, and that EuroCopper would soon be gone—and with it, Slade's little fiefdom."

"Do you know what the end of the story is going to be?" Roberts asked.

"The end of the story," the doctor repeated, mantra-like. "Perhaps you can see the end of the story tomorrow morning. I think I finally lost my reason entirely. Over the past five years I've seen a new kind of illness. You've heard of AIDS. Well, in all my years of practicing medicine, I have never witnessed the spread of a plague like this HIV disease. And of course, I've seen sickness in its most horrible light—children starved, adult males murdered and women ravaged—but never anything like this. And so I came to my own personal and professional crisis some months ago when this camp began to fill up with villagers suffering from AIDS, when the abandonées began to walk into camp obviously suffering from HIV infection. I began to see my own integrity in light of this plague, and when I did that, I saw how little it meant. I decided that I would do anything to increase my own ability to stay here in this compound and see to my patients. I reasoned that EuroCopper had behaved abominably toward their workers. I reasoned that Slade had acted devilishly. In this way I compromised myself and did a terrible thing."

Roberts had been listening while clouds piled up on the horizon, lighted by a hidden moon. He had momentarily forgotten the strange dense heat. "And what was this terrible thing?" he asked. He thought he already knew.

"I arranged my own kidnapping," the doctor said. "That is to say, I pretended to be kidnapped, when all the time I was quite safe, here in my own quarters." The doctor stood and took a few steps nervously. "I knew that EuroCopper had a policy of insurance against such an eventuality. I knew also that Slade probably couldn't become involved in such a matter, because of the amount of money at stake. So, I pretended to go off in the bush and disappear. I sent a false message to the company in Kinshasa making it clear that I had been kidnapped and naming a ransom. I asked that a representative be sent to the New Stanley Hotel. But I left the name of the group responsible quite ambiguous, so that no harm came to any other person or tribe. I thought that someone would come with the money and that I would arrange a harmless exchange. Nobody would be physically in danger and I would have money to run the clinic after the company left Zaire. Even Mr. Slade would be gone from Zaire as well. It was really bloody nonsense. But I was quite desperate."

"Did Adam know about this plan?"

"Yes he did. I told Adam and Marie, and one or two others. People who have been with me for many years." The doctor sadly smiled, and sat down next to Roberts on the wooden bench. "You must not blame Adam for all this. When I sent the note, the company responded by asking that somebody be sent from the compound to Kinshasa, so as to lead their representative upriver. I asked Adam if he would go, and he agreed. I think his moral perspective is something like mine. His integrity is very vital to his life, but I think it is nothing compared to all this suffering." The doctor put down her wet rag, and touched Roberts lightly on the thigh. "That isn't to say the end justifies the means. Far from it. But something else is going on here that I can't explain. I've seen EuroCopper take so much from the people of Zaire and give nothing back. I just wanted to see a tiny fraction of it come back. I thought that if I could get one-hundred thousand English pounds, I could invest it in some safe place in Europe, and that the interest would come to ten or fifteen thousand a year. That would be enough to keep us going here. That much would be as much as the company ever sent back to Zaire in its best years, when they made so much profit from copper. Oh, we would never be rich, but we could keep the clinic functioning, keep the compounds open to the sick, help the people die with dignity at least. It was silly and immoral but I did it."

"How did you expect the ransom exchange to work?"

"As I told you there are perhaps five or six men on the compound grounds who know of the plan. I thought that somebody like you would come out to the compound and these men would show themselves, make a drama out of returning me, you would be satisfied and give the ransom to them, and then go away with a job well done, nobody the wiser. Of course, there would be no violence."

"And what happened?" Roberts asked.

"You happened," the doctor said.

"I'm not quite sure I understand."

"When Adam came into camp he told me how ill you were. He explained everything about you. He told me how much you'd done for him and for the clinic, all without being asked. He told me of your concern for me personally and how hard you'd worked to bring the ransom here, although there were great dangers. And so what could I do?"

"You came out of hiding?"

"I'm afraid not right away. I thought that perhaps I could still keep my secret. You were brought to my quarters and we went to work on you. But gradually, the people in the compound learned that I had been seen and the secret was out."

"Did Adam tell you about the diamonds?"

"Yes. He told me you purchased them in Brazzaville, and that Marie had them in your valise at the leper compound."

"You could have let me die."

"That was never in question."

"Of course, I'm sorry."

The doctor looked away, then back at Roberts. Roberts realized she was fighting back tears. "But then Tom Slade came into the compound and everything went badly."

"Slade has been here," Roberts said, suddenly excited.

"Please don't excite yourself," the doctor said. Roberts felt tired and light-headed, and so they went back inside the hut and Roberts lay down on the bed while the doctor washed his face and arms.

"Is Slade the one who beat up Adam?" Roberts asked after a while.

"Yes, it was Slade. He came into camp and confronted Adam. He demanded to know what was going on and where you'd gone to. Adam wouldn't say anything. By then there was a rumor in the compound that I was back and Slade demanded the truth. Again Adam didn't tell him anything. Finally the man lost his temper and took it out on Adam."

"Where is Slade now?"

"He went back to Kisangani, threatening to return here. He was told you'd gotten cholera, and that cooled him down for a while. I don't think he has a stomach for all this disease and poverty."

Roberts lay back in bed. "What do you think I should do?" he asked.

The doctor sat in the rattan chair and studied the light patterns on the jalousie. "Do what you must," she said. "I wouldn't blame you for whatever you do. And I have no moral claim on your actions. I'm sorry you became ill with cholera. To some extent, that is my fault. But you will recover completely and you will be as good as new. All I ask is that you not blame Adam and Marie."

Roberts closed his eyes and let himself be carried along by the night sounds, bats sliding through the darkness, the sound of the coffee trees whispering in the breeze, thunder out over the cuvée. Something enormous was happening out there, a plague and a seething political disconcertion, something just beyond his ability to understand. But Roberts was too tired to think just then, and he could feel the doctor placing an embrocation on his head, her soft hands on his hair. He didn't have to think about sleep. It came over him swiftly, evenly, leaving no trace. Somewhere in the night he woke up to find that Adam had come inside the hut and was sitting in the rattan chair. The man was crying softly, trying not to make noise. Roberts touched his hand, and slept again without dreaming.

3

A BRIGHT, HOT MORNING SHOT through the open jalousies. Mbenga had brought in fresh boiled eggs, some matoke and a cup of coffee, and Roberts had sat up in bed feeling half-alive again. He had eaten most of one egg, part of the matoke and he drank the coffee greedily. After that he got down two glasses of lemonade, and then he put on some washed khaki pants and a clean white cotton shirt. He could hear a strong wind beating through the coffee trees. It would rush in and out of the groves like ocean waves, and Roberts thought that there must be a storm brewing somewhere east, somewhere over the huge trees of the Ituri Forest, back down the Stanley cataracts, where the river was unnavigable. As he sat up in bed getting dressed, he thought he could hear human sounds in the compound, men and women at their morning chores, beating the wash, mashing manioc, herding goats uphill toward the lush elephant grass steppes above his quarters.

When Roberts finished his breakfast he got out of bed by himself and took a walk around the room to test his legs. He did it without becoming dizzy, and he was pleased, and so he and Mbenga went outside and sat down under the huge tamarind tree, resting in the shade while a red haze of laterite dust rose up around them.

Mbenga steadied himself against his leg brace. "Your temperature is very much down, mzungu," he said self-consciously. Roberts replied that he felt very much better, that his head didn't ache, though his joints were sore and the pustules on his arms and legs itched terribly. Roberts knew they were both marking time, and that it was the moment to talk about serious things. "The doctor is making her morning rounds," Mbenga said, still dissembling against the necessity to speak of their mutual troubles. "I believe she would like you to see all of the clinic today . . . if you feel able. Perhaps you will be leaving us soon."

"I'll feel well enough," Roberts realized. "But tomorrow morning I have to go into Kisangani. I have to deal with the situation. There isn't any time to delay."

"I am sorry for all this trouble, mzungu," Mbenga said. "I never meant any harm to come to you, or to anybody. When I saw what happened to you in Brazzaville, and in Kinshasa, with the Kikongo, I was very depressed. I did not know what to do." Mbenga moved closer, hauling his brace.

"The doctor explained everything to me last night."

"But I have said nothing," Mbenga said forcefully. "I feel it necessary to explain my own feelings to you directly." Mbenga looked down the hill where two women, leading goats and dogs, had emerged from coffee trees. Dust had powdered Mbenga's face, streaking his cheeks where there might have been tears. Roberts thought the man looked as if sorrow had ripped him open like a tamarind pod, and pain was pouring out into the wind. Mbenga was wearing his bright beaded skullcap, a knit shirt and plastic sandals. Roberts thought he looked very tired. "You must not think badly of me, mzungu. I couldn't stand it if you did."

"I understand everything, Adam," Roberts said. "You

mustn't worry. But did you think you could pull off this kidnapping scheme?"

Mbenga shrugged. "I am devoted to the doctor. She has saved many lives, and she had dedicated her own life to this place. I have no way to know why she does this thing, no? And she did not force me into this position. I come by my present difficulties with free will and an open mind. I told you how I came to be at this clinic, and how I came to be who I am. In my own simple way, I believed that some naive Westerner would arrive in Brazzaville, and I would lead him up the river with the ransom and then the money would change hands and my Westerner would go away and leave us alone. Then Mr. Slade would leave Zaire, and EuroCopper would leave Zaire, and everything would revert to darkness, except that my doctor would have one-hundred thousand English pounds. Such a small amount of money in England or Switzerland, and such a huge fortune here." The two women came by leading their goats and dogs, and were joined by five or six ducks. The dogs chased the ducks, which flew up, and the women shouted in Lingala. "I think we all have our own moral or political values which are sometimes tested. My own were tested by this thing. Perhaps I have failed."

"I don't think so somehow," Roberts said.

"But at any rate," Mbenga continued, "I did not mean for you to come to harm or to be in any danger. And now you have come to harm and I know that you were in constant danger, perhaps still are in danger."

"Slade you mean," Roberts said.

Mbenga shrugged the question away and then folded his hands. A cloud of swallowtail butterflies rode through the courtyard and the two men let the butterflies pass. "When we met," Mbenga said, "you were only a means to an end to me.

It did not take long for that to change, for you to transform yourself in front of my eyes into a real human being."

"When did that happen, Adam?"

"When you called down to those Kikongo from the quay. I remember hearing your French. Your accent was terrible, by the way. But I knew that it was something very few men would have done. And I realized then that you were not a messenger, but that you were something else entirely. That you were, perhaps, one of us."

"You saved my life," Roberts said, something out of sequence again, but very important in the big picture. "And the doctor has come out of hiding to treat me. She told me that the people have seen her, and that it is no longer possible to claim that she has been kidnapped. Not even Slade would believe it. I know she did this to save me."

"This Slade is very difficult. A bad man."

"So, I think we're even. I think all of us are equal now, we've all given up something important for the other. We have a clean slate."

"A clean slate?" Mbenga said, puzzled.

"Tout compris," Roberts said. "Everybody is paid in full. We owe nothing and we have no fear. It is a mutual friendship that has been earned."

Mbenga smiled, a big grateful grin. "But this Slade is still a difficult man."

"What did he say to you?"

"When he saw me here last night he knew you were somewhere in the compound. He asked me to take him to you. I refused and he questioned me. I told you you were contagious with cholera. This seemed to satisfy him, or to frighten him. He went away right after."

"But he hit you."

"Yes, several times. I let him do it. It means nothing to me, and perhaps it gave him some satisfaction."

"And Marie has the diamonds and guns?"

"They are safe in the leper compound."

"And the rhinestones in the tooth powder tin?"

"In the doctor's quarters. In your black valise where your clothes are packed."

"Along with the plastique."

"Before you go away, mzungu," Mbenga said, "you must try to see our clinic. To see what all this trouble is about." Mbenga tested out a tentative smile. "I only want you to see that we are not bad people. We tried this terrible fraud only because of extreme need. *C'est une mal idée.*"

The doctor came through the coffee trees wearing a white smock and a hair net. She walked uphill through the laterite dust and fallen leaves, and stood directly behind Mbenga, one hand on his shoulder. Even though it was early morning she looked weary, sweat-soaked. Mbenga told her that Roberts had eaten, and that his temperature was below one hundred Fahrenheit.

"I've done my morning work," she told Roberts. "Would you care to see the compound?"

"I'm going into Kisangani tomorrow morning."

"This is very dangerous for you. You may not be strong enough. But I know you must leave us soon. I just don't wish you to think of us as moral freaks."

Roberts walked between the doctor and Mbenga. Roberts felt vaguely weak, yet exhilarated too, just to be outside and walking around, a semblance of being alive. They reached a clearing surrounded by palms. Around the clearing were six wooden huts on stilts, just off the ground, dirty washed mahogany and hardwood, with torn screen windows and raffia roofs. There were women in front of each hut washing clothes, tending goats and children, and some compound dogs chasing ducks. Green hills rose up behind the huts and disappeared into clouds. The wind was whistling over the coned hills and Roberts could hear it click in the palms. A rutted road led out of the clearing and into acacia bush and smaller deciduous trees covered by vines. There was a Land Rover parked in shade beside a cookhouse.

As soon as Roberts came into the clearing he was surrounded by a dozen children, most naked, who began to shout in Lingala and laugh and make a circle around him. The doctor shooed them away at last and they went across the clearing where the smell of matoke was strong. Mbenga went back across the clearing with some of the children and Roberts followed the doctor into one of the huts, a long low rectangle that was dark and hot and filled with iron beds, and cheap Army-surplus cots. The room was thick with flies. The whole room was full of sick children, some of them lying together two and three to a cot, head to toe, some in blankets on the floor. Perhaps Roberts had expected there to be noises, crying and shouting, something to indicate the existence of pain, but it was quiet. Most of the children were stick-thin with bloated bellies and reddish hair, the unmistakable stigma of malnourishment, and they said nothing, but only stared into an empty space just in front of their eyes.

"These are our abandonées," the doctor said. "They filter in from the bush when their parents disappear." The doctor leaned down and touched the forehead of one of the children. Roberts looked at the child, but he couldn't tell its sex. These images were riveting him, shooting him through with white hot wires of despair. Before, he had seen this on television, and it had seemed remote, but being here felt urgent and real. Now he couldn't take his eyes off the frail girl-child lying so quietly on her wet cot under a thin cotton gown, eyes empty and liquid, without a hint of emotion. Perhaps Roberts had expected them to supplicate or beg, cry and pray, or squeal for pardon, but they didn't. The whole room was immersed in silence, with only the buzzing of the flies as counterpoint. "These children are the last signs of a dying culture. Twenty years ago you couldn't imagine an African abandoning his child. Now it is very common. It is the ultimate breakdown."

"What's going to happen to them?" Roberts asked.

"These children are new to us. We don't know if they will survive or not. Some of them will be all right once they have some decent food. But others have illnesses we haven't begun to diagnose. When we discover if they are ill, and what they have, they will be moved to one of our other wards where they will be treated. Some will be saved. Some will have measles or yaws or worms, or worse. What can we do?"

Roberts had to turn his back to the searing outside light, just so that he could have some connection to the air. Some of the children who had surrounded him were huddled across the clearing, staring at him. Roberts felt both anger and pity. "How many of these kids do you have?" he asked, turning back inside.

"One more hut full of them. More come every month. Perhaps one hundred now. I couldn't tell you the exact number. Here the healthy tend the sick."

They left and walked a short ways across the clearing to what the doctor called the dispensary. It was a single-story building of whitewashed stone with store-bought windows and a red tile roof. The floor was octagonal tile and the walls were freshly painted. The doctor led him through the dispensary, then outside through a back door to the gardens where there was a small herd of cattle, then down to a rain pond where there were fish being raised to eat. Farther uphill they came to another hut, raised off the ground on stilts and open to the air on two sides. Once inside, the doctor showed Roberts twenty or thirty patients lying on cots, some on the floor. They were adults, but like the children, they had no expression.

"This is the AIDS compound," the doctor said.

"AIDS," Roberts intoned. Even the word had magical and frightening connotations for him.

"There is no need to be frightened. You can't catch the virus from these people. It is transmitted only by blood or by fluids." The doctor turned and stood just outside the door so that her words would be caught by the wind. "These people are here to die. Most will be gone in a few days or weeks, or at most a few months. If you wish to see our cemetery, I can show it to you."

"You didn't mention this last night."

"I wanted you to see this for yourself. There are three more huts up the hill just like this one. Some of them have children and pregnant women inside. This disease does not respect any person. I am sorry. I do not mean to shock you, but this is part of our reality. The reality of Zaire."

Standing there just inside the hut where the smells were so intense, and the silence so awesomely complete, Roberts felt weak, as if his blood had suddenly thinned. He tried to make eye contact with a young African male who was lying on a cot near the door. The wind had blown away the cotton blanket that had covered the man, and he was naked, his body riddled by sores. His hair was patchy and his lips cracked, and he made no motion, nor did he acknowledge Roberts' gaze. Suddenly one young man across the room sat up on his cot and coughed and pointed his finger aimlessly in the air. The doctor was standing just behind Roberts, on one of the steps that led up to the door, and she had taken off her hair net and was ruffling her hair, trying to comb it with her fingers.

"I had no idea," Roberts said, turning around.

They went down the stairs and found some shade on the side of the hut. Roberts sat down on an empty oil drum.

"Where the hell did all this start?" he asked.

"All the signposts say Africa. We can't know for sure, and perhaps it doesn't matter. But the only rural part of Africa with a real epidemic is a region around Lake Victoria."

"These people come across the border?"

"Some do. Some of these young men have been smugglers taking goods from eastern Zaire into Uganda and Rwanda. Some of these people you see have fled from Amin. All I know is that during the fall of 1982, seventeen people in Kasensero in Uganda came down with fulminating AIDS, the first reported cases in that country. They were thieves and smugglers who had intercourse with rural women and brought back HIV with them. Then they infected their wives, and so on and so on." The doctor sat down on the oil drum beside Roberts. "You saw those people in the hut who had carcinomas? You saw how skinny they've become. Well, the Africans call this disease *slim*. And this *slim* moves fifty miles every year, through villages and towns, inexorably. We're seeing the disease in its original primeval form right here."

"What is this all about? How can we understand?"

"All about?" the doctor said. "It's all about a retrovirus. A parasite of the cells, a freeloader something like an amoeba. But a virus is different. It's a packet of information wrapped in a protein covering. It is very small, only about one ten-thousandth the size of the body cell. The virus does not eat. The virus does not respire. The virus cannot reproduce without the help of its host cell. Some scientists aren't sure the virus is alive. Beginning in 1970 the virus began to appear in Kinshasa. There was a Danish doctor named Grethe Rask who had worked in Zaire since 1964. I think her clinic was in a primitive provincial capital named Abumombazi, in northern Zaire. She became ill and lost weight. Her lymph glands swelled and eventually she died, perhaps the first one to die of AIDS. And that was the beginning. Only now, after all these years, are we commencing to scratch the surface of our knowledge of the retrovirus's place in the ecological niche between mammals and their environment. All I can say is that urban Africans are at great risk for this *slim*. The citoyennes come to Kinshasa and sell their sex. The disease spreads wildly."

"I've seen the citoyennes outside the Hotel Intercontinental in Kinshasa."

The doctor made a sweeping gesture. "All the patients you've seen have the typical symptoms. In early cases there is Kaposi's sarcoma, primarily an African cancer and rare in the West. And of course there is diarrhea, infestations of intestinal parasites like salmonella and shigella, also common to poor rural Africa. There is Burkitt's lymphoma, tropical in its setting, common in the lymphoma belt of Africa between fifteen degrees north and south of the equator, which is also the epidemic space of Kaposi's sarcoma."

"Can't anything be done for these people?"

"This is a complicated issue," the doctor said. "Would you like to go across the clearing and sit at a table and have some lemonade?"

"We could do that," Roberts admitted, tired and hot. They went back to the dispensary and sat in the shade of an acacia. They were on a slope, just inclined above the other huts, where they could see the garden plots and some cows, children playing in the red dust. The doctor poured lemonade and they emptied the glasses quickly.

"I could tell you about this," the doctor said. "But I don't want you to think I'm doing public relations."

"No," Roberts insisted. "I want to hear."

The doctor unbuttoned her smock. The wind had dropped now that morning was over, but Roberts could hear it in the high trees. Heat ticked off the tin roofs. "It's different when you see it," the doctor said.

"Very different," Roberts agreed. "You hear about it. You see commercials on TV. The reality never sinks in."

"The reality probably started in the '60s and '70s for Africa. At that time the population of eleven cities in Africa suddenly swelled to more than a million each—a huge mushrooming of people away from their traditions and their families and their religions. At the same time there was universal war and famine, armies marching everywhere from Angola to Eritrea. More danger and infamy than we'll ever know. Perhaps it was then that HIV slipped out of its rural hiding place near Lake Victoria and set upon the cities. There was a wave of promiscuity. Health services in the cities had already collapsed, and at the same time there was a sexual revolution on a continent that was already very sex-positive. Put together a sexual revolution in Zaire, anarchy and terror in Uganda, and a burst of population in Rwanda and you have the conditions the virus seems to desire, its *raison d'être*."

The doctor poured some more lemonade. The sky was a terrific high blue, but behind in the east were the first thunderheads of the day. "For an epidemiologist it is very easy to track," she continued. "There was an outburst of hemhorraghic fever in southern Sudan in 1976. In 1983 a wave of hemhorraghic conjunctivitis spread from West Africa, to Brazil, to Panama and Malaysia. Both of these were caused by HIV-related viruses. There are many more examples of contemporaneous scourges that were signs that a new virus was breaking out into the open, so to speak."

An old man herded some cows past them. The doctor called to him in Lingala, and the old man returned her greeting.

"This was my original impetus for coming to this clinic," the doctor continued. "In the '70s, there seemed to be continual outbreaks of tropical diseases that were being created by a constantly mutating virus. The virus would mutate into existence, and then just as suddenly it would mutate out of existence. At the same time, many African diseases that were thought to be under control before Zairian independence began to come back in more virulent forms. There was a cholera epidemic in 1977 and an outbreak of shigellosis in 1981. Right now tuberculosis is raging throughout central Africa, along with leprosy, sleeping sickness, bilharziasis, onchocerciasis, a river blindness. When I came here I thought I could use my specialty in tropical disease to really help with these outbreaks that were beginning to cluster themselves into Zaire after the breakdown of the central authority. But after I got here I found out I had more on my hands than outbreaks of old-style diseases with unknown causes. I had malnutrition and its attendant congenital abnormalities, goiters leading to cretinism, mental retardation, infant mortality. And I had AIDS." The doctor stopped and got her breath. "Some of this is happening because of bad health habits, of course. Some of it is lack of medicine and supplies, the destruction of the country's infrastructure, lack of roads and hospitals. Did you know that there hasn't been a new hospital built in Kinshasa since independence? Back then the city had a population of three-hundred thousand souls. There are now nearly eight million. And not one new hospital."

Roberts studied the milky sky, looking for answers, relief from the heat, anything. The blue was gone and thin clouds had waved over. Everything was damp and hot. A few vultures fell away on air currents, and he thought about the whores in front of the Hotel Intercontinental. "I don't understand all this suffering," he muttered. "Why the hell is this happening?"

The doctor shrugged, something familiar and portentous. Her hair was limp with the heat, and her cheeks were hollow. "The retroviral map of the world," she said weakly, "looks like a medieval mariner's chart. Huge portions are blank. Some are described as being infested with demons. Some of the coastline is vague. It is much too early to draw serious conclusions about this virus and its origin. As I told you, many have thought that it originated in Africa, but the data are not yet there to prove it." The doctor took a coffee bean and began to chew it. "One of the problems," she said, "is that there are two viruses, HIV-1 and HIV-2, both isolated at the Pasteur Institute in Paris in the mid-'80s. You can make a strong case that HIV-2 originated in Africa because its genetics are similar to a virus discovered in green monkeys. These monkeys are quite common to Africa, and the theory is that the virus crossed over."

"I've seen these monkeys. On the boat upriver."

"I'm sure you have. They're the most common monkey on the entire continent."

"The people would roast them over the diesel exhaust. They'd burn off the monkey's hair and then sell the carcass."

"I suppose I've been in Africa so long these things don't impress me any longer."

"So this virus comes from the monkey?"

"Well, the human virus is different from the green monkey virus. For one thing, the human HIV has a long latency period. And in their transmission, through blood or sex, this virus is more like the hepatitis B virus. We don't know when, but perhaps one hundred years ago, the HIV-1 crossed over from monkeys. Some scientists believe there is a cloud of strains between HIVs. But this human virus mutates more quickly and is more virulent than even the flu virus."

"Why stay here? What can you do?"

"I'm a doctor," she said flatly. "It would be no different in the West. It seems that the West made an amazing discovery around 1983 that there was a general epidemic of AIDS raging in central Africa. This was followed by the discovery that its main mode of transmission here was heterosexual intercourse. Now you find in the West a creeping fear that their epidemic will resemble ours, that the plague will spread to the general population, no longer infect only gays or drug users. So, it's natural for Americans to believe that AIDS comes from Africa. But Africans are equally convinced that it was introduced to them by Europeans or Americans. On both sides there is much ignorance and superstition. Our own beloved President Mobutu theorized that the disease came into Zaire from canned food donated by Western charities. All at once he promoted an "Eat African" campaign, which only succeeded in producing starvation. The truth is that every continent is attacked, there is no place to hide."

"But what about you personally? Surely you can do more good back in some think-tank, a research facility."

"Oh, there is no place to hide, don't you see? And for me, I am an African doctor. I made my commitment years ago, and now that this plague is creeping over all of Zaire, it would make no moral sense to abandon my original commitment. Research is only one function for modern medicine. Perhaps my role is to make death easier." The doctor noticed that there was no more lemonade. She placed her hands flat on the table in front of her and seemed to study them for a long time. The vultures had come back over and were roosting at the edge of the clearing, riding out the afternoon heat. "It's only Africa and her people," the doctor said quietly. "There are mostly young people on this continent and they are all sex-positive. So, one looks to education to break the grip of the disease. But there are no schools since the breakdown. Lack of education leads to a greater promiscuity. A vicious circle. And this disease is killing off the educated elite as well. It is killing adults who work in transport and mining. What you've seen is just the tip of the iceberg. Because of premature death and disease, Zaire is going backward through time, to a place beyond even anarchy. I have no name for such a place, but it is just beyond the horizon, over there." The doctor gestured east, to where the forest rose up into hills and gray cone-shaped clouds.

"And so you concocted the kidnapping scheme," Roberts remarked. He was waiting for the rain to come. He could see its promise in the sky.

"Don't think me naive," the doctor said. "Desperate per-haps, but not innocent. I knew what I was doing was wrong. But there are many people in this clinic I can actually help. If I have food and medical supplies, I can save many of those children you saw today. I don't know what I'll save them for, but they are human beings, and they deserve to have love touch them once in their lives. And I thought that if I had this money, I could at least provide a place for my AIDS patients to die. Nothing more and nothing less. The point of my scheme was that I knew I could not rely any longer on the outside world. That world no longer exists for Zaire. It is the same thing in Haiti. In the Philippines. Soon there will be nothing left."

"It seems so hopeless," Roberts said.

"It has long been one of the vanities of modern science," the doctor said. She smoothed back her hair. "At least in wealthy countries, we doctors have boasted that we will conquer infectious disease. But now comes the retrovirus and its extraordinary complexity. Now we are exposed in our pride, our hubris. Now we know that nature is not conquered. We know that nature is our very being."

The doctor stood up and helped Roberts to his feet. He was feeling tired and drained. They had been sitting in one spot for a long time, and now the sun was coming around the corner, burning down on them. They walked back through the clearing and uphill toward the doctor's quarters. He noticed the cookhouse again, and a long structure that was probably the mess. Every once in a while, he heard a dog bark and some children laugh, but the mid-afternoon had taken on a silky aura, a texture of finitude just before rain and storms. The doctor took him back to the hut and put him to bed, and almost at once he went to sleep in his clothes. When he awoke it was late afternoon and there were six goats in the clearing beneath the tamarind. He realized that he had been undressed and washed, and that somebody had turned down the bed and put up the mosquito netting. His traveling bag was open beside the bed, and his clothes had been washed. The circular fan stirred and the jalousies banged in the breeze.

"Good evening, mzungu," Roberts heard Mbenga say from across the room.

"God, I've slept all afternoon," Roberts replied.

"This is good for you." Mbenga walked over and sat down beside the bed.

"The doctor showed me the clinic."

"I know. She said you were a good student."

"I have a lot to learn."

"I think you do not hate us, no?"

"I couldn't," he said honestly. "It never crossed my mind."
Roberts didn't know how he could explain his feelings to
Adam, or if he should even try.

"Good, I am very glad."

"But I have to go to Kisangani tomorrow morning."

Roberts had prepared himself for something like a small
collision of wills. Instead, Mbenga bowed his head and was as
quiet as a child. Roberts looked across the room at his clothes
and equipment, all laid out in a definite symmetry. Finally
Mbenga said, "The doctor has spoken to me about your
desire to go to Kisangani. It is possible if there is not too much
heat or stress." Mbenga stood up and looked at Roberts, who
had gotten his feet on the floor. "And I must tell you that Mr.
Slade has come again."

"What about Mr. Slade?" Roberts said, surprised. Too
many things were going through his head at once and he
couldn't think. Now that it was late afternoon, insects were
swarming in the pink sunlight, banging against the jalousies,
and the wind had raised itself through the coffee trees. "What
do you mean he came around again?"

"While you were sleeping," Mbenga said flatly, as if the
tension had drained away. "He drove up from the town in his
rented car with a driver. He insisted on seeing you and made
a demand to see the doctor. He has heard the rumors. He
knows the doctor is back."

"What was he told?"

"He was told you were contagious. He was very angry and
impatient, but this time he went away without violence."

"But you think he knows about the doctor."

"Yes, he knows. It is common knowledge now." Mbenga
suffered a painful smile. "Everyone is very happy, but Mr.
Slade is the exception."

Roberts got out of bed and drank some tepid lemonade.

He washed his face and took a couple of vitamin pills. Mbenga took his temperature, and was quite satisfied. They went outside and sat down under the honey-colored tamarind tree which was full of pied crows, and even a parrot or two. With the sound of the birds and the wind and the barking of the compound dogs, it was difficult to concentrate.

"Now, we have to go to Kisangani tomorrow," Roberts announced. Mbenga agreed, telling Roberts they could go at first light, taking the Land Rover which still had plenty of petrol even though there were shortages everywhere. Slade would be easy to find at the New Stanley, as there hadn't been a dozen white men at Kisangani in six months; most of those were foreign workers closing Western businesses, some World Bank functionaries and an aid mission from Germany. The town was a burned-out hulk of its former self, and even the wealthy Zairians had fled to Kinshasa or out of the country to Kenya.

"The road is difficult," Mbenga explained. "It is only six miles to Kisangani, but it may take an hour."

The sun was coming in flat over the coffee trees just beyond their range of vision, and the air was swarming with red dust. It reminded Roberts of that afternoon in Brazzaville when he'd met with Raymond on the public square just across from the People's Palace, a vivid strange color in the air, filtered through a thousand sounds.

"I want you to know something," Roberts said, motioning for Mbenga to remain silent. "The doctor explained her whole plan to me this morning. It doesn't matter whether I approve or disapprove really. What matters is that you know I have absolute faith and trust in both of you, and in Marie. I know the doctor came out of hiding to treat me, and in that way put herself in great jeopardy, and her clinic as well."

Mbenga shifted nervously as a lizard darted across the

courtyard. "I am glad, mzungu," he said. "This has worried me since that day on the quay. And after we said goodbye to the assassin on the fire escape I knew you were doing something extraordinary for us. And I did not want you to think that it had turned out to all be false." Roberts opened his hands, a new gesture. "There is no falsity in my feeling for you, mzungu."

"That's settled," Roberts sighed, slightly embarrassed. "But there's something else. You have to help me think it through."

"Anything you wish."

"Do you remember my hotel room in Brazzaville, how the African came in and surprised me and asked me for the diamonds we'd just purchased from Raymond?"

"I remember this very well."

"We decided this guy was sent by Raymond to steal back the diamonds."

"Undoubtedly."

"And later we confirmed it because this same guy was following me down the street away from the hotel, and I gave him the slip in the Ouzey market?"

"A very good trick."

"And how did we know he was sent by Raymond?"

"Very simple," Mbenga said. "You had just come from Raymond. There had been only a few hours' gap. Raymond knew where you were staying, and he was the only person in Brazzaville who knew you had diamonds."

"Absolutely, yes. And so when the African came into my hotel room and demanded the diamonds, we knew he was sent by Raymond."

"I am sorry about this Raymond. He was my idea."

"Yeah, we took care of him."

"Yes, that was very good."

"But what about the assassin at the Intercontinental in Kinshasa? Who sent *him?*"

"Well, it must have been Raymond."

"We thought it was Raymond. We *assumed* it was Raymond. But was it really Raymond who sent him?"

"I don't understand, mzungu."

"There was an African in my room when I got back from my meeting with Tom Slade. It wasn't the same African who came into my room in Brazzaville."

"No, it was not the same man."

"Let me tell you something else. When I came into the room the guy had already gone through the place. He'd turned everything upside down. He'd opened all the drawers, looked in the closets, checked my bags, overturned the bed. He'd looked in the nightstand and he'd gone into the bathroom and looked in the medicine cabinet. He was very thorough."

"And Raymond would have assumed you were staying at the Intercontinental. All Westerners stay there. There is no place else."

"That doesn't matter. What matters is this. There was a tooth powder tin in the bathroom. It wasn't touched. There were film canisters in my bags. They weren't opened. I had half-a-dozen small packets of medicine, and some vitamin pills and other small vials, and none of them were opened. I had some shaving cream in a can. It wasn't touched. I had a razor kit that was about the size of a Bible. It wasn't opened, or even looked at."

Mbenga thought for a moment. "I am beginning to see your point," he said.

"It turns out to be simple. I was so stunned by the attack and by killing him that I quit thinking. If Raymond had sent the assassin to my room in Kinshasa, the man would have known I was carrying diamonds. He would have looked at the tooth powder tin and he would have emptied it. He would have opened all the film canisters, and he would have looked in my shaving kit and he would have opened all the medicine bottles. After all, the African who searched my room in Brazzaville did just that. But the man who searched my room in Kinshasa wasn't looking for diamonds."

"This African was looking for cash."

"You're getting me now."

"And this would mean what?"

"Well, just before I went back to my hotel room I'd been at the Sozacom Building talking with Slade. I told him I had the ransom. I didn't tell him it was in diamonds because I didn't want to tell him anything more than I had to."

"Mr. Slade is not a good man."

"I talked to the doctor this morning about him, too. For years this guy has been stealing supplies from the clinic and dealing them on the black market. It's one of his sidelines."

"It's true," Mbenga said.

"And after my meeting with him at the Sozacom Building, you and I went out for some food. There was a long time when I wasn't in my room at the Intercontinental. And in addition to that, Slade has tried to find out everything about my mission from the first. He's taken more than a friendly insurance man's interest in what I've been doing. At first I thought he was just a meddling bastard who probably didn't trust me."

"And you think he was behind our troubles."

"I think Tom Slade sent that assassin to my room in Kinshasa. I think he was supposed to steal the ransom money and I think he was supposed to kill me doing it. Then Slade could report to the insurance company that I'd been robbed and murdered. Then he would have the money and he would live happily ever after. The bastard."

"This makes the situation very complicated," Mbenga said.

"It does indeed," Roberts said. "Now that I know he's been here at the clinic asking for me, and that he's even hit you in order to get information, I don't think he's finished yet. I think he still wants the money. I still think he's planning to disappear with it. Only now that the doctor is back, he'll probably tell the company that this whole thing has been a fraud, and that the doctor and I have stolen the money in a scheme to cheat Lloyd's. He'll probably take the money and then report the doctor and me to the authorities, and hope we disappear into a Zairian prison. He may already have paid bribes in Kinshasa to do just that."

Mbenga seemed to tremble, but he said nothing. There was faraway thunder, and the pied crows rose up out of the tamarind in a single cloud, and then settled back, like volcanic ash raining down. Now there would be the brief gold twilight, and then full night. Already the first few insects were powdering down. Mbenga helped Roberts get inside the hut and change into his cotton robe. The man went down to the kitchen and came back with a tray of boiled fish and some rice. Roberts ate his dinner in the dark and then said goodnight to Mbenga.

It was only later that Roberts knew what he had to do. He put half a pound of plastique under the bottom leather of his black valise and he rigged detonators to it. He timed his transmitter so that he could explode the plastique by radio signal from as much as three or four miles distance. Then he put Marie's rhinestones in the valise, along with some towels and handkerchiefs. He had no idea of time, but it was late when he finally went to sleep.

4

SLADE WAS ON THE TERRACE of the New Stanley Hotel, sitting at a corner table where the Avenue Independence intersected the hotel gardens. Roberts came up the marble stairs, put down his black valise and watched the man unfurl a *Paris Soir* and order breakfast from the African waiter. Across the street in the Place de Martyres dozens of squatters were building their morning charcoal fires under blooming mimosa trees. There was another colonial hotel across the square, but its windows were broken out and the lobby gutted, and it looked as if squatters had taken it over. Laundry fluttered from its green-shaded windows and most of the intricate cornices had been torn down for firewood. Slade sipped his coffee when it came and shooed the flies away from a basin of margarine. He looked absentmindedly at the square, and then went back to his breakfast and his paper.

Roberts and Mbenga had driven in the Land Rover. They had gotten up before dawn and Roberts had washed himself in a tin basin in the courtyard, and then he had eaten some matoke and boiled rice, and some brown sugar coffee. The doctor had come up to the hut and said goodbye, and Mbenga had spoken a few words with Marie, who was living in the leper compound in a grove of coffee trees and sugar cane, about two hundred yards across the steppes.

Despite his continuing weakness and his headaches, Roberts felt reasonably well, although he was surprised at how hot it was, even though it was technically night. It didn't surprise him that it took an hour to drive into town, but the enormity of the damage to the road did surprise him, and he began to become nauseated and feverish with the constant pounding. There were fallen trees blocking the shoulders, and tremendous stretches of red laterite mud they had to circumnavigate. Maybe more surprising, and distressing, were the hundreds of squatter families living in shelters and lean-tos beside the road, men and women and children huddled around early morning charcoal boiling their few grams of rice with some tinned milk. To their left—north—bush stretched out flat toward the river basin where every one of the hardwood trees had been cut down for firewood or shelter, or to sell downriver, and there were deep gorges cut in the hills where rainwater ran down into open sewers where the people defecated and washed. Sometimes they would come to open clearings in the bush where fisherman had set up racks and were drying fish, and the stink was enormous—a smell of baked bandages. The closer they came to Kisangani, the more they began to see concrete bunkers and sere red hills on which were perched more shacks and lean-tos. They saw a few men and boys riding bicycles, but almost no cars and no police, and no soldiers either, which relieved Roberts. This town was different from Kinshasa because there were no whores visible. But then again perhaps it was too early in the day.

Finally the rutted road turned into a warren of lanes lined by burned out concrete sheds covered by mildew and mold, some hastily constructed shanties made of tin and plywood, cardboard lean-tos heaved up onto the top of garbage piles. Off in the distance Roberts could see the wharf area and its big cranes that looked like dead spiders, and one or two glass office buildings that made up the downtown, arrowing up out of the flat river bottom of palm trees and graffiti-covered signboards. Closer into downtown there were shops, but they were all shuttered closed by steel blinds, and there were a few sooty buses jammed with Africans carrying bundles of household goods and food. This town was too quiet, Roberts thought, not at all like Brazzaville, which produced a healthy musical buzz as soon as the sun came up. Once they got into town, the sky clouded over and it threatened rain, but nothing happened, except that the heat sank inside everything, a torpor beyond words.

They drove once around the Place de Martyres. Mbenga found an inconspicuous spot beside the burned out colonial hotel, and Roberts walked across the square and saw Slade at his early breakfast. Roberts went into the lobby of the New Stanley and bought a package of Belgian cigars, made in Belize, and lit one and went out onto the terrace and watched Slade for a long time. There were two Africans having breakfast on the terrace, and Slade, and fifteen empty tables. Below the terrace, on the Avenue of Independence, some vendors were setting up their wares in an impromptu marketplace. Roberts walked over to Slade and sat down at his table without being asked.

The man looked up in astonishment. "For God's sake," he said, "you've had cholera."

"Don't worry," Roberts replied. "I'm not contagious." Roberts puffed on his cigar, which was making him distracted and fractious. Nevertheless, he thought he needed an edge on Slade, something to divert attention. Roberts had put the black valise under the table, and he tapped it once with his foot for effect.

"What they said was true then?" Slade asked. "You've had cholera."

"Oh yes, it's true. But I'm not contagious."

"Well, well," Slade said contemptuously. "You don't look contagious. But you do look yellow."

"It's been a trying couple of weeks."

"I must say," Slade remarked without meaning. Slade began to drum the table with his knuckles. It annoyed Roberts, but it was probably intended to annoy him. Across the street in the Place de Martyres an argument was consuming the attention of about twenty squatters who had drawn in a circle and were shouting in Lingala. Roberts expected soldiers at any moment, but none came and the argument ebbed and flowed under the fine sooty filth of charcoal smoke. "But I am glad to see you," Slade continued. "At any rate, I've been up to the clinic to see about you."

"Your concern for my health is touching."

"Come now," Slade said. "You volunteered for this bloody assignment. Did you think Zaire would be a picnic? Did you think you'd have checkered tablecloths and fine Montrachet?"

"Oh, I have no problem with the assignment," Roberts said. "It's only the artificial interference that bothers me. You neglected to fill me in on all the details."

Slade was wearing a white shirt that had turned yellow from the laundry, and was soggy with sweat already. He leaned forward across the table, balancing on his elbows. His deliberate black eyes focused on Roberts. "See here, Roberts," he growled, "you're working for me. I won't stand for any of this cheeky little schoolboy nonsense. And besides, I don't know what you mean."

"We have to clear up some things."

"The only thing we have to clear up is the ransom money. It belongs to the company. There is a rumor that the doctor was never really kidnapped. By my reckoning, that would make these stories I've heard part of a deliberate fraud. In fact, I've been up to the clinic and I've heard these rumors myself. You'd do well to return the money and get on with it. You've earned your fee."

"My fee," Roberts said. "I've earned half of it."

Slade laughed. "I knew it would come down to this. You're holding me up for the other half of your fee. Well, you'll have to talk to London about that."

"No, I'm not going to hold you up."

"It wouldn't be wise. There are people here in Kisangani and in Kinshasa who are prepared to assist me in gaining the return of the ransom. Dangerous people. Authorities as well."

"You're threatening me," Roberts said wryly.

Slade paused and broke a crust of croissant. The flies were terrible, and he had to swat them constantly. "Oh, now let's be reasonable," he said. "You were to receive half your fee in London and half when you did the job. It's an open question whether you've done half. And besides, it isn't up to me."

"So I chat about it with the home office?"

"That's right old boy," Slade said, trying to soften his tone. "I don't have the authority to tell you anything one way or the other. Presents a rather interesting legal riddle, don't you think? But then I don't know the facts."

Roberts was smoking his cigar now to keep away the flies. Out in the Place de Martyres, the argument had erupted into a fight. "Before we get to the issue of the ransom money," Roberts said, "I'd like to clear up a few things."

"Look here old man," Slade said, feigning weariness. "I've had an airplane ready at the field across town for three days. I've had to pay matabish every bloody day just to keep my permission to take off. If I can get off the ground this morning, I can make it to Kinshasa late this evening. You have no idea of the risk involved at this time of year. There isn't any place to land for fifteen hundred miles and the weather is nasty and unpredictable. In this season you can hit a line of thunderstorms that stretch for sixty or seventy miles, thirty thousand feet high. Try getting through an equatorial storm in a King Air. I'd bloody well like to see you try."

"It sounds dangerous," Roberts admitted. "But I only want a few minutes."

"You're in danger too. You won't like flying back in this weather any more than I."

"I'm not going back with you," Roberts said.

Slade was surprised now, open-faced. "You're staying in this forsaken place?"

"I'm just not flying back with you. I'd find it distasteful and annoying."

"Suit yourself old man. But I do want the company's money if you don't mind."

"Just a few questions."

Roberts lit another cigar. He wanted to keep busy as a way to divert everything away from its interior tension. "Make it very brief," Slade said.

"Back in London you didn't tell me you'd been involved in Zaire for many years."

"It wasn't important, was it?"

"I know you handled clinic affairs for a long time."

"How did you know this? The doctor?"

"Yes, I've spoken to her."

"Then it's true," Slade said, obviously delighted. "Then you have the ransom."

"Oh, you'll get your money back," Roberts said. "But when I spoke to the doctor she told me the history of the clinic and its connection to the insurance company. She explained how you've been pilfering supplies and drugs from clinic shipments for years and selling them on the black market."

"Did the doctor tell you she'd been padding her reports to defraud the company?"

"Yes, she told me."

"Then what difference does any of this make, even if it were true?"

Thunder had begun in the east, far away over the river up-country and forest. "I'll tell you the difference," Roberts said. "The doctor was trying to help her patients. She just wanted to get an extra box of penicillin, maybe two or three dozen bandages. Nothing outrageous. It was a kind of payback for years of neglect by people like you."

"For God's sake man," Slade said. "You've seen the country. You've been in Kinshasa and now in Kisangani. This bloody place is a nightmare and getting worse. Ten years ago when I came here you could buy an entire government ministry for five thousand U.S. dollars and the minister himself would take you to lunch with a prostitute. Ten years later and the price has gone up and the ministers revolve every six weeks, but otherwise there has been no change." Slade gestured across the street to the Place de Martyres. "And take a look at these buggers yourself," he said. "They'd cut your throat for a shilling. Less than that. They don't give a damn about themselves or anybody else. There isn't an honest man in sight. And what about a few bloody boxes of penicillin? There are hundreds of thousands of sick and dying out there in the bush, and more every day. They come into Kinshasa by the thousands. And you have the gall to talk to me about some boxes of bandages. You'd better take a good look around and come to your bloody senses."

"That's it?" Roberts said. "This country is a bloody mess and it's okay to cut yourself a profit from its misery?"

"Don't lecture me on morality. You know better than that. You came down here to earn a fee. You didn't come down here for nothing. If you hadn't been paid you'd have never laid eyes on the place. You have your moral arrangements and I have mine."

"And the doctor? Where does she fit in?"

"You don't think she padded her figures? I know she did. I've been looking at her claims for years. It became a bloody game between us. She would make a false claim, and I'd process it for her. She needed two cases of bandages, she orders six and claims there's been a fire on the mine site. Why don't you put this into your moral calculator and tell me how it computes?"

"Have you seen the clinic?"

"Several times."

"I don't mean in the past two days."

"No need, old man."

"Well, I've had a good look around. In fact, I spent yesterday morning going through all the wards. In one there are about fifty kids with AIDS. And down from there are two or three huts full of abandonées. There is a leper compound and and pregnant women with German measles, and mothers who can't feed their babies and families who share worms and monstrous amoebic infestations. The doctor and five or six other people try to deal with that every day."

"You talk as if that were my fault."

"Not your fault, your *concern.*"

"All a part of the whole, that sort of rot. The whole bloody country is a lunatic asylum. Everywhere you look. You came upriver by boat?" Roberts admitted he had. "Then you were impressed by the humanity you saw? Were those the kinds of people you'd have me wash with my concern?"

"You're a cold man, Slade," Roberts said.

"It doesn't really matter in the whole scheme of things, does it Roberts? I have a job to do and you have a job to do, and neither of us have any connection, really, to Zaire or its bloody problems. Concern has nothing to do with it. Why am I having this bloody conversation with you anyway? If you want a gold watch and a commendation from Geneva for your humanitarian concern, I'll see what I can do. As for me, I want the ransom money because I've got to take off."

"But there's something else," Roberts said.

"Make it bloody quick. When I finish my breakfast I'm getting out of here. And if I don't have the ransom by then, we'll call my friends or the police. You wouldn't want to deal with them and I've already paid them off. You wouldn't stand a chance."

Roberts picked up the valise and placed it on the table. Slade took a deep breath and smiled. "The money you wanted. The ransom. It's inside."

Slade opened the valise and rummaged through it. He sat there holding the tooth powder tin and some towels. "What the hell are you talking about?" he asked.

"Diamonds," Roberts said. "There are diamonds inside the tin. I'd say thirty-five stones.

"You brought diamonds into Zaire?" Slade said, more a comment than a question. "How did you manage that?" Slade opened the tin and filtered out a powdery stone.

"It doesn't matter now," Roberts said, hoping the man wouldn't take much time with the stones. Slade closed the tin. "Bloody clever wasn't it?"

"Very clever indeed," Slade agreed.

"You didn't think of that when you sent that chap over to my hotel room at the Intercontinental did you? The guy was looking for cash because that's what you thought I had. Did you know I killed him? Did it make the morning papers, or did you just look the other way when the guy didn't come back to the Sozacom?"

"Don't be a fool," Slade snapped.

"Just tell me about it. That's all I want."

"I said, don't be a fool."

"Did you plan this in London? Or did it just come to you when you knew I'd be cashing a check at a French bank in Brazzaville. Did you have a way to get the cash out of the country?" Roberts snapped his fingers. "Of course, you're a pilot. You're going to fly it out."

"I'm warning you," Slade said. "You'd best shut your bloody mouth. I was going to take you down to Kinshasa by plane and get you out of Zaire. You stay here and you could be stuck for months in this hole. You might never get out. Boat traffic is unreliable, and you'd never get a seat on the plane, not now anyway. Take my word for it, some of my friends downriver are looking for you. So I'd advise you to come along with me and be friendly. And to keep your mouth shut. You might survive if you do that."

"You plan to toss me out of the plane? Or will the authorities be at the airport in Kinshasa?"

"I said, shut up."

"All right Slade," Roberts said, slumping backward in fatigue. "I don't really care what you do with the diamonds. They aren't mine anyway. And I wouldn't want to try to get them out of the country myself. But if you just disappear, Lloyd's will look for you."

"Let this be," Slade said.

"Just tell me why you knocked Adam Mbenga around? What was the use of that?"

"Oh that?" Slade laughed. "Bloody beggar was holding out on me. He knew where you were, but wouldn't say."

"That took some courage, knocking him down with his braced leg."

"An African," Slade said distastefully. "He wouldn't tell me where the company money was, and he wouldn't tell me about your situation, or where the doctor was. I'd heard a rumor that the doctor was back in the compound. He got cheeky and wouldn't talk. What did you expect me to do with this kind of money at stake?" Slade took the valise and walked around the table. "Forgive me," he said, "but I have to go now. These clouds are building in the east and they'll be chasing me all the way down the river and across the *cuvée*. Besides, my plane is gassed and the bribes are paid. And you wouldn't want me to have to pay another round of bribes tomorrow, would you? We wouldn't want to waste company money, would we?" Slade walked away toward the hotel lobby and stopped. "Don't be surprised if you have a difficult time getting out of Zaire," he said. "Some of these African officials can be difficult, yes?"

Slade disappeared inside the hotel lobby. Roberts hurried after him and caught him at the front desk. Slade turned and glared at Roberts.

"Just one more thing," Roberts said.

"One more thing."

"Come out to the clinic with me today."

"See here. I've told you I have to fly out of here today. You can see the clouds already."

"Do you know how many sick and injured the doctor takes care of?"

"You've told me."

"Four hundred at least."

The light in the lobby was gray.

"Look at those Africans in the square," Slade said. "There are millions more like them. When the four hundred at the clinic die, there will be four hundred more to take their place. And then when those four hundred die, there will be a thousand. There isn't a single thing about all this suffering that impresses me, except its futility and awkwardness."

"Give me the ransom. Let me donate it to the clinic."

"Not a chance," Slade laughed.

"I'm giving you the opportunity to do something here."

"Nothing doing."

"But I know you'll keep the diamonds yourself."

"Bloody hell," Slade said, walking away. He was standing in a dark foyer, waiting to go upstairs.

Roberts went out of the lobby and down the steps and walked across one corner of the Place de Martyres. Some children tried to beg money from him, but he kept walking to where Mbenga had parked the Land Rover. Roberts got in the car, and Mbenga started the engine.

"You've talked to Slade?" Mbenga asked.

"I've seen him. We've talked."

"Will he tell about the doctor when he returns to Kinshasa? Will the police come and take her?"

"I don't know," Roberts said. Inside himself, Roberts felt a dead spot growing and expanding, from his heart to his head, like a stain. "I know he's gone off with Marie's rhinestones, though."

"But he will discover his mistake quite soon. And he will come back."

Roberts had to laugh. He told Mbenga to drive to the airport, which was a mile across town, near the forest edge of river bottom where cataracts cut into swamps. "I think maybe our friend Slade might try to sell these diamonds to Raymond," Roberts joked when they cut into the warehouse district.

The airport was two hundred acres of palms on a red

laterite field surrounded by barbed wire, some customs huts, and a single weather station. Soldiers played cards in the shadows of some barracks. The sky back east had begun to darken in irregular patches of cloud, and you could smell ozone in the air. Mbenga drove around a circular track and parked just outside the gates of the ticket office, behind a line of idle cabbies. The concrete walls were shot with mildew and garbage lay uncollected on the lawns. Roberts put the transmitter in his shirt pocket and began to get out of the car.

"What are we doing at the airport, mzungu?" Mbenga asked.

Roberts leaned inside the window. "We're saying good-bye to Slade. Nothing to worry about. And tomorrow morning I have to arrange to leave the country."

"You can take a boat."

"No, I want to go east. Maybe get out through Burundi or Uganda and catch a plane in Nairobi. How hard will that be?"

"Difficult," Mbenga said. "Three hundred miles to the border and all the roads are bad. You cannot go out through Kinshasa?"

"Not through Kinshasa. Some obscure border station."

"Then we can do it. Only you must be prepared for inconvenience and worry. Petrol is a problem. But I know the roads and I know some of the towns too. It might take us a five or six days' journey."

"You can get back by yourself all right?"

"I can do that," Mbenga said. *"Pas de problem."* Mbenga smiled now, as if he had assimilated Roberts whole. He was posting his real friendship in language, and it was working.

A taxi pulled to a stop and Roberts watched Slade get out, then work his way inside the terminal with two bags and the black valise. Roberts followed him through the terminal and watched the man cross a long patch of tarmac. Roberts was behind barbed wire when he caught up to Slade.

"You are persistent," Slade said. "Changed your mind about coming along?"

"Just giving you one more chance to do the right thing."

"This is ridiculous."

"You sent the African to my room, didn't you?"

"What if I did? What difference does it make now?"

"I'd just like to know."

"You know I'll deny everything if you make that ridiculous charge. Besides, who would you report it to?" Slade edged away from the barbed-wire fence and began to walk across the tarmac toward his King Air, which was parked under a line of ragged banana palms.

The wind was from the east, and Roberts knew that Slade would taxi into it and bank out over the bush and cataract country, and make a long arc back north, across the river, and then turn back west with a good tailwind. A line of thunderstorms looked to be trailing a front about twenty miles due east of the airport, with plenty of dark clouds and sheet lightning. Roberts saw Slade put on some dark glasses and wave to him, about two hundred yards away across the tarmac. Roberts lit a cigar and watched Slade check the airplane, and then crawl up onto the wing and get inside the cockpit. The engines started with a tiny puff of gray smoke, and Slade taxied back west on the single runway, and then commenced a long run due east, rising gently just over the palm trees. The plane wobbled and rose, and then buffeted over the forest edge. Roberts could feel his heart pounding and his palms were sweaty as he took the transmitter in his right hand. Now the dead spot in his body was growing larger, and he felt numb.

The King Air was due north of the airport at about five hundred feet. It tipped up, starting its climb when Roberts touched the switch.

A silent red rose bloomed just behind the cockpit window. There was a puff of white smoke and a flange of flame, but then nothing for ten seconds while the plane angled up. Then the wings tipped down, and the plane glided silently toward the tops of the forest trees, and then disappeared. Roberts walked back inside the terminal and out to the circular drive where Mbenga was sitting in the Land Rover running the engine. They drove away from the airport and got on the road back to the clinic.

"There's a chance that Slade won't come back," Roberts said.

"That would be good."

"Then the doctor will use the diamonds to make an investment in Europe. The clinic will have money for some years to come."

"A nice thought. But Slade is a very bad man."

"We'll see," Roberts said.

They were on a hill above the river when Roberts looked back and saw a trail of smoke rising through the forest far away near the airport. He turned and put his arm on the seat behind Mbenga and tried to turn off his mind, which was one way he had of dealing with reality. When he looked around again, another mile down the road, they were too deep in the bush to see any smoke at all.

5

THEY MANAGED FIFTY MILES OF ungraded gravel road from Kisangani to Lubutu in just under five hours. Up before dawn, and on the road before the sun had crept over the canopy of forest, Roberts and Mbenga were supplied with a spare fifty gallons of petrol stored in an oil drum in the back of the car, and enough food to last a week—cheese, bread, bananas, water in animal skins, tins of Spam and some thermos jugs of lemonade. Pretty soon they realized that the road shoulders were going to be flooded, with water standing nearly up to the hubcaps of the Rover, and two or three times that first morning they were forced off the road because of huge unmanageable downpours from tropical thunderstorms out of the east. Thunder would rumble and crash down around them and sheet lightning would sear across the black sky, and then the rain would roar down horizontally, borne by stiff winds. Mbenga would charge off the road and find a large umbrella tree on a small rise, and they would wait out the rain. It would rain for an hour or more, and then the sun would stab out of the clouds and everything would be enveloped in vapor; the insects would begin to rise from the puddles, and they would begin again, weaving in and out of washed out sections of road, crashing around downed trees, making detours and losing their way, finding it again, bypassing swamps and morasses.

There were almost no villages between Kisangani and Lubutu, and the few they passed seemed deserted. The road itself had some isolated foot traffic from fishermen and vendors, and the occasional family packing out toward Kisangani, with their goods and food in sacks, heading toward their future as squatters in the big city, seeking something from Zaire that it could not give them. Around noon, Mbenga stopped for lunch.

The fifty miles to Lubutu took the rest of the day. At one point Roberts thought that the road was going to become impassible, and he began to lose heart. But they pushed on and through the mud, and found that they had come into territory where the villages were abandoned and ruined, with nobody in sight. Now there were no people on the road at all, and when he saw the first ruined village of smoking huts and abandoned shacks, Roberts realized he was witnessing the future of a whole culture. And then once, when he spotted an ancient German Mercedes diesel coming toward them out of the gloom, he was cheered. But as it passed by, he was disappointed to see that it was carrying only human cargo, dozens of families and their belongings clinging to its parts, they too headed for Kisangani and hopeless squatter status. All these women and children, and a few men, one or two goats, feeling their way toward nothingness depressed Roberts, and he fell silent for a long time. The only commerce here, he realized, was the traffic in human despair.

They spent the night at a dirty hotel in Lubutu which had formerly been run by a Belgian couple, but which was now under ambiguous African ownership and control, and was infested by cockroaches and despicable flying beetles crawling over its mildew-stained walls. The toilets were clogged by raw sewage which had backed up and spilled onto the floor, over the tile, and down the main hall, advancing toward the stairs. That night Roberts' fever increased by two degrees and he was unable to eat the thin corn gruel sent up from the kitchen, along with the thigh of a boiled monkey that seemed to be green with age. And even later, when he tried to sleep he was unable to do so, partly because of his fever, and partly because of the noise of dozens of drunken men who had gathered in front of the hotel on the main square, to drink palm wine and build bonfires and dance until dawn. Roberts was too sick to feel threatened by the crowd, but he was glad to be on the road the next morning at dawn before the men could rise up from their stupors.

That day, and the next, they rode up through heavy forest and bush, making first twenty, then thirty, and finally fifty miles, onto plateau country. It reminded Roberts a little of northern New Mexico, except for its snow, where the fields showed evidence of slash and burn, overgrazing, and where the hills had been reduced by erosion to gullies and bare vistas of carved barrancas. There were long stretches of scrub acacia and more ruined villages, and sometimes Roberts would see children peering out from their bushy hiding places, spying on the Land Rover as if it were a mechanical monster from Mars driven by aliens. Mbenga did not stop, nor did they stay in any of the villages, or even near them, even when it seemed that perhaps one of the ruined huts might contain a family who had remained behind. In that way, the two of them made Bukavu on the Burundi border on the third day, nearly three hundred miles from Kisangani, a journey that Roberts knew Mbenga would make in reverse.

Bukavu, which had been called Costermansville under the Belgians, had some altitude and fresh air. Even though they were only a few degrees south of the equator, they could see slashes of evergreen dotting the hillsides. Mbenga drove straight through the town without stopping, and along a dirt road that led uphill to the border crossing station. He stopped the Land Rover about two hundred yards from a customs hut on the border of Burundi. The road itself was a morass of mud that tilted up through conifers and fern meadows. It was mid-morning and the rain would not be commencing for another few hours, and just now it was cool and there were clouds of fog slipping through the Mountains of the Moon in the near distance and dark cuts of granite in the passes and cols. Roberts sat there in the Land Rover and put on a long-sleeve shirt and studied the customs shed two hundred yards away.

There were three soldiers dressed in olive-drab uniforms sitting around a makeshift table. They were wearing dark glasses and seemed to be smoking and playing cards. Roberts got out of the Land Rover and sank up to his ankles in red mud.

"I don't know what to say," he told Mbenga.

"Do you believe we will see each other again?" Mbenga asked.

"I do believe it. I expect you to write me letters to London. Whatever happens, take care of the doctor. She'll need plenty of help."

"Do not despair of these impassible rivers," Mbenga said then, taking a slow deep breath. "This life we are living is all poetry and danger."

Roberts walked around the Land Rover and hugged Mbenga from outside the driver's-side window. He could see how tired the man looked after his three-day ordeal. Then Roberts trudged fifty yards up the road toward the customs shed. He would try to pass over into Burundi and then take the Goma train to Kampala and on to Nairobi. If he was lucky, he would be in London within the week. He stopped and turned back and saw that Mbenga had gotten out of the Land Rover and was standing beside the muddy ditch. *"Bakie nzuri!"* Mbenga shouted over the wind. His words echoed faintly in the hills. Roberts knew the Swahili now: *Stay well.*

He waved and when he turned back toward the customs hut the soldiers had already seen him coming and were picking up their rifles.

HIV ADDS ONE MILLION VICTIMS IN NINE MONTHS
Geneva, Switzerland.

The United Nations World Health Organization, in a chilling assessment of the spread of AIDS, predicted that the disease would soon become the main cause of premature death in many Western cities and would leave as many as 10 million African children orphaned by the end of the decade.

AP